Lives En

Enchained He

Acknowledgements

To Katy Katt Brooke, who has worked so hard to get me
and my books out into the world. I appreciate it so much.
With Love

x

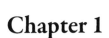

Chapter 1

~Cassie~

My palms were sweating.

I laid on that narrow bed, with Alex next to me, and my witch of a mother in front of him.

It was only the second time Alex had set eyes on Suzanne Bellingham. The first time was a disaster, only a few days ago.

My parents had decided that it was time to interfere in my life after Grandma Ruby had spilled the baby beans.

They'd shown up at our penthouse, full of false happiness and cringeworthy gifts, like monogrammed toothbrushes for each of us. Ugh. She might as well have admitted outright that she didn't approve of us sharing a bathroom, and our lives, with each other.

It had made me sick.

Okay, well, everything made me sick. My morning sickness hadn't abated and, now, my parents just continued to exacerbate it.

Looking at my husband now, I could tell that he was startled by her looks. For my sins, I looked exactly like her. And I mean *exactly*. If any of my men wanted to know what I would look like in twenty years' time, all they had to do was look at my mother. I could see Alex casting glances in between the two of us out of the corner of my eye.

It was bugging me.

I was nervous and that is what really annoyed me. Not Alex. He was the sweetest, sexiest, most amazing man. Well, one of. I was the luckiest woman in the world.

"So, you really don't care who the child belongs to?" she barked out at him.

"No, of course not," he said smoothly, taking my hand and gripping it tightly.

"Humph," she muttered. "I think it is insane. *I* would have to know."

"Yes, well, we aren't you," I replied tightly.

Where the hell were Rex and Lachlan? We needed them here. The doctor was due any minute.

"Isn't *that* obvious in more ways than one," she commented nastily, with a flirty look at Alex that made my skin crawl.

If he noticed the sparkle in her eye, he didn't acknowledge it.

"You don't have to be here," I snapped at her, completely losing it now. I didn't need her here making things worse.

"Of course I do," she said haughtily. "That is my grandchild." She indicated vaguely at my slight bump. "Not that anyone would believe I look old enough." She shook her shoulders, her raven locks bouncing. Then she ran her hands under Alex's suit lapels in a really flirty way and licked her lips. "I hope it's you," she whispered, leaning into him. "Imagine those eyes!"

Alex gave her a wide-eyed look of disbelief, taking her hands and removing them from his chest.

I shot him an apologetic look, which he caught, and had him grinning at me. "This child will be perfect, no matter what." He said just the right thing in the moment, and I couldn't love him more if I tried.

"Hmm," Suzanne drawled and then looked at the dainty watch on her narrow wrist. "I am going to chase down that doctor. I have places to be."

She looked so thoroughly put out, I would have laughed, but then that was just sad, so I grimaced at her and let her leave.

I breathed out.

"She is a piece of work," Alex whispered to me, his eyes flashing with laughter.

"You have no idea," I murmured back.

My serious tone had his face clouding with worry. "I can make her leave, if that's what you want," he said, curling my hair behind my ear.

"No, let her stay. Hopefully then she will lose interest and be done with this farce."

He nodded and stepped back as Suzanne came back with the doctor.

"Ready?" he asked.

"As I'll ever be," I replied, squeezing Alex's hand tight.

Where the fuck are Rex and Lachlan?

No sooner had the thought entered my head, they swept in, apologies on their lips. They both ducked to kiss my forehead and then Lachlan turned to my mother.

"Suzanne, how nice to see you," he said, kissing her on both cheeks.

Such a smooth mover. I rolled my eyes at him.

He grinned back at me.

Rex, on the other hand, just glowered at her.

She returned it, tenfold.

I sighed.

She took an instant dislike to him, as he did to her.

Not that I cared in the grand scheme of things, but right then, I was so nervous, it wasn't helping.

I watched with a growing trepidation as the doctor prepared the enormous needle for the amniocentesis. I wasn't sure that I wanted this, but it was the responsible thing to do, as we didn't know who the father was, so we had no idea about any family history that had been passed down. Rex and Alex never knew their fathers and Rex's mom was dead, so any potential questions had died with her. I didn't want to ask Alex to contact his mom, because what was the point when we couldn't get a full history? This was the best way. It just meant that I had to have a massive needle stuck in my belly.

My mother gave the doctor a knowing look and then he approached me with caution.

Lachlan came around the bed and took my other hand, while Rex hovered next to Alex, looking petrified.

I gave him a reassuring smile, which did little to alleviate his nerves. He was so overprotective; I knew this must be killing him. Anything that caused me hurt or even anxiety, had him ready to thump something. Right now, the doctor was in the firing line.

"I'm okay," I said to him.

He grimaced and nodded, but kept a watchful eye on the doctor, nonetheless.

I closed my eyes and said, "Do it."

I then went to my happy place.

The four of us, running and laughing through a meadow of daisies. Collapsing, eventually, to make love in the flowers.

I felt myself relax and then I heard the doctor say, "All done."

I opened my eyes and breathed out in relief.

"Bed rest for a few days. I will call you with the results."

I gave him an odd look at his brusque attitude. He'd been quite friendly earlier, but his whole demeanor had changed.

"Is everything okay?" I asked him.

"I'm sure everything is just fine," Suzanne interrupted, bustling her way closer to me by elbowing Rex and Alex out of the way.

Both men were well-muscled and much larger than my mother, but you wouldn't have known it, as they gave way to her like they were made of paper.

Lachlan, stayed on my other side, kissing my hand reassuringly.

"I will see you later, Cassandra," she said, giving me an air kiss.

"Sure," I murmured, and watched in relief as she left me and my husbands to get me off this damned bed and back home.

~Rex~

I WATCHED AS SUZANNE left the hospital room. I disliked that woman more than words could say. The way she had treated Cassie was despicable, and now she'd just walked in acting like she had a right to be *anything* to this child.

"Rex?" Cassie asked, drawing my thoughts away. "Everything okay?"

"Yeah," I replied with a small smile. "Perfect." I stooped to give her a kiss and then took her hand to lead her out.

She walked gingerly, mindful of the doctor's orders, and it was killing me. I ignored her protests as I scooped her up and carried her the rest of the way to the car.

I knew that it was the right thing to do, having that test, but I also knew the risks. Cassie wasn't going anywhere for the next few days. We would wait on her hand and foot, whether she liked it, or not.

My phone buzzed in my pocket. I ignored it. I felt eyes on me as we headed to the car and I ignored that too. Whoever was threatening me could wait until I was sure Cassie was okay. Lachlan and Alex were quite capable of taking care of her the way I would but seeing her safe and home was something I needed to do before I could think about looking at my phone.

Alex and Lachlan sat with Cassie in the back of the SUV while I drove us all home. Carefully.

"What? Are you driving Miss-fucking-Daisy?" Cassie snapped at me when I, once again, halted at a traffic light way too soon.

Alex snorted into his hand as Lachlan outright laughed at me, but I didn't care. Cassie was what mattered.

"You are precious, Cassie. I'm not taking any chances with you and our baby." I glared at them in the back seat through the rear-view mirror.

It shut them up.

My phone buzzed again and, this time, Cassie asked, "Who *is* that?"

I shrugged nonchalantly. "Work, probably. I'll answer it when we get home."

"If you have to do a job, go. We can take care of Cas," Lachlan piped up from behind me.

"No," I stated with such finality, it put an end to the discussion.

"I don't need taking care of," Cassie grumbled a few minutes later.

"Yes, you do," we all said in unison.

The rest of the drive went by in stony silence. Cassie was giving us the cold shoulder, but that was okay. Her moods never lasted that long, and this was just her being stubborn and independent.

I pulled up into the underground parking lot and I got Cassie upstairs and into bed. She was already coming around, giving me a bright smile.

"I love you," she murmured to us before she closed her eyes and promptly fell asleep.

Lachlan chuckled at her, but then grabbed me by the elbow and ushered me out of the room with Alex hot on our heels.

"What is going on?" he demanded in a low tone as soon as we were back in the living room.

"What do you mean?" I asked carefully. I wanted to keep the other men out of this. They didn't need to know. I would take care of it myself.

"The texts, Rex," Alex whispered. "We know something's up."

"It's nothing. Work," I lied, knowing it was futile, but I had to try. They were like two dogs with a bone.

"Oh, please. Work doesn't get you all antsy," Lachlan barked at me as loudly as he dared.

"I am *not* antsy," I commented, slightly insulted. I prided myself on my calm exterior, despite the raging going on inside. It was why I'd been able to do the work that I had.

"Is someone threatening you?" Alex asked astutely. He had that instinct that drove me nuts. He saw problems before most and then went about fixing them.

I sighed.

"Cassie? If it's Cassie, I will..."

"It's nothing," I lied again, interrupting him and giving him a vicious stare. One that usually had him backing down. Not this time. He knew me too well now and it pissed me off.

"Look, Rex. We are in this together, remember?" Lachlan tried a different tactic to sway me. It wasn't going to work.

I folded my arms across my chest and glared at him.

"If you can't tell us about this, then what the fuck are we doing?" he asked me seriously. "Don't you trust us by now?"

Asshole.

He knew that I did. He knew that it took all the strength and courage that I had to drop my guards around him and Alex and let them into a part of my life that I wanted to keep away from them all. Without them, I would have cracked under the pressure of lying to Cassie, my *wife,* about my former occupation. It ate me up inside, added to my guilt. It'd never bothered me before, but since I'd entered into this relationship with Cassie and her other two men, it was all I could think about. The face of every one of my victims haunted me now. I knew that I had to let Lachlan and Alex in further, to tell them about this, but it was difficult for me to accept that this was one problem that I wasn't sure I could handle on my own.

Especially now that we had a baby coming.

I was still struggling with that knowledge. The fear and guilt over the possibility that the baby was mine was something that I could never share with any of them. They would never understand that it was my worst nightmare to pass along my darkness, my utter *brokenness,* to an innocent child. I would accept the baby as my own completely and truly, but if I was the biological father, I knew that it would push me over the edge of the cliff that I teetered on every minute of every day.

I gulped and shook my head.

"It's nothing," I stated and turned towards the elevator to leave. I had to get out of the penthouse and away from them before I broke down and told them everything.

~Lachlan~

"DO WE LEAVE THIS?" Alex asked me.

I was still staring after Rex. He'd just fucked off, ducking out of this conversation like we'd meant nothing to him. It fucking hurt.

"Lach? Do we go after him?" Alex pressed desperately. He ran his hand through his hair as I looked back at him.

"No, let him do his wounded bird thing. We've got him when he gets back."

He nodded and then turned to the hallway when Cassie appeared.

"Where's Rex?" she asked, looking around.

I rushed to her. She shouldn't be on her feet.

I scooped her up and she giggled at me. She would always protest to Rex because she needed him to know that he didn't have to watch her every second, that she could take care of herself. But, with me, she was more vulnerable. I loved it about her. "What part of bed rest don't you get?" I asked her, walking her back to the bedroom.

"The rest part," she commented. "I get bed..."

The deliciousness of those three words had my dick going so hard it nearly busted my zipper. "You are so wicked," I murmured to her, dropping a light kiss on her lips as I lowered her to the bed.

She grinned at me, but then it turned into a frown. "Rex?" she demanded.

"He had a job," Alex said, following us into the room and stripping off his suit jacket.

I saw Cassie watching him with fire in her eyes.

"Careful, Suits," I drawled at him, "You're getting her worked up."

He chuckled, enjoying the nickname as much as he enjoyed Cassie's lust for him.

"When will he be back?" she asked briskly, drawing our attention back to the fact that we'd lied to her *again* and that we'd have to continue to do so, in order to protect her from the truth.

"Not sure," Alex shrugged. "He'll message when he knows," he added lightly.

There was a short, uneasy silence while she took that information in. "Fine," she huffed and looked out of the window, a faraway look in her eyes.

My heart thumped.

I glanced at Alex, who looked as stricken as I felt.

"He won't be long," he blurted out.

I shook my head and rolled my eyes at him.

"You know he can't be without you for very long," I said, kneeling at her side, gripping her hand tightly.

She snorted. "Do you...have you noticed that he is being even more skittish than usual?" she suddenly asked us.

We exchanged a fearful look.

"I—I'm sure..." I started.

"I think he's freaking out about the baby!" she wailed, tears springing to her eyes. "I'm so worried he doesn't want this."

Relief flooded me, to be quickly replaced by sympathy for my wife. She was really scared about this and had clearly been sitting on it for a while now.

"Don't be ridiculous," I chided her gently. "He is as excited as the rest of us."

"Of course he is," Alex piped up, climbing onto the bed next to her.

"Then what is the problem with him?" she asked, frustrated.

We both saw as realization dawned on her as her face went grim.

"It's because we can't play, isn't it?" she spat out. "Is that it? He is getting frustrated because he isn't getting any."

I bit my lip.

Well, it probably wasn't helping whatever was going on with him right now. But I would die a thousand deaths before I told Cassie that.

"We agreed no play until you've had the baby. He is fine with that. Don't worry so much."

"*You* agreed," she said forcefully, jabbing me in the chest. "I went along with it, because I had no choice. I want to play too. I know that's why he is being shifty. He *needs* it."

She implored me by clutching at my shirt.

I didn't disagree, but no way was I clamping up those ripe nipples and taking a whip to her when she was expecting our baby.

"Perhaps, if we came up with a plan...something to ease his need," Alex said carefully, not wanting to admit it might be a problem, but being the problem-solver, he was known for. Oh, and also for deflecting the real issue...which we still weren't clear on.

I nodded approvingly at him and then smiled at Cassie. "Yes, tie him up and flog him. I am sure he will love it."

She chuckled through her tears. "It won't be enough. He needs to dominate me as well."

"Absolutely not," I barked at her, startling her. "I am putting my foot down about this, Cassie."

"But..."

"No buts! Now get some rest and stay in bed. The doctor gave you orders." I stood up to show her I meant business.

She tilted her head back to glare up at me, but I folded my arms across my chest, unmoving.

"Fine," she huffed eventually, but I knew this wasn't the last we would hear about it.

I bent down to kiss her forehead. "I love you," I murmured to her.

"Talk to him," she whispered back. "Make sure he's okay."

"We will," I told her and then stepped back so that Alex could kiss her.

We left her, a stony silence growing between us.

"We *do* need to find out what is going on with him," Alex whispered to me. "He is sliding."

"No shit," I muttered.

An even more morbid atmosphere descended upon us.

I left Alex to stare out of the windows. I was more worried about Rex than I was letting on. I had noticed, probably at the same time as Cassie, that Rex was being shifty. I, too, had thought it might be about the baby, but I knew now that it wasn't. Something else, or *someone*, was causing it and I intended to find out who was messing with him and take care of it, once and for all.

~Alex~

I SAT AT THE BREAKFAST bar, my back to Lachlan, staring at the oven. Cassie's words rang a bit too true for me. Not for Rex though, but for me. *I* was nervous about this baby. I had never really thought about having kids before. I'd had a shitty upbringing, so it wasn't something that'd ever occurred to me. Certainly not with any of my previous girlfriends. When Cassie told us, I'd been shocked, stupidly so. With so much sex going on, despite the Pill, the possibility had been strong. No form of protection was ever a hundred percent. I just didn't actually think about it until she'd told us.

I was happy, of course, but it didn't stop the fear that I would screw up somehow.

Added to that now, was what Suzanne had said earlier about hoping it was mine.

I *did* hope it was mine.

I had no idea if the other two men felt that way, but I did. I couldn't help it. I would love the child more than anything, even if it wasn't mine, but if it was...I breathed in deeply to stop that train of thought. We'd agreed we wouldn't find out until it became obvious.

I'd wanted so badly to shout out to the doctor to do a DNA test, but I had to hold my tongue.

We'd agreed.

I sighed. Having more than just one other person to consider was hard fucking work.

I loved being in this relationship, I did, but sometimes it was overwhelming. I wanted to talk to Cassie about it, but

I never found the right time. We hardly ever got time to be alone, and it wasn't something that I wanted to discuss with Lachlan or Rex. Not yet anyway. I trusted them with a lot of things, but, to my shame, I didn't trust them with this. If they turned against me because of my thoughts, I would be devastated. I was starting to love them. They were more than just best friends. We were *family*. It was something that I had very little of, and even less experience with. The men were just as much a part of my heart as Cassie was.

Rex and Lachlan were polar opposites, but I loved them both in a way that I never thought I could love. I was close to succumbing to that love, that *desire*. I knew Lachlan wanted it. It had been months since we'd got together and I hadn't gone further than a kiss with him, without tongues. I was too scared, or too embarrassed. It was hard to tell which was worse. I wanted to give in. I just needed to get over myself and fall into it.

I'd watched Rex and Lachlan together and it turned me on. It turned me on to watch Cassie watching them, but *they* set off sparks of lust in me as well. I wanted to give in. I wanted to see what it would be like to have Lachlan take me in his mouth and suck me so hard, I came in an explosion while Cassie's eyes had that look of pure hunger in them.

I stifled my groan as my dick went hard just thinking about it. My thoughts had gone into a tailspin.

The thing I had to focus on was Rex. Something was up with him and we had to find out what soon. Cassie was growing suspicious and we couldn't let anything stress her out.

"What you thinking?" Lachlan asked, striding over to me and standing so close to me, my thoughts immediately went back to his mouth around my dick.

"Nothing," I lied. If I told him what I was thinking, he wouldn't hesitate to drag me into the bedroom and have my pants off in front of Cassie in record time. I needed a bit more time to get used to these new feelings.

"Don't give me that bullshit," Lachlan said. "You have that face on, when you are absorbed in your thoughts."

I had a thoughtful face? And he knew what it was?

He wasn't making it any easier to take this new aspect of my sexuality slowly.

"Rex," I said eventually. It was the truth. Part-truth, whatever.

"Obviously," he drawled. "What are we going to do?"

I stood up to face him. Staring into his hard pecs while I was seated was a bit more than my brain could handle right now.

"We are going to confront him. Away from here. Demand he tells us what the fuck is going on with him. I won't have Cassie, or the baby, put in harm's way, because she is stressed over him, or worse."

Lachlan gave me a surprised look at my vehemence, but then nodded his approval.

"Gotcha," he said. "When?"

I shook my head. Cassie was on two days bed rest, enforceable by us, but then she was back at work.

"When Cas goes back to work," I stated. "We will have to sit on it until then and pretend everything is fine. If he comes forward before then, we deal, but otherwise, we strategize over the next two days on how to get this out of him."

The lust in Lachlan's eyes did not go unnoticed by me.

"Anyone ever tell you; you are fucking sexy when you get all authoritative?" He gave me that lazy smile of his that I knew made Cassie go wet.

"No," I said, deciding in the spur of the moment to flirt back with him, and giving him, what I hoped, was a seductive look. "Say it again."

His breath caught in his surprise over my overt come on.

"Careful where you go with that, Suits," he said huskily. "A fella might get the wrong idea."

"Doubtful," I replied, my heart thumping. I wanted to lean forward and kiss him with tongues, before I lost my nerve, but without Cassie there, I wasn't sure about the lines. It seemed wrong to do it without her there, so I settled for lowering my eyes to his lips and then back up to his eyes.

"Fuck me," he whispered. "You're ready, aren't you?"

The seriousness of his question made me pause. If I led him along now, it would be really shitty of me. I needed to decide what I was going to do.

"Yes," I replied, going with my gut.

His sexy smile grew. "Oh, Alex," he said, using my actual name in a rare moment. "You have no idea how much I am looking forward to this."

"Me too," I replied, enjoying his words.

"And don't even get me started on Cassie," he added wickedly.

"She wants this," I croaked out, my palms starting to sweat. "But so do I."

"About time," Cassie murmured from the hallway.

She gave us a sassy smile as we turned to glare at her.

"Back to bed, for fuck's sake!" we both snapped at her, the sexual tension dropping.

"Boo," she pouted. "I was hoping to see some action."

"Later," I said briskly. "When Rex is here." It was a great excuse to give me time to prepare myself.

She chuckled at me and let me pick her up, cradling her carefully and walking slowly back to the bedroom.

"Thank you," she murmured in my ear.

I blushed. I couldn't help it. She made it sound like I was giving her the best gift in the world. It made me feel bad for denying it to her all this time.

"It's time," I said shortly.

She gave me a smile full of promise as I lowered her to the bed.

"Now stay the fuck there before we have to tie you down."

She let out a loud guffaw as Lachlan groaned.

"Now you've done it, Suits," he said, shaking his head at me.

We laughed together, falling back into the easy atmosphere that I had come to love.

The only dark spot was Rex's issue.

We needed to nip that in the bud as quickly, and as effectively, as possible before Cassie found out something she shouldn't.

Chapter 2

~Rex~

I had been walking around for about an hour. I knew the men would be worried about me. I was a bit surprised they hadn't followed me, but this wasn't something that involved them. It was *my* shit and I had to deal with it *my* way.

The texts were sent from a burner phone. Impossible to trace, even for me, but I had experience with stalkers. They *stalked*. It was their whole M.O. I had to keep a watchful eye out, but nothing had come across as overtly suspicious so far.

But I had been distracted.

With Cassie and the baby and this test and her parents showing up a few days ago, it was all a bit overwhelming.

Suzanne Bellingham was a first-class bitch. I disliked her intensely. I knew the feeling was mutual. As soon as she'd set eyes on me, I could tell. I didn't give a shit. She could fuck off out of Cassie's life and never return as far as I was concerned. Cassie though? As much as she talked about hating her parents, if she truly didn't crave their approval, she would have kicked them out the second they'd strolled into the penthouse like they'd owned it.

Damien was a curiosity for me. He's Teddy's — the Captain's — brother.

They looked similar, but where Teddy was more jovial, despite his murderous undercurrents, Damien was uncaring and distant. He hadn't even pretended to be happy to be there.

Suzanne, on the other hand, had swept in with icy smiles and offensive gifts.

I needed to keep my eye on her; she was a snake. I should know. I was one too. I was trying, desperately, to be a better man, but it was a hard struggle every day. Especially, since Lachlan had made the decision for all of us to forego any play. It was the only thing that kept me sane, well, *saner*. I got that Cassie couldn't be dominated, but why she couldn't dominate *me* was something I was going to have to address. There was no harm in it for her or the child.

The child.

I gulped as that thought re-entered my head.

I hoped that the baby was Alex's or Lachlan's. It couldn't be mine, it just couldn't. I wasn't someone a child should have as a father. At least not a biological one. What if my tendencies were hereditary? What if my mothers were? She was a crack addict whore. If that got passed down to my own child, I wouldn't be able to go on.

I sighed and took in a deep breath.

It was time to go back home.

Alex and Lachlan were going to kick my ass if I stayed out any longer.

It was as I stepped off the curb to cross the road, that I saw the black SUV lurking. It pulled away quickly, too quickly, when I glanced over.

I watched as it drove past, the blacked-out windows making it impossible to see inside.

If that didn't confirm it for me, then nothing would.

Whoever was in that car, was my stalker.

They knew what they were doing. The car was stripped of its plates. The SUV was a common one. There must've been thousands of people who had one in the state. Hell, *I* had one.

I needed something to track this fucker down. Just one little clue and I could unravel the web. I needed to be more vigilant. Cassie's safety, and that of the baby, were in jeopardy if someone was after me. I couldn't let anything happen to them.

I needed to find out who it was before I smashed them out of existence for threatening me. I might not be a murderer for hire anymore, but I wasn't going to sit back and have anyone threaten my family and the shred of happiness that I had eked out for myself in this world.

With that resolved, I stalked over to the door of the apartment block that we lived in.

I nodded to the man on duty. He worked for me. They all did. In fact, every aspect of Cassie's life was covered with security. She may not know about all of it, but even a handful of her staff at work were put there to protect her.

As I'd half expected, one of the men was waiting for me in the lobby.

"Cassie know you're down here?" I drawled at Alex.

He was pacing up and down and looked relieved to see me.

"No," he admitted. "She's finally gone to sleep. Lachlan is watching her."

"Look, Alex." I huffed at him.

He put his hand up to stop me. "I'm just gonna say this. Whatever it is that is bugging your ass, we've got you. Okay? You can trust us, you know that."

He surprised me by turning from me, stalking over to the private elevator and stabbing the button.

I followed after a beat and stepped beside him when the doors opened. "That it?" I asked, staring straight ahead.

"Yeah," he replied, also boring a hole in the doors with his gaze.

I nodded. I knew he saw it in his peripheral vision as he nodded back.

"Thanks," I muttered quietly as the doors slid open a few moments later, opening up into the penthouse where Lachlan was pacing in the living room like a caged tiger.

He stopped and glared at me when we exited the elevator.

"He tell you?" He pointed at Alex.

"Yeah," I said.

We looked at each other in a rare awkward moment. I wasn't ready to tell them. I needed to know more first. They would get involved with it and probably alert the stalker to our investigation. They didn't know how to do it covertly and with stealth. But why should they? They'd never had to skulk around in the shadows like I had.

The flash of resentment I felt was unfounded and made me feel even more guilty.

I grimaced at them and turned towards the hallway. I needed to see Cassie. She'd always had the ability to calm the raging inside me.

"Don't wake her," Lachlan called quietly after me. "It took us a fucking age to get her to submit to sleep."

I snorted with amusement. I could imagine.

I stopped and turned back to the men.

They were standing close together, very close. An air of sexual tension was wafting between them. I wondered what I'd missed.

"What's changed here?" I asked curiously, approaching them with a hawk-eye.

Lachlan chuckled. "You are way too observant for your own good. Now, don't be jealous, Angelwings, but Alex has decided to let me sex him up."

"What?" I spluttered, an actual genuine smile passing briefly over my face. "In your dreams would I be *jealous*," I then growled at him. Asshole. "I am with you because *Cassie* wants it."

"Sure, keep telling yourself that," Lachlan joked. "I know how I make you feel."

Well, he had me there, but no way was I adding to his super ego.

"Interesting development," I added under my breath. I hadn't expected this. Alex had always been very aloof. Watching, but not joining in. Not even slightly. Not as observant as I thought, then. Must do something about that. I needed my wits about me more than ever. "Go easy on him," I added as an afterthought.

Alex spluttered, going bright red. "I...*we* need to discuss boundaries."

"So, I'm good enough to take your cock in my mouth, but not to give it to you in the ass?" Lachlan asked, mock insulted.

I bit my lip. I wanted to burst out laughing, but it just didn't come out. It never did. The feeling was there, but never acted upon. I was incapable of the easy joviality that came to these men.

"I didn't mean that!" Alex defended himself.

I sat down to watch them decide amongst themselves what was acceptable to them both.

I was glad that Alex hadn't asked me to join in. I was comfortable with Lachlan taking me on, because he knew what he was doing, he knew what I needed and he...he loved me. He'd said the words and he'd meant it. Alex was just testing the waters. I wasn't prepared to take *that* on. Especially, if he decided to reject me halfway through. I couldn't bear it. I had feelings for these men that still shook me when I thought about it. I didn't think that I loved them. I didn't think I was *capable* of loving anyone but Cassie. But I felt a lot for them. I *did* trust them, and I *did* care deeply about them. In my own way. I hoped that they knew that.

~Cassie~

I GROANED, WAKING UP, stifled under the duvet. My head was aching from taking a nap during the day. It was always the case, which was why I tried to avoid it, but my husbands were insistent.

I heard them talking in the living room, an occasional laugh and a shush.

I rolled my eyes and was about to climb out of bed when I heard Rex's heavy footfalls coming down the hallway. His biker boots thudded on the tile, that's how I knew it was him.

He tentatively stuck his head around the door.

I smiled at him and he approached me, his lips curling up briefly in a tight smile, before a tormented look crossed this face. It tore at my heart. I wished that I could ease that pain in him, but he wouldn't let me in far enough. It was something that I would have to rectify before the baby arrived. I needed to know what was going on in his head before we brought a child into this world and raised them. He kicked off his boots and then came to kneel at the side of me, taking my hand and laying his head on my chest.

I tangled my fingers into his hair and then fisted them tightly. He groaned in relief, the pain giving it to him. I knew exactly what I needed to do, and Lachlan would just have to accept it.

"Go to the playroom," I whispered to him. "Strip and wait for me."

His head shot up, the look of adoration in his eyes confirming that this was what he needed.

He stood up, but then he frowned at me.

Before he could say anything, I brought my foot out from underneath the covers and poked him in his hard stomach with my toes.

"Go," I ordered him.

He nodded and left without a word.

I climbed carefully out of the bed, but I felt fine. I got up and stalked over to the closet. I opened the secret door at the back and dragged out a flogger. I wasn't going to dress up for him. He wouldn't even notice the effort I put in. All he wanted was a release and I was going to give it to him.

"Oh no!" I heard Lachlan roar, as I assumed, he saw Rex heading to the playroom. "Not happening."

There was silence and then I heard him storm into the bedroom.

"Cas!"

"I'm fine," I reassured him, turning to him, flogger in hand.

His eyes zoomed straight to it and lit up, as I knew they would.

"If at any point, I become *un*-fine, then I will say, and you can put me to bed for however long you wish."

"Promise?" he growled at me.

"Yes," I stated and then pushed past him.

"You're doing this?" Alex muttered to me as I passed him, eyes on the other side of the living room, where the hallway to the playroom led.

"Yes. Watch, or not, I don't care, but he needs this. He needs *me*."

"You cannot have sex with him," Alex whispered desperately. "You can't..."

"I have a mouth, don't I?" I snapped, turning to him.

"Erm..." he stammered and looked to Lachlan for help.

He shrugged and, with a sense of triumph, I stalked over to the playroom. Rex had left the door ajar, so I kicked it gently open.

The sight before me had a shot of lust burning through me.

He was naked on the daybed, his head bowed, one wrist already chained to the bed, and waiting for me to cuff the other one.

I caught my breath at the beautiful sight of him. He was completely vulnerable and at my mercy. It made me want to jump on him and ride him all night long, but I knew that I shouldn't.

He kept his eyes down as I slowly approached him with my bare feet. I suddenly wished that I had made the effort to dress up for him. I was in the least sexy outfit, ever. Leggings and an oversized top. They'd told me to dress comfortably for the procedure, but maybe I'd taken it too far.

I paused, wondering what he would do if I left him there while I changed.

I decided almost straight away that it was cruel.

I felt, rather than heard, Lachlan and Alex approach. They were both barefoot as well, silent and stealthy, as they joined us in the room.

I snapped the flogger suddenly into the silence, the crack making the men jump.

"Do you want them here?" I asked Rex.

He kept his head down as he whispered, "Yes."

It was a soft croak that made my heart pound. I crept closer to him and leaned down to whisper in his ear, "Do you want them to see me punish you?"

He groaned and it stirred his cock. I wanted it inside me more than anything, but I restrained myself with effort.

"Yes," he replied.

I pulled away from him and indicated to Lachlan that he should cuff Rex's other wrist to the bed.

He did it roughly, making me gasp, but Rex took it as he always did: silent and unmoving.

I shot an annoyed look at Lachlan, but, again, he just shrugged and then stepped back.

I circled Rex, slowly, taking my time, making him wait.

I didn't know how much time passed, but the tension in the room was heavy when I finally stopped behind him and brought my arm up to crack the flogger against his back.

He braced himself against the second lash, and the third.

The fourth made him moan. The relief in it was noticeable to all of us.

"More," he rasped.

I stopped.

"You don't order me," I barked at him and went back to circling him.

He was panting.

He was so aroused it was hard not to look at him.

I flicked the flogger at Lachlan, gesturing that he kneel in front of Rex, which he did with a wicked smile.

"Take him in your mouth," I whispered to him, placing my hand on the back of his head and pushing him down.

He grunted at me. He wasn't into being submissive to me. Despite his ownership of Corsets & Collars, New York's hottest sex club, he wasn't into playing that much. But when he did, he needed to be on top. That was fine. I switched. I enjoyed it because I could take out my dominance on Rex. Alex was still very new to all of this. He watched and learned what it was all about.

I hoped that he would be ready soon and that he would decide that I could chain him up and flog him like I was doing to Rex.

I saw him come closer, watching Lachlan's mouth fill with Rex's cock. He was holding his breath. He was as turned on as much as I was by watching this.

Rex groaned and I let go of Lachlan to return to his back, flicking the flogger gently over him, teasing him, before I brought it down with more force, causing him to grunt and spurt his load into Lachlan's mouth.

"Fuck," Alex muttered.

Lachlan pulled back, a lascivious smile curving his lips up, but he didn't say anything. He moved out of the way as I came around to face Rex.

"That was naughty," I murmured. "I wanted you to come in *my* mouth." I lashed gently at his chest.

He breathed in deeply, his eyes tightly shut. "Sorry, Mistress," he mumbled.

"Hmm," I sniffed and trailed the ends of the flogger over his cock. "I expect you ready again in two minutes."

It was an order that he knew would be bordering on impossible for him.

"Yes, Mistress," he said, opening his eyes, the dark depths boring into mine, accepting the challenge.

I stepped back and admired his rock-hard body. I still nearly drooled at the angel wings tattoo adorning his lower abdomen. A much, much larger version of the ones that I had on the back of my neck.

I couldn't help but murmur to him, "You are fucking gorgeous."

Lachlan stifled his snort, knowing that I'd broken play by being Rex's wife, not his Mistress.

"Can't argue with that," Lachlan said quietly, leaning over and running his hand over Rex's shoulder blades. "You are a god."

Rex whimpered.

This entire situation had just spun out of control, but he wasn't turned off in any way. In fact, it was working to stir his cock again.

I flicked the flogger gently over his semi, watching it grow harder.

His head was bowed again, so I raised the tip and placed it under his chin to lift his head, so that I could see his eyes again.

"Are you ready?" I asked.

He nodded.

"Do you want me?"

Again, he nodded.

"Do you want them to watch me suck you off?"

"Yes," he croaked.

"Uncuff him," I demanded my other two husbands. Rex's eyes met mine in protest. "And then hold him down," I added.

"Jesus," Lachlan breathed, shifting uncomfortably in his jeans. The bulge was enormous.

I gave him a slow smile and then reached over to lower his zipper, pulling his engorged cock out and sliding my hand softly over it.

He batted my hand away and was naked in under five seconds.

I bit back my laugh at his eagerness.

I dropped the flogger and turned to Alex. He was a little slower to undress, his eyes firmly on mine.

I lowered myself to my knees and placed my hands on Rex's thighs.

"No coming until I say so," I told him.

Lachlan and Alex climbed on the daybed and shoved him backwards, hands on his shoulders, holding him in place, while I took him in my mouth.

He writhed under their hold on him as I gave him the most torturous blowjob I could. I licked him. I grazed my teeth over him, nibbled gently at his tip, before licking the tiny hole and then taking him into my mouth in a deep throat that had all of them groaning.

I repeated the process over and over again until he was almost weeping with restraint.

"Please," he eventually begged me.

I looked up from my arduous torture to see Alex and Lachlan were both jerking themselves off with their spare hands, their eyes on me.

"You don't beg," I said to Rex slowly, surprised that he had capitulated. He had never once asked for mercy.

"I wasn't talking to you," he panted, causing the other two men to look at him in surprise. It soon turned to unbridled lust as they furiously worked themselves into a frenzy over the top of Rex.

I smiled and then ducked my head back to his cock. He was like iron. I licked my lips and then proceeded to work my mouth around him, making sure to give him a fantastic blowjob as he watched the other men shoot their loads all over him with loud grunts of satisfaction.

It pushed him over the edge, and he came in my mouth shortly afterwards.

I swallowed it all and then I stood up, leaning over him, my hands on his sticky chest. I dug my nails into him. Hard. He moaned but took it as I scraped them down his chest, down his abs, leaving red scratches in their wake.

I grabbed his soft cock in my hand.

"I didn't say you could come," I growled at him.

I could feel Alex's wide eyes on me. I knew he was startled by the pain I had inflicted upon Rex, but I ignored him.

"What should your punishment be?" I asked idly.

"Whatever you decide," he murmured to me, still held down by Alex and Lachlan.

I stood up straight and stripped off.

"Cas..." Lachlan warned me, taking his hand off Rex to stop me from climbing onto him.

"Oh, I'm not going to fuck him," I commented breezily. "I want him to want it so badly and not have it."

He hissed and closed his eyes tight shut.

"You are evil, woman," Lachlan chuckled at me. "Do you want him restrained?"

"No. Leave him free. But if he touches me, break his fingers."

Alex choked back his shock at my awful words.

But that was all it was. Lachlan knew that. He knew I would rather break my own fingers than hurt Rex. Well, *really* hurt him like that.

"As you wish," Rex croaked out and proceeded to glare at me as I gave him a sexy lap dance, mindful of doctor's orders, that had him all riled up and ready to pounce on me before I got up and walked away.

Chapter 3

~Alex~

I watched Cassie walk out of the playroom with narrowed eyes. I leapt off the daybed, and with a cursory glance at Rex, I asked, "You okay?"

"Yeah," he said, sitting up. His shoulders seemed less tense, even though Cassie had worked him up to the point where it had looked like his cock was going to burst.

I nodded once and then followed our wife out of the playroom.

I found her lounging on the bed in all her naked glory, her inked nipples erect and ready to pop. It took everything that I had not to pounce on her and ravage her.

"Enjoy yourself?" I asked her instead, climbing onto the bed next to her.

"Immensely," she said with a happy sigh. "Is Rex okay?"

"He's fine," I told her.

She didn't look overly concerned as she leaned back with her eyes closed, so I assumed that was something they had done before.

"Although..."

"What?" Her eyes snapped open and dared me to say my next words.

I hesitated. I had no idea really what the deal was here, but in my way of thinking, letting him go unfulfilled was only going to exacerbate his tension.

"Speak up," she barked at me.

"Uhm, won't he be, you know, frustrated now?"

She snorted at me and closed her eyes again. "That's what makes him relax," she said.

I didn't say anything.

She opened her eyes again. "If I thought it would make him worse than he has been, I wouldn't have done it. It's what he wanted. He wanted me to take control of him. However I do that is up to me. He will do whatever I want, because that is what *he* wants from me. It's what he needs from me."

I nodded slowly, sort of getting it. It was a mental thing and I was just thinking about his body and what *I* would want to do if she did that to me. Clearly, I didn't know the half of what went on in his head. Not that I claimed to, mind you. Shady fucker.

"For the record, if you gave *me* a lap dance like that and walked away, I would have to do something about it," I said lightly.

Her eyes opened again, and she considered my words seriously. "I would never do anything that you didn't want me to," she said eventually.

I wondered if I saw that brief flash of disappointment, or if I'd imagined it.

"Rex is fine," she reassured me. "Trust me." She looked towards the door. "Tell him," she added.

I turned to see Rex and Lachlan appear in the doorway.

Rex's dark eyes bored into mine, full of curiosity. "I'm fine," he said shortly. "In fact..." He stretched his arms out and above his head, linked his hands and brought his arms down, cracking his back and neck. "Never better."

I couldn't help but glance at his raging hard-on.

It didn't go unnoticed by him *or* Lachlan.

Or Cassie.

"Oh, yes," she drawled, looking between me and Lachlan. "Didn't you two have something you wanted to do?"

I gulped, ready for it, and looked at Lachlan, but he was looking at Cassie.

"Not today. You are in no way to get involved right now and I want you so wet when he pulls his dick out of my mouth and slides it into you while I watch."

"Oh," she said faintly, licking her lips.

I breathed out, only slightly relieved, but it was marred with disappointment as well. I wanted to do this, I just needed to get on with it.

Rex looked at Cassie and she held her hand out for him. A fleeting smile passed over his face before he climbed into bed with her, drawing her gently to him.

Lachlan also climbed onto the bed when my phone, ringing in the kitchen, interrupted whatever had been about to happen next.

"I'd better get that," I muttered, receiving a glare of annoyance from my wife. She loved having us all surround her.

I slipped off the bed and picking up a pair of sweats off the chair in the corner, I headed towards the kitchen. I scooped up my phone from its usual place near the fruit bowl, when I spotted Rex's phone, keys and wallet dumped on the counter. He must've ditched them before he'd headed for the playroom.

I glanced towards the bedroom and put my phone on silent as I listened. They were talking and laughing quietly about something. I looked back at Rex's phone.

It was a betrayal of his trust to even think about snooping.

I debated with myself and then picked it up gingerly and pressed the Home button. It came as no shock to see that there was a passcode lock on it. If I expected it to be anything else than a ten-digit one, I was a fool. I would never guess it in a million years, so I threw it back on the counter and looked at my own phone. I walked over to the windows in the living room and called my assistant, Stacy, back.

While I was waiting for her to answer, Rex walked into the room.

His eyes went straight to his phone.

He must've realized that he had left it there all alone.

His eyes narrowed as he snatched it up and then brandished it at me.

"Snooping now?" he barked.

I cringed. Of course he would know it wasn't placed exactly as he'd left it.

"I was not," I stated, as I ended my call. This was far more important.

"So, everything you said downstairs was bullshit?" he hissed at me.

"No, it wasn't," I said, brandishing my own phone at him. "But whatever is going on with you affects Cassie and the baby. Don't you see that, man? It is my duty, *our* duty, to protect them and we can't do that if we aren't working together."

I swallowed as his face went so dark, I was sure he was about to punch me through the penthouse windows, to plummet to my untimely death on the sidewalk.

"I know that," he growled at me. "I just need a fucking minute to deal with this on my own."

"And what is *this*?" I hissed at him.

We were now face-to-face. It pissed me off that I had to look up slightly at him.

He knew and he used it.

He stepped even closer, glaring down at me.

"*This* is something that I need to deal with on my own first," he said in a completely normal tone, before he turned and walked over to Cassie.

How he knew she was there, and I didn't when I was facing the direction in which she appeared, would forever be a mystery.

"Everything okay in here?" she asked, the suspicion in her tone unmissable.

Lachlan came up behind her and gave us both a furious look.

"Fine," Rex said, stalking over and chucking his phone back on the counter before he crossed to Cassie. "Back to bed."

She scowled at him and then at me as he ushered her back to the bedroom.

Lachlan lingered, glaring at me.

"What?" I asked with a shrug. "I didn't do anything."

"You pissed him off. All of Cassie's work has just been undone."

"For fuck's sake," I growled, running my hand through my hair. "The world doesn't revolve around him!"

Lachlan stifled his noise of amusement. "No, it revolves around Cassie. And a pissed off Rex is not what she needs right now."

"Then we need to bring forward this timeline. We need to speak to him *tonight*."

Lachlan sighed. He knew I was right. This was festering and causing friction between us. It had to end.

"Fine," he said after a beat. "Give me a minute to think of a reason why we all need to leave Cassie."

I nodded. He could come up with that plan.

I just wanted to know what the fuck was going on with Rex and be prepared for whatever fallout I knew was headed our way.

~Lachlan~

IN THE END, I MADE a lame excuse to Cassie about where the three of us had to go. I told her, and Rex, that it was a surprise and that it needed all of us to go. She was suspicious, obviously, but she didn't question it when I told her it was for the baby.

What a dick move that was. Now we had to come back with something huge for the baby that it took three large men to go and get.

"You really are a fucking idiot," Alex moaned at me an hour later.

"I know," I said through gritted teeth as we stood in the middle of the exclusive baby shop, not far from the penthouse, looking at cribs for the baby.

Rex looked slightly enamored and was studying them all as if this was actually a thing we were supposed to be doing. Although, seeing as that is what I'd told him, as far as he knew, it *was*. Little did he know, Alex and I were about to gang up on him, intervention-style, and he was going to kick our asses to New Jersey and back.

"This one," Alex said, kicking out at the one he was standing in front of. It was small and a light brown wood.

Rex glowered at him. "Don't be ridiculous," he scoffed. "It has to be the best one and that isn't it."

Alex scowled at him and folded his arms across his chest. "Can we just get this show on the road?" he complained.

I was in agreement, but we had to play along, especially as the store assistant had just sidled over with a knowing look on her face. "Which one of you is the daddy?" she sang at us.

"We don't know," Rex commented with a frown at the crib he was standing in front of.

The woman looked like she was about to have an apoplexy, which made me snort into my hand.

"Oh," she spluttered. "I see."

Clearly, she didn't see, but who cared.

"How safe is this one?" Rex asked her, pointing at a massive affair in white with lace and bows and all sorts of fancy stuff all over it.

I tuned out, as did Alex, when the assistant went into great detail with Rex, and he asked every question he could think of regarding the safety of the crib and the adornments.

"Jesus," Alex whisper-snapped at me. "We should just get one with Kevlar all around it. Might satisfy him."

I looked back at Rex, who was giving the woman the third degree now, and chuckled. He was spectacular. "He is taking this seriously, because he doesn't know it was a ploy. We are going to seriously piss him off when we gang up on him later."

Alex sighed and also looked over at Rex. "Yeah. But we're doing the right thing. Aren't we?"

His worried look back at me made me feel a rush of love for him. He could be the most confident man in the room when he wanted to be, but this vulnerable side of him was very attractive. I knew that it drew Cassie in hook, line and sinker, and I understood why.

"Don't second guess yourself," I said, slapping him on the back. "Yes, we are doing the right thing. He needs to let us in. He needs to learn how to do that *now*."

He nodded and then we were interrupted by Rex storming over to us and giving us ferocious glares. "Don't you even care about this?" he demanded.

"Of course, we do," I said, "But you are doing a great job. We trust you." I gave him a bright smile.

He growled at me, knowing what I had done there. "We'll take it," he spat out at the woman. She looked plain terrified now, but that magnificent man had caught the attention of every other person in the store. Man and woman. All eyes were on him as we made our way to the checkout.

The women were practically drooling on their shoes and the men were puffing themselves up, trying to compete with him.

He didn't notice a damn thing.

It made me love him even more.

We waited at the checkout while Alex paid an exorbitant amount that made his eyes water. But he was the one that pulled his wallet out first.

Sucker.

"How are we going to fit this in the elevator?" Alex asked. "I don't fancy carrying it up a thousand flights of stairs."

"Hmm, one of us will have to go up, then we'll send the crib up and then the other two will follow, yeah?" I said, thinking that was an excellent plan.

The other two men nodded in agreement and then we all stared at the woman as she came out of the back, pushing a very large, flat-ish box towards us, while another woman had her arms full of a bundled-up package.

I blinked at the box.

That couldn't be it. Could it?

I looked back at the crib that Rex had wanted on the shop floor and then back at the box, as did the other two men.

We all groaned in unison.

We had to build the fucking thing ourselves.

"Can't we have that one?" Alex was bold enough to ask, pointing at the display model, I supposed it was.

The woman gave him a sickly-sweet smile. "No," she said and shoved the box in his direction.

Her friend stifled her laughter into the bundle, which I assumed was the lacy, bow-ridden bedding.

"Great, just great," he mumbled, giving me a death stare.

Rex, of course, was already hauling the humongous box towards him, but soon realizing that even he was going to need help with it.

With a sigh, I shoved Alex towards it.

"Oh, no," he said, shaking his head. "I paid."

"Fine," I grumbled and helped Rex pick up the box. "You get the bow-y bundle of lace."

I choked back my laugh at his face, so did Rex, as we headed for the door.

It was all so easy again after the stress of the last few hours, but I knew we had to ruin it.

Alex was right. It had to be done tonight.

"So," I started as we maneuvered out of the shop door. "You gonna come clean?"

"About what?" Rex snarled, glaring at me over the box I was suddenly glad was in between us. He looked fucking mad.

"About whatever it is that is bugging you," Alex piped up from behind the safety of his soft bedding bundle.

"We already talked about this," Rex stated with finality, walking backwards, but then stopping. "Sideways on," he added.

I agreed.

We turned and didn't care how much sidewalk we were taking up. It was easier this way.

"That was before you nearly hit me earlier," Alex said, falling into step next to me.

"I wasn't going to hit you," Rex sniped, and then heaved such a massive sigh, I suddenly felt really bad for him. Whatever it was, he didn't want to be pushed into telling us. I was about to suggest to Alex that we drop it, when Rex said, "Look, if I tell you, do you promise to just let me handle it?"

"Yes," Alex said immediately.

"Yes." I had no choice but to agree, now that Alex had. The whole point of this was to *help* him with it.

"Someone has been texting me saying that they know about my past employment," he said quietly. "They are threatening to tell Cassie everything."

I stopped walking, jarring him to a stop as well. Alex walked on for a few paces, before he realized we weren't next to him anymore. He turned and dropped the bundle lower, so he could look at Rex.

"We can't let that happen," I said fiercely, dropping the box, so full of rage suddenly, that I actually saw red.

"Obviously," Rex commented. "She can never find out about what I used to do. It would destroy her, and me along with it."

My heart lurched at his words. If she turned from him, it would kill him. We couldn't let that happen. Not ever.

"What do they want? Money? Revenge? What is it all about?" Alex asked the practical questions.

"They want something from me, but, so far, they've been coy about revealing what," Rex replied.

"So, they are trying to make you paranoid enough to give it to them? Whatever it is?" Alex asked.

Rex shrugged but said nothing.

"No leads?" I asked.

"None. Yet."

"Have they only contacted you by text?"

"So far," he said, but I didn't believe him.

"What aren't you saying?" Alex asked, also picking up on the vibe.

Rex sighed again. "I've seen them watching me. Just once. Earlier."

"Fuckers!" I spit out. "On your own, or with Cassie?"

"On my own. You know I would die protecting her!" he lashed out at me.

"Let's hope it doesn't come to that," I muttered back and picked up my side of the box.

He picked up his side and we walked back to the penthouse in a somber silence that only grew with each step we took.

Chapter 4

~Cassie~

Four months had passed since my husbands had brought home the crib and it had yet to be built.

I was huge, due in less than a month.

So, there was only one thing for it.

I had to build it myself.

I opened the box and laid all the bits and pieces out. I got the instructions and sat down in the middle of the floor to look at them.

It seemed fairly simple, but the men had been putting it off. We had been so busy with one thing and another, this had gotten overlooked.

I was thankful that my parents had decided to take an extended vacation in Europe seven weeks ago, so they hadn't been around to annoy me. To my horror, I had found my mother snooping around our penthouse a couple of days after I'd gone in for the amnio. I'd come in from work early, having felt like crap and I'd found her in our bedroom. My first thought had gone straight to the secret cupboard at the back of my closet, but it hadn't looked like she'd found it. I hadn't known what she'd been looking for.

Anyway, Rex had hit the roof when I'd told my husbands about it, unsurprisingly, and he'd forbidden my mother entry into our apartment again. I'd agreed readily and then she'd gone away, so I hadn't seen her, or my father, in ages, to my relief.

"Hey," Rex said from the doorway.

I looked up with a smile.

"You shouldn't be doing that," he added with a frown, coming into the room and sitting down next to me.

"Who else is going to do it?" I replied sassily.

He snorted. "Yeah, we've passed the buck on this one. We are terrible husbands."

I gave him a gentle look and reached up to cup his face. "No, you are the best husbands a girl could ask for."

He returned my look and leaned in to kiss me. I got swept up in it, as he did, and soon we were clawing at each other's clothes.

Breathlessly, I pulled away, much to his disappointment.

They had all tried, repeatedly, to get me on my own to have sex just as two, but I wasn't going for it. We were in this relationship together. We made love *together*. It was as simple as that for me.

He sighed, but I knew he would be okay. Since I'd started dominating him completely, he had relaxed so much more than I'd ever seen him. He clearly wasn't into switching like he'd made out in the beginning. He'd done that for me, I was sure. He wanted to be submissive to me and that suited me. When I wanted to be tied up and whipped, Lachlan would be there to do it after the baby was born.

Alex *still* hadn't ventured very far into our playtime, but he was getting closer. It'd been difficult with my advancing pregnancy. I'd had complications a few months ago and the doctor had told us to limit our sex life. Clearly, he was under the impression that I had three times as much sex as the average girl. But just because I had three men, didn't mean that it was *more* sex. Just that it went on longer and in all three of my holes at the same time. But try explaining that to your OBGYN and his nurse.

However, the men had taken him at his word and had refused to do any more than a quick in and out. It was bordering on offensive at that point.

Not to mention, this 'keeping it to a minimum' was driving all of us nuts. Except Rex. He was quite happy with his end of the bargain.

Lucky fucker.

As soon as the baby was born, and I had the go-ahead, my men were fucking in for it. I needed to let loose in the worst way. Whips, chains, my best Domme outfit, blindfolds, masks, heels with killer spikes, the fucking lot.

Soon.

I couldn't fucking wait.

"I love you," I murmured to Rex, so that he knew I wasn't rejecting him exactly.

"I love you, Cassie. But I want time on our own together. They do too. We can work something out."

It was the first time one of them had actually said it out loud to my face. Why didn't it surprise me that it was Rex? The others had probably made him, seeing as he was the most alpha out of a group of alpha males.

But I wasn't budging.

I shook my head and then went back to fitting the crib together. He helped, silently, and soon, it was all pieced together.

Rex heaved it into place while I went to fetch the bedding from the closet.

A sudden pain ripped through me, making me gasp, but it was gone just as quickly as it came.

Rex was on me in the next breath. "Are you okay?"

"Fine," I said. "Braxton Hicks."

He nodded at me, but I could tell he wasn't convinced. I needed to distract him from his worry.

I drew him to me and held him close. His strong arms went around me. I felt safe and loved.

"Cassie," he started, but I kissed him, getting as close to him as the bump would let me.

I thought he was starting to accept that I was okay, when it all got shot to hell and back. Another contraction ripped through me, surprising me with its sudden vehemence.

"Ahhh," I groaned, panting. I gripped Rex's arms, digging my nails into him.

"Cassie," he said, his tone perfectly calm. "Let's get you to the hospital."

I nodded and he led me out of the nursery. He stabbed the elevator button and then said, "I'll get your bag."

He disappeared as I circled my bump with my arm. I was worried. It was a bit too early.

The elevator doors slid open and I stepped inside, leaning on the doors to stop them from closing, while I waited for Rex. He reappeared with my hospital bag, packed only yesterday, and took me in his free arm to hold me close.

"Breathe," he muttered to me.

"Call Lachlan and Alex!" I cried suddenly. "I need them with us."

He nodded and pulled his phone out as we stepped out of the elevator and headed for the SUV. He helped me in and closed the door as he started talking. He was furious as he climbed into the driver's seat.

"What?" I asked in dread.

"Lachlan is on his way, but he reminded me that Alex is upstate in meetings all day. He's going to keep trying him."

"No!" I shouted. That wasn't news I wanted. I needed Alex there. I needed all of them.

"Don't stress," he said. "Everything will be fine."

"No, it won't if Alex misses this!"

"We don't even know what this is yet," he responded to my panic with a soothing tone. "It might be nothing."

I grunted as another contraction hit me, glaring at my husband for his stupid man-words. "Tell that to my uterus," I growled.

He threw me a worried look, which quickly turned to a bland expression in typical Rex fashion.

"What can I do?" he asked seriously.

I gave him a tight smile. He was a problem solver, but this wasn't something he could help me with.

"Just get me to the hospital. Soon," I gritted out, and then we fell into silence.

As I sat there, staring out of the car window, I hoped and prayed that Lach could get a hold of Alex. I'd remembered him telling us at breakfast that he was out all day today. Rex must've forgotten, which was why he was angry when he'd got into the car. I couldn't do this without all of my husbands. I knew it was the real deal. I could feel it.

"Fuck," I moaned, wishing we could hurry the fuck up.

Rex slammed his foot down, to my relief, and soon we were at the hospital. Lachlan was pacing up and down outside, waiting for us, so Rex pulled up and let me out into Lachlan's care while he parked.

"Let's get you inside," Lachlan ventured.

"We wait for him," I snarled. "And where the fuck is Alex?"

"I've tried," he replied desperately. "It keeps going to voicemail."

"Leave a mess..." I roared.

"I have!" he interrupted, snapping back at me, but then gave me an apologetic look and took my hand. "I have. Several of them."

"Thanks," I muttered. "When all of this is over, I promise you can get to do that thing you want to do."

His eyes lit up and he grinned at me. "Thank *fuck*. Ever since he mentioned it, I have been going nuts thinking about it. I didn't think it would ever happen at this rate."

"Sorry," I muttered back, my cheeks going pink. "I know things have been stressful for you over the last few months. I want it to be perfect for you, for us, and this situation hasn't been. I'm frustrated too. I need a good fuck like you have no idea, not this gentle crap you've all been putting me through lately."

He snorted with mirth and I chuckled too, but then the pain wiped it all away and I was back to being grim and pissed off.

Lachlan had not taken it well when I'd told him and Alex to put a pin in their evolving relationship. I'd thought at one point that he was going to snap and tell me to go and fuck myself, but they have stuck to it. I had my reasons. I needed to watch it and then have them both ravage me. It was selfish and I felt like a bitch at the time, but I wanted it how I wanted it. Not 'mind the bump' and 'be careful' but hot, savage sex that ended up with us devouring each other entirely. I wanted the pain that came with such brutal sex and it wasn't going to happen with me being pregnant.

He ducked his head from his towering height advantage and kissed me chastely. "I can't wait," he murmured, and then grabbed me as another contraction tore its way through me.

"Inside. Now," he demanded, leading me in the direction of the door.

Rex caught up with us quickly and commandeered a wheelchair from a passing nurse to her loud protest, but he didn't care. He glared at her and she shut it pretty quickly. I hid my smile. He had such a menacing air to anyone who didn't know him, but he was like a soft teddy bear with me and my other husbands. I loved him so much.

I took his hand and kissed it as he helped me sit, and then I was off at racing-car speed to the maternity unit, Lachlan jogging to keep up with us, still desperately trying to get a hold of Alex.

~Rex~

WE HURRIED TO THE MATERNITY unit, with Cassie growling like a rabid dog. Something wasn't right. I'd read the books. It was supposed to be a gradual thing and not this early. Her contractions were coming fast, and I was worried. Lachlan was remaining calm. It was his thing. He very rarely got riled up.

I stayed with her while he got our wife all booked in and then we were kicked out while she got changed and the doctor examined her. I wanted to stay, I needed to make sure she was okay, that the baby was okay, but she told us to fuck off. That was a direct quote.

I loved Cassie like no other person on earth. She was feisty and a fighter. I knew deep down that she could take care of herself, but I worried about her every second of every day. I knew it irritated her sometimes when I got overbearing, but I couldn't help it. If anything happened to her, I wouldn't be able to go on. She had given me something to live for and I needed her to breathe. Especially in the last few months where she had been taking complete control over me. It was what I'd always wanted. I couldn't bear to hurt her in any way. It killed me when she wanted me to give her that pain. Being her submissive is what I wanted. I had never felt quite so relieved, quite so light in all of my time on this planet. I was dreading her wanting to go back to what we usually did. I didn't want to. I needed to mention it to Lachlan. See if he would give her the pain she craved and leave me out of it. I couldn't see Alex stepping in to fulfill that desire for her anytime soon. He was skeptical. He watched everything with a hawk-eye, but never ventured into the play.

"Hello, boys," a sarcastic voice drawled from behind me.

I grimaced and turned, not bothering to adjust my features.

"Suzanne," I sneered. "Back from Europe so soon?"

"Hmm," she sniffed, dismissing me and finding Lachlan to cozy up to instead. It made me sick. Why he indulged her was a mystery. One I should probably get to the bottom of. I watched them air kiss, her hands running up his chest, before he gently pushed her away. She lingered, though, making it obvious she fancied the fuck out of him.

"How did you know to come?" I snarled at her.

She turned to me, her eyes flashing. "I was with my mother when Lachlan called. I came straight over, of course."

"Of course," I drawled back, matching her sarcastic tone.

It hadn't escaped my notice that the threats against me had stopped as soon as Suzanne and Damien had disappeared onto their yacht in the South of France. Was it a coincidence or not? That had yet to be determined. I was sure that Teddy wouldn't snitch on me, he had just as much to lose if he did, but if it *was* Suzanne, how else could she have found out about my past? I would know for sure, if the threats started up again now that she was back.

Her green eyes, so much like her daughter's, bored into mine, but my gaze was unflinching. Something she clearly wasn't used to. She raised her perfect eyebrow at me, the sneer deepening on her face.

"Where is Alex?" she asked, turning back to Lachlan.

"Work," he replied. "In fact, I need to try him again." He took his phone out of his pocket and started to dial.

Great. That left me and Suzanne to glare at each other.

I folded my arms across my chest as she sidled over to the nurse's station. "When can I go in?" she barked at the nurse on duty. "I am her mother."

"When Cassie says you can," I answered for the nurse, who shot me a relieved look.

"Humph," Suzanne muttered. "Well, it doesn't surprise me that she wants a bit of privacy. I am sure it's in short supply, what with your...*living arrangement*. Besides, I think you men should stay out here. It will be too crowded in there." She lifted her nose up in the air in obvious distaste.

"Why are you even here?" I asked her, needing to know why she was bothering if she found her daughter's life so unsavory. "And it's not a 'living arrangement'. We are married."

"Yes, I am aware, even though I wasn't invited to the big event," she commented and then gave me a curious look as she came closer. I stood my ground, even though I wanted to back away. I was sure that whatever was about to come out of her mouth was going to be big and hurtful in that veiled way she had perfected. "I don't understand it, though. I mean, you men are all married to *her*, but what about each other?"

I drew in a deep breath. If she called us 'you men' one more time I would strike her. I had no qualms in that area. I had taken my hand to plenty of women in the past, some far less deserving than this bitch.

She did have a point, though, when I looked past the disdain. Alex, Lachlan and I had no commitment to each other. I wondered why that was. Cassie was the center of our relationship, but, perhaps, something to solidify us together wouldn't be such a bad idea. She smirked at me as I stayed silent. She thought she'd gotten the better of me, but it was, in fact, the opposite. I planned to have a talk with Cassie about that soon. I wondered what she would make of it. I wondered what the other men would think.

"We are all committed to Cassandra and each other," I told her anyway, even though I knew it would send another smirk in my direction.

I wasn't wrong.

"Sure," she said and turned from me, as Lachlan returned from his phone call.

"Finally spoke to him. He is already on his way," he said.

"Oh, you should have said," Suzanne replied, running her hand up his arm. "I would've sent the helicopter."

I glared at her. Why hadn't she mentioned that before Alex got on the road? I shook my head at her and her false offer.

Lachlan grimaced at her. He tried to make it a smile, but I could see how tense he was.

"Boys!" a loud voice boomed behind us and we turned to look at the newcomer. Now I didn't have a problem with this part of Cassie's family. Her grandfather, William, was a force to be reckoned with, even in his advanced years, and her grandmother, Ruby, was a kind and generous woman. They both loved Cassie, which was more than could be said of her own parents.

"Where are we at?"

"Not sure," Lachlan said, stepping forward to shake William's hand, then bending down to give Ruby a kiss on her cheek. "We're still waiting."

"Where's Alex?" William demanded, his ice blue eyes scoping out the waiting area.

"Stuck upstate," Lachlan gritted out. "He's on his way."

William's eyes landed on me. I nodded once at him and he nodded back. It was our way and he accepted it. I did step forward to give Ruby a light kiss on her cheek. It was unnatural for me, but she'd always insisted on it. It'd become easier for me to initiate the contact, than to have her swoop in on me unprepared.

She gave me a glowing smile and patted my arm.

"Fuck's sake," William growled. "Why didn't anyone say? We would have sent the helicopter."

I resisted the urge to roll my eyes, but at least *William's* offer was genuine.

Lachlan took him at his word, though, and soon they had arranged a place for Alex to pull up where the chopper would land and pick him up.

That life wasn't for me. I didn't know how the other men coped with it. I was just glad that Cassie preferred to keep things as simple as her station in life allowed her.

Suzanne watched all of this with a growing sense of annoyance. She felt my eyes on her and turned to look at me, not even bothering to cover it up.

Silence fell as the nurse hurried towards us. Behind her, we could see Cassie being wheeled off on a bed in a hurry. Lachlan and I stepped forward, nearly knocking the nurse over to get to our wife.

"Cassie!" I called out to her, but she was already through the double doors. I spun around and approached the nurse, my fists clenched. If they did anything to her, or the baby, I would kill them. I felt Lachlan's hand on my arm, and it brought my swimming head back to what the nurse was hurriedly saying to us.

All I got was "complications", "surgery", "C-Section" and "consent form".

"Why didn't Cassie sign it?" I gripped the nurse's arm.

She grimaced in pain, but I kept it there until she answered me, her words sending my heart plummeting.

"She wasn't able to. She lost a lot of blood..."

I let go and stumbled back from her. My stomach clenched into a tight ball. I felt sick. If anything happened to her...

"She'll be okay," Lachlan murmured to me, taking me by the elbow and leading me away from Cassie's family. "She's strong and she won't let anything happen to herself, or the baby."

I blinked, my entire being going numb.

"Well, at least this is moving forward quickly," Suzanne said, looking at her watch and then clicking her fingers at Derek, her asshole henchman. He handed her a small hip flask that she took a tiny sip out of before she handed it back to him. "Tell the Butlers I should be able to make the dinner after all," she told him, and then, "Hopefully this baby will come out looking like one of you, so we can *finally* find out who the father is."

I took a step forward, intending to throttle the life out of her. But, again, Lachlan stopped me.

"Ignore her," he murmured to me and turned me to face the other way. "We have bigger things to worry about than that bitch and her comments. I hope Alex hurries the fuck up now," he added under his breath.

I clenched and unclenched my fists, trying to get the blood flowing again. It felt like ice in my veins.

Cassie is a fighter. She'll be okay.

I kept telling myself that, hoping that it was true.

Only then did the reality of the situation sink in.

We were having a baby. A child that belonged to one of us, but that we would all love unconditionally.

I hoped even more then, that it wasn't mine.

I felt the panic set in again.

The darkness that I had been able to shove aside since Cassie had started to truly give me everything that I'd needed to survive, started to creep back over me.

I gulped.

Lachlan frowned at me, gripping my elbow tighter and steering me towards a hard, plastic chair. He shoved me down and sat next to me.

"Everything will be fine," he murmured, taking my hand and lacing our fingers together.

I felt Suzanne's eyes on us, but I didn't give her the satisfaction of pulling away.

Lachlan must've felt it too, because he gripped me tighter, bringing my hand up to his lips to kiss lightly, before he let go.

"Say it," I croaked out, needing to hear it now more than ever.

He knew exactly what I wanted from him and he gave it to me.

"I love you," he whispered.

I closed my eyes and controlled my breathing. I wanted to say it back to him, but I just couldn't get the words out, because I wasn't sure if I'd really mean them.

I opened my eyes and looked into his brown eyes that were sparkling mischievously. He knew my inner debate, but he didn't push it. He wouldn't. I could count on him not to.

Perhaps it was that knowledge that made me lean over and kiss his lips, to his surprise.

I heard Suzanne splutter and choke on her martini, or whatever the hell was in that hip flask, but I didn't care.

"Cassie will be fine and so will the baby," he said to me earnestly when I pulled back. "And when we are all settled back home, safe and well, you can finish what you just started."

"Get me through the next few hours first," I murmured to him, hoping it didn't sound like I was begging.

"Count on it," he replied.

Then there was much ruckus, as apparently, a helicopter had landed on the roof without authorization, which signified the arrival of Alex, to mine and Lachlan's relief.

Chapter 5

~Cassie~

I woke up with a start and tried to sit up. A firm hand on my shoulder stopped me.

"Easy there," Lachlan said.

His face swam into view, smiling at me. "Hi," he added.

I brushed my hair out of my face and swallowed. My mouth was as dry as dust. I blinked and then grabbed him by his shirt front as everything came rushing back to me. Getting changed, the doctor coming in, and then so much blood gushing from between my legs.

"The baby!" I snarled at him.

"She's just fine," he said soothingly, taking my hand in his and pulling it off his shirt. He looked over to the opposite corner where Alex was cradling a blanketed bundle with a look of sweet awe on his face.

"She?" I croaked, relief flooding me.

"Yes, baby Ruby," Alex said with a big beam that Lachlan also gave me as he helped me to sit up. I felt like I'd had my insides ripped out.

"Gimme!" I growled at my husband, annoyed that he was hogging my daughter. My daughter. My breath caught in my throat as he placed her gently in my outstretched arms.

"Oh, she's beautiful!" I exclaimed, searching her face for signs of her daddy. I couldn't help myself. I was sure the men had all done the exact same thing secretly.

"She looks just like you," Lachlan said, cupping her head and giving her a soft kiss. It melted my heart.

I gave him a big smile and then looked at Rex squashed into the furthest corner away from me.

He looked terrified.

"I'm okay," I said to him, holding my hand out for him. He came to me instantly, warily, as if I might suddenly disappear from his sight.

He gripped my hand tightly, making it go numb.

I wanted to ask him if he'd held her yet, but my Grandma popped her head around the door.

"Oh, you're up!" she cried and came into the room. "Thank you, dear," she added to Lachlan, who'd got up out of the only chair to offer it to her. She gazed longingly at my daughter and, after a moment's hesitation, I handed her over. I watched, with a smile, as she cooed at and kissed her namesake. It was very sweet.

I was just about to ask what the hell happened to me, when a nurse bustled in with a clipboard and a terse smile.

"Ms. Bellingham," she said.

"Wait," I interrupted, putting my hand up. "What happened? I don't remember anything."

She frowned at me. "The doctor explained this to you in recovery."

I shook my head. I'd been in and out, I didn't remember anything at all.

"Hm, okay," she said and examined her chart. "It appears that there were complications with your delivery, a placental abruption, and you were rushed to surgery. The baby was delivered by Caesarean section. You lost a lot of blood and we gave you a transfusion, as was agreed on your consent form. Luckily, they didn't need to remove your uterus as the bleeding was contained."

I spluttered at that comment. "What?" I barked at her. "Was that even an option?"

She glared at me for apparently defying her. "Your mother agreed to it on the consent form if it was needed."

"What?" I demanded, my blood pressure shooting through the roof and making me lightheaded.

"Your mother?" Alex suddenly spat out at me. It was one of the only times I'd heard such venom in his voice. "Why did your mother sign it? Why didn't one of you?" He glared at Rex and Lachlan.

"We didn't get the option to," Lachlan stammered.

"If I may," Grandma interrupted. "Cassie's mother has Power of Attorney over her, which includes Medical Power of Attorney, until she turns twenty-five and inherits the rest of her trust."

Alex's eyes became even more furious. "The *rest* of your trust? I thought you had it all."

"Just a third," I squeaked. "I get the rest when I'm twenty-five. I didn't know that Mother had the Power of Attorney. I thought it was Granddaddy." I glared at my grandmother.

"Oh, no, dear. He can't do it. It had to go to your mother." She just shrugged as if it was no big deal. I should've paid more attention to it, but it had never concerned me. Anytime I'd dealt with the trust, I'd gone to my grandfather. I bit my lip in consternation.

"Well, you can get rid of that right now!" Alex practically shouted at me. "How dare she have that kind of control over you, over us! If this baby doesn't turn out to be mine, Cassandra, I want to conceive a baby with you. I'm sorry if that isn't something that you want to hear and, yes, we should discuss it, but it is what I want. And Suzanne swoops in here and potentially takes that away without a thought to us. No fucking way." His cheeks had gone bright red and he was panting.

He threw my grandmother an apologetic look for swearing, but then his gaze went hard again at me.

I gave it back. This isn't my fucking fault, after all.

He backed down, surprisingly. I thought he'd been all guns blazing. It brought delicious submission thoughts to mind at the most inappropriate moment known to man.

"I'm not angry at you," he said, taking my hand. "But you should have told us this. It matters, Cassie."

"I know," I wailed at him. "But I didn't know it was her. I don't want her having control over my trust, or my life. Grandma, we need to change it." I looked over at her and she bit her lip.

"I will talk to William," she said eventually. She handed me baby Ruby back and stood up. "I'll go now."

She exited quickly, not that I blamed her. This was clearly a sore spot with at least one of my husbands. I dared not even look at Rex yet. I chose instead to look at Lachlan. He looked grim, but not shocked. He knew more than Alex or Rex about trust funds and their complications.

I pursed my lips at him and shuffled uncomfortably to look back at Alex. "I hear what you're saying, and I accept it. I will get my mother removed as my Power of Attorney. About another baby..."

"We don't have to discuss that now," Lachlan stepped in, taking back his chair and holding my hand lightly. "You've just had major surgery, Cassie, not to mention, a massive trauma. You need to rest and not have any stress."

The tears welled up. I couldn't help it. "I want to go home," I sobbed. I couldn't even lean forward to hug him. It hurt too much. I was an active person, so this was going to be really difficult. I was trying not to even think about the scar it would leave. That made me sob even harder.

It brought all of my men to me, awkwardly hugging me carefully, so as not to crush the baby, or my delicate body.

I cried harder.

"I'm sorry," Alex murmured to me as the nurse bustled back in and stopped dead to see us all in a group hug.

She stared at us, until Rex glared at her and she backed off, dropping her eyes as she came further into the room with pain killers and her stupid chart.

"We will talk about this later," I promised them and then asked them to leave. I was getting overwhelmed and I wanted a minute with my baby. I needed to look at her properly. Take in all of her tiny features, feed her and change her and...

"It's time for you to get up," the nurse interrupted my thoughts.

"Excuse me?" I asked her. I could barely move, and she wanted me to stand up? What the fuck?

Her look turned sympathetic for all of a moment, before she became brusque again. "I'll help you," she said and took the sleeping Ruby off me, placed her in the plastic crib on wheels, and then proceeded to boss me about for the next half an hour, until I was unsteadily and painfully on my feet, showered, dressed, and back in bed ready to feed my baby for the first time.

~Lachlan~

"YOU'RE A FIRST-CLASS dick," I spat out at Alex, only half meaning it. But he needed to know that his words to Cassie had been harsh. She'd just been through a traumatic situation. Cut open, a baby pulled out of her, sewn up, and pumped full of blood and drugs.

"I know," he muttered back, running his hand through his hair.

I sighed.

"Just the thought of that...*woman* having control of Cassie like that really scared me and I just blurted it all out."

"I know. We were here, we should've paid more attention."

We both looked at Rex. He was silent and brooding in the small plastic chair outside of Cassie's room. We had been out here for a while now and he hadn't said a word.

"You okay?" I asked him, sitting down next to him.

"Hmm," he said and looked up at us. "Come with me."

He got up and started to walk away, so, after a quick glance at each other, Alex and I followed him. He led us to an empty cubicle a short way away and pulled the curtain closed. He turned and folded his arms across his chest, his shoulders hunched.

"What is it?" Alex whispered, the tension getting to him. He was anxious. His hair was sticking up on end, he had run his hand through it that many times.

It was pretty damn hot.

Rex grimaced at him. He did hate it when he was pressured into talking. He much preferred to do things in his own time, his own way.

"I find it one hell of a coincidence that, since Suzanne arrived back home, the threats have started up again," he growled at us in a low tone that would have sent chills of fear down my spine, if I didn't love him so much. As it was, it just fucking turned me on. I felt my cock stand to attention and cleared my throat as I tried to get it to go down.

I was so horny all of the time now. Having to be gentle with Cassie had done nothing to calm the raging lust in me that I had for that woman, or these two men. We hadn't been able to take her all at once for months, instead, taking it in turns. Which meant I'd lost out two thirds of the time. Time that wasn't all that often, as we were all so scared of hurting her and the baby.

I blinked as he glared at me and my lack of a response to his statement.

Wait...

"Are you saying that you think it's *Suzanne,* that's threatening you?" I asked as Alex gaped at him.

"Yes," he hissed. "I might have had an inkling when she went away, and the threats stopped. I didn't share it, because it was unfounded and just a hunch. But now...?" He took his phone out and brandished it at us, waving it vigorously in the air.

I snatched it off him and looked down at it.

He gave me a sardonic look and snatched it back, unlocked it, and handed it to me.

"So mistrustful," I murmured to him. "You know *my* passcode."

"Only because you insisted on giving it to me," he pointed out.

Alex snorted as he remembered that particularly painful conversation. Rex could be so stubborn and unconcerned about shit like that sometimes. To me, it was important. It showed both of them, and Cassie, that I had no secrets, nothing to hide, and they were free to go through my phone if the need arose. I wouldn't hold it against them.

Alex had agreed and had also given up the goods, but not Rex, and we hadn't pushed him. We'd just hoped that, in time, he would trust us enough.

I glared down at the message sent from an unknown number:

Time is running out. I will tell Cassandra everything unless you give me what I want.

"What do they want?" I asked.

He sighed. "I still don't know. I wish they would get it over with. As soon as they reveal themselves, I can do something about it." His tone, while so sexy before, had turned ominous and I wasn't the only one who caught it.

Alex cleared his throat. "What does that mean?" he croaked out.

Rex gave him a look that would kill a houseplant. "Do you really want me to spell it out?"

"Yes," I interrupted before Alex got in way over his head. I knew how to handle killer Rex. I had dealt with him in the past. Okay, so I hadn't known what he was back then, but I knew his dark side, more than anyone. I had seen the damage he could cause when he was on one of his dark benders. I shuddered as the memories of several trips to the E.R. with his sex victims in tow, caught up in the wrong place at the wrong time with the wrong man, resurfaced like the proverbial bad penny.

He turned those black eyes to me. They were cold and dead, just like they used to be before Cassie had come into his life. "You know what I am capable of," he stated. "I will not let anyone threaten me, or Cassie."

"We have a baby to consider now," I reminded him, hoping that would soften his killer instinct.

It might have.

Who knew?

His face remained exactly the same.

"Even more reason to take out this threat. As soon as possible," he answered.

"You really think it's Cassie's mother?" Alex asked into the silence that fell.

"It tracks," Rex said shortly. "Plus, it is obvious that she hates me. She must know about my past. Teddy must've told Damien," he added thoughtfully, his darkness retreating slightly at the conundrum.

"She doesn't hate you," Alex said, trying to placate him.

Rex choked back a noise that could've been a laugh. It was hard to tell. "I don't really care," he drawled. "I can't stand that bitch, so if I have a reason to get her out of our lives, then even better."

"Let's just back up a bit," I said, stepping in again. "You can't seriously be talking about taking Suzanne out, can you? Cassie would be hurt. She is *still* her mother, even after all the shit she has put her through. And, God forbid, she found out that it was *you*," I added with a whisper.

His withering gaze did nothing to get rid of my hard-on. "I know how to cover my tracks. I have been outed by Teddy. He was responsible for *your* knowledge, after all." The challenge came head on, hands on hips, black eyes hard.

"We don't know anything yet," Alex interrupted us, just in the nick of time. Rex was close to losing it on my ass. I had never had that kind of tussle with him, but I was pretty sure his complete ruthlessness would give him the edge on an, otherwise, even fight.

"It might be a coincidence for all we know. Or, a set-up, even." He landed on that with a triumphant gleam in his eye.

"You've been watching too much TV," Rex said scathingly.

"Not necessarily," I said, playing Devil's Advocate. "Alex might have a point."

"So might I," Rex countered. "That woman is a first-class bitch. Why do you find it so hard to believe that she would stoop to this?" His eyes flashed dangerously. "Or, don't you want to believe it, because you are secretly having it off with her?"

His words hit me in the pit of my stomach like a sledge-hammer.

Alex's sharp intake of breath was all I heard as I saw red.

"How dare you!" I hissed at him, bunching my fist and throwing the punch, before I knew what I was doing.

It landed right on his nose, breaking it, blood gushing down his face.

"Whoa!" Alex said, stepping in between us, before Rex got over his shock enough to flatten me. "What are we doing here? That cunt does not come between us. Back to your corners. Now."

It was only his use of the 'c' word that brought me back to my senses. It was said with purpose and it worked. We both looked at him in surprise at his vile verbiage. He hated that word. We both knew it. I wasn't a fan of it either, but he'd hit the nail on the head, there was no denying it.

"Well?" Rex snarled at me, holding his nose, but not advancing any further. "I see her flirting with you every time she is within sniffing distance, and you give it back to her as good as you get."

I gritted my teeth. The thought of it made me sick to my stomach. That he actually thought that about me, was even worse.

"I love my wife," I said quietly. "It hurts me that you think I am such a disgusting asshole that I would fuck my mother-in-law."

"Just telling it like I see it," he growled back.

"This is getting us nowhere," Alex interrupted again. "Rex, he would never do that. You know that."

"Humph," he muttered and turned his back to us.

"We cannot divide now," Alex continued. "We just had a baby. Cassie is in turmoil and overwhelmed with it all. We need to stop this shit and be there for her and the baby. Right now. This is a non-issue, as far as I am concerned. I know Lachlan wouldn't do anything with Suzanne. He's a big flirt, we all know that..."

"Hey!" I growled at him.

He just shrugged and carried on, "We need that. We need at least one of us to keep on her good side, because, while I may not think she is a threatening stalker, she sure as shit is a snake and she is up to something."

I had to agree with that. She had been acting shifty around us ever since she'd found out about our relationship with her daughter, which had also been the same day she'd found out Cassie had been expecting a baby that belonged to one of us.

"He's right," I said grudgingly. "Sorry I hit you."

"*Not* forgiven," Rex snarled as he turned back around, looking so much of a mess, it made me want to kiss him. "But I agree with your assessment," he added to Alex. "I will keep an eye on her, but if *I* turn out to be right, then I deal with it *my* way. Now, if you will excuse me, I need to get my nose fixed."

He gave me a death stare and then, shoving the curtain aside, he stalked off.

I watched him go. He was seriously pissed with me. Probably because I'd gotten the jump on him. I was sure not many men could say that. He would get over it.

"I'm going back to Cassie," I told Alex. "Whether she wants me there, or not, I need to be near her."

"Same," he said, and we headed off back to the room. I probably wasn't the only one wondering what the hell we were going to tell Cassie about Rex's absence *and* his broken nose when he finally reappeared.

Chapter 6

~Alex~

Cassie was sleeping when Lachlan and I arrived back in the room. She was pale with dark circles under her eyes. I couldn't help but bend down to kiss her lips, hoping that I didn't wake her.

The baby was nowhere in sight, so we both assumed she had been taken back to the nursery.

The door opened and a nurse came in. Not the one from before, but a different one. Perky and pretty.

"Which one of you is the father?" she whispered to us.

We shrugged and waited for the judgmental looks to begin. But it didn't come. She just smiled and said, "We took baby Ruby back to the nursery. Cassandra needs to sleep. She's had a rough time." She gave Cassie a sympathetic look. Then, her eyes went to Lachlan and lit up. I was about to roll mine when they shot to me and lit up even more. She licked her cherry red lips and pushed her chest out a little bit further.

"Ahem," I cleared my throat. What was happening here? Did this woman not know that we were married men?

"So, how does this work with you three?" she purred.

"Four," Rex barked, as he stepped into the room, his eyes black with bruising and a bandage across his nose.

He looked terrifying.

I hid my smile as her eyes went even wider and her mouth formed an 'O'.

"I see," she said. "Well, she is a lucky woman, having three hot guys all to herself."

You didn't need to be a genius to hear the envy in her voice.

"How did you, you know, do it?"

She asked that to me. I blinked back at her.

Lachlan snorted and said, "He was the last one in. *I* suggested it to Cassie and asked her to bring Rex in." He nodded at Rex, who glowered back at him. Lachlan was definitely still 'not forgiven'.

I gave Lachlan a stern glance. Why did he feel the need to explain our relationship to this stranger? I point-blank refused to acknowledge such violations of our privacy. It was no one's business but ours.

"Hmm," the nurse mused and then brushed past him, tits pushed out, to get to Cassie's chart.

"When can we take her home?" I asked.

She glanced up. "Depends. The baby needs a check-up and the doctor wants to see Cassie. Tomorrow, at the earliest, but we advise a three-day stay."

"She wants to leave," Rex blurted out.

"I'll pass it along," the nurse murmured and put the chart back.

I could tell she was dying to ask more personal details about our relationship, but she refrained and disappeared quickly. I was not a betting man; I *knew* that Rex's presence had everything to do with it.

"You two good?" I asked briskly. "Because we have shit to do."

"I'm fine," Lachlan said breezily. "As long as he apologizes for his disgusting insult to my fidelity."

"You give me every reason to suspect you," Rex snarled at him quietly. "Always cozying up to her."

"It's called being polite," Lachlan snarled back. "Besides, she is the one doing the cozying. Clearly, she wants a piece of her daughter's husband. Filthy bitch. Furthermore, I don't hear you bitching to Alex for the same thing."

"*He* doesn't take her on," Rex said, defending me.

"Neither do I," Lachlan started, but then Cassie woke up and this stupid argument was put on hold.

"What the hell?" she asked, hoisting herself into a sitting position that looked very painful for her, her eyes fixed on Rex. "What happened?"

"I punched him," Lachlan admitted, to my surprise. "He was being a dick."

Cassie bit her lip and blinked. "You okay?" she asked Rex, holding her arms out for him.

He slid into them quickly, desperately, clinging to her as if his life depended on it. "Of course," he scoffed. "He hits like a girl."

"Oh, come over here and say that," Lachlan exclaimed, but he caught Rex's slight smile and he relaxed.

So did I.

This whole situation had been fraught, and I needed a bit of normalcy.

"The nurse said you might be able to go home tomorrow," I ventured, approaching her slowly, in case she was still annoyed with me and my spouting earlier.

She grinned at me. "Yay," she said, and then grimaced, as the pain got a bit too much for her.

"I think we should have a naming ceremony. At the penthouse," I mentioned the idea that had been brewing in my mind for a while now. "We can invite a few people and celebrate Ruby's birth."

"Oh, I think that's a lovely idea!" Cassie exclaimed, sinking back into the pillows. "We'll set it up for a couple of weeks from now, when I'm back on my feet properly."

"Great," I replied. "I'll start making a list. I suppose we should invite your parents?" I hoped she said no.

Her face went tight. "I suppose so," she said shortly. "It will only piss her off if we exclude them, and I really can't be bothered with the drama. It's probably safer this way."

"Okay," I said and then my phone rang.

It was work. I had to take it. I was the project manager and this account had to be locked down. The fact that I'd disappeared without a word, as soon as I'd received Lachlan's first voicemail, without a doubt, had gone down like a lead balloon.

"Sorry," I murmured. I answered it, leaving the room, as I got an earful from the director, wishing that I could stay.

TWO DAYS LATER, WE had Cassie and the baby home, safe and sound. Rex had gone around and baby proofed the entire penthouse, even though she was nowhere near the age of being able to open a cupboard or stick her head down the toilet.

"I've been thinking," Cassie said, when she was settled on the sofa, with Ruby in her crib. "We need to start looking at hiring a nanny. I need to get back to work soon."

"What?" came the resounding reply to that statement out of the blue.

Cassie was looking a bit shifty, which immediately set all of our alarm bells ringing.

"Why?" I asked, before Lachlan or Rex could.

They both gritted their teeth, desperate to grill her, but not wanting to verbally attack her as soon as she had returned home from bringing our child into the world.

She sighed. "It's nothing," she lied. "I just, you know, need to go back." She picked at the throw that Lachlan had tucked her up in.

"Who is messing with you, Cassie?" Rex asked bluntly.

Lachlan elbowed him in the ribs, but he ignored him and gave Cassie that penetrating look that would make her come clean even if she didn't want to.

She obviously didn't want to.

She avoided his eyes and mumbled something like 'takeovers' but I couldn't be sure.

"Are you saying that someone is trying to oust you from your own company?" Lachlan asked incredulously.

He sat down next to her and took her hand.

"Not exactly. They can't do that. Granddaddy made sure. But I do still have a board and if I get enough opposers, they can make it so bad for me that I will want to leave."

She burst out crying and we all went to her to console her. I wasn't used to seeing her so fragile. She was strong, feisty and a fighter.

I put it all down to hormones, not that I would ask her to confirm that, for fear of having my head bitten off.

"Who is it?" Rex growled at her a moment later.

"Look, just leave it. They are called sharks, because they think I am weak, and they can prey on me. They can't. I have to show them that they can't, which is why I need to go back to work as soon as I can walk properly!" She was nearing hysteria, so we all just agreed to her request, but with an exchanged look that made it clear the three of us were *not* on the same page as she was.

Ruby let out a loud howl, having been disturbed by all the noise her mother was making. I was closest to her, so I scooped her up and beamed down at her. She was precious. Not for the first time, I hoped that she was mine. I wanted to have created something so beautiful with the woman that I loved.

"She's hungry," I commented softly. "Give me a bottle."

To my surprise, it was Rex that handed me one. He had been a bit distant with the baby since she'd arrived a few days ago. I wasn't even sure that he'd held her. In order to test him, I held her out for him to take.

His eyes went wide and then narrowed into two slits as he glared at me. He knew what I was doing. He had absolutely no choice now but to take her or show Cassie that he was scared. That is what I deduced from the look of sheer terror on his face when he shakily held his arms out to take her. I placed her gently in his arms and watched as she snuggled into him.

He glanced down at her in surprise, which quickly turned to awe.

"Sit," I said to him. "Give her the bottle."

"I—I don't know how," he said, sounding very unsure of himself.

"It's easy," I said. "Just put it in her mouth. She will do the rest."

Cassie smiled through her tears at him, but, for the first time ever, he was completely unaware of her.

He was enamored with our baby daughter.

It was the most amazing thing to see, as his face softened completely and he smiled, a happy, genuine smile that reached his eyes.

I cast a glance over at Lachlan who was watching him with love in his eyes.

I sat on the coffee table in front of Cassie and took her hand. "Thank you," I whispered to her.

She looked over at me in surprise. "What for?" she asked.

"For making this miracle and bringing her into the world. You are truly amazing."

She grinned at me; her earlier woes forgotten.

Our four had become five and I couldn't wait to expand our growing family. I knew she felt the same.

~Cassie~

I WAS HEALING UP NICELY from the surgery and settling back into life without being pregnant. It had only been
a couple of weeks, but I felt more mobile and less sore. I
knew my husbands were against it, despite their words, but I
was planning on getting back to work next week. I had spent
the last couple of days scouring the city for the best nanny
money could buy. I thought I had found her. I was just waiting for her to arrive for her second interview and meet Ruby. My husbands didn't know, yet, but they were also going
to meet her today. They were going to be so mad with me,
but I was pretty sure I could coax them into seeing things my
way. I wasn't overly worried about the sharks at work. I knew
I kicked ass. I was simply having a crisis of confidence after
the baby was born and the flood of hormones had made me
reveal my feelings to my men. However, there was no getting
away from the fact that the longer I stayed away, the more
they would circle.

As I waited, I looked again at the list for the naming ceremony. It was this weekend, only two days away. I only kept
looking at it to convince myself that I *couldn't* remove my
parents from the list. I had barely seen my father since Ruby was born, and Mother had shown her face once while I'd
been awake and once while I'd slept. I had much preferred
the visit while I'd slept.

She had always been a cold-hearted bitch. I'd tried so
hard when I was little to get her to notice me, even just a
small gesture would have gone a long way, but she hadn't
been interested then, and she wasn't now. All she wanted

was to show up here and make comments, flirt with my husbands, throw death stares at Rex and generally be a horrid witch.

I sighed and chucked the list onto the coffee table. I was fairly sure this would be the last time that I asked them to come over. Unless things changed on Saturday in a drastic way, I was washing my hands of them. They had one last chance to make things right with me.

I didn't care that my daughter would grow up without her maternal grandparents. She had Lachlan's parents, my own grandparents, three fathers who dote on her. That's all she would ever need.

The buzzer on the intercom brought my attention back to the matter at hand. I hauled myself to my feet and answered it.

Confirming it was the potential nanny, I let her in and went to the front door to wait for her.

She knocked a few minutes later and I let her in.

"Aurora," I said with a smile. "Please come in."

"Thanks," she beamed at me. "I just love your place so much," she added, looking around.

"Thanks," I murmured, leading her to the sofa. Baby Ruby was sleeping in her crib and I watched as Aurora went over to her and cooed softly down at her.

"She's gorgeous," she whispered.

"I know," I said with pride. "She's just perfect."

She turned back to me with an expectant look.

I gave her a smile. "I know you are probably wondering why I called you back here today. I am happy with your references and our first interview made my mind up about you. However..." I stopped speaking as I heard the elevator ding.

Aurora slid her eyes over to the doors and then probably wished she hadn't.

Rex came storming out like a bat out of hell. "Who are you?" he snarled at her.

The poor girl nearly wet herself.

"Rex, wait." I went to him and put my hand on his arm. "She's here with me."

His black eyes met mine and softened slightly, but not as much as I'd expected them to.

"Get away from my daughter," he grit out, turning back to Aurora.

"Rex, let me explain," I tried again. "She's the new nanny."

Aurora gulped as Rex nearly went apoplectic.

He spun to me and shouted, "Are you fucking joking?"

"No, I'm not," I replied calmly.

"You went behind my back and did this?" he yelled.

"Behind all of our backs," Lachlan said snidely, sliding into the room like a freaking ghost.

Where the fuck did he come from?

I turned around to see him approaching me, with Alex on his tail, looking like a raging bull.

Okay, so I'd known it wouldn't go down well, but I'd assumed with the woman actually standing before them, they would've been a bit more rational about this.

"Sit!" I barked at them, fully expecting them to obey. Sadly, the only one who did was Aurora.

She parked her ass, clutching her bag to her like a shield.

"Give us a minute, will you?" I said to her, giving her a tight smile.

She nodded as I shoved Rex towards the hallway. He snatched the baby monitor up with a forceful glare at Aurora, letting her know he was watching. Lachlan and Alex followed us and soon we were standing in the nursery, glaring at each other.

"What are you doing?" Alex asked me.

"I told you, I needed to get back to work. I have been very thorough about the background check on Aurora. She comes highly recommended from a granddaughter of one of my grandmother's close friends. She has everything, from a degree in childcare, to impeccable credit history, and she is qualified in infant first aid."

"So, you have decided that this is the right thing for our daughter?" Lachlan asked. "You going back to work and her being raised by a nanny?"

Wow. Harsh.

"That is not what is happening here. But I need to get back to work. You will be around and so will Rex. She is here to make sure that there is full time care."

"Way to make me feel bad about having a normal day job," Alex grumbled at me.

I threw him an annoyed look. That's all he had to say?

"I invited her here so that you could meet her before I made it official. You have probably terrified the crap out of her."

"You should have run this past us first," Rex said. "It is *our* decision to make."

"So, go out there and decide," I snapped at him. His eyes went to mine in query.

Oh, yes. I'd pulled out the Mistress card and he would obey me.

"On your knees," I said quietly.

He took in a deep breath, as Lachlan and Alex gaped at me, disbelieving.

He hesitated for only a second. Then he shoved the monitor at Alex and dropped to his knees, his head bowed in submission.

I inhaled deeply, reveling in the power that rushed through me. It was a bold move and it could never be used again. I'd pulled this out as a last resort, because I wanted Aurora to help care for our child and I needed to get back to work. It wasn't just about a job; it was my *legacy*. My grandfather had built his empire from the ground up and entrusted it to me to take care of and then pass on to the next generation. I had to honor that and ensure that when my daughter was ready, I would pass the baton to her to take over. I would do anything to ensure its safety. To do that, I needed to be there.

I leaned down and stroked Rex's hair, my hand stilled on the back of his neck.

I dug my nails into his skin, harder when I heard him grunt with the bite of pain. It was all I had at my disposal to discipline him with.

"Cassie," Lachlan warned me.

"Quiet," Alex muttered to my utter surprise. But I didn't let it stop me.

"Are you going to agree with me on this?" I asked Rex quietly.

I knew it was going against everything in him to just agree to this because I was Domm'ing him into it.

But he would agree.

Of that, I had no doubt.

I dug my nails in harder.

"Yes," he whispered back.

"Yes, what?" I barked.

"Yes, Mistress. She stays."

"That's better," I said quietly in his ear.

Bending over was becoming a massive issue for my surgical scar, so I straightened up again and retracted my nails from his neck. I stroked his head again, like a dog sitting at my feet.

I saw his shoulders sag.

He was enjoying it.

I was treating him just the way he wanted to be.

Part of me didn't like to treat my husband like a pet, but the domineering side of me was loving it.

"Good boy," I murmured.

We heard a gasp in the doorway, and all looked over at the same time. Even Rex.

Aurora was standing there cradling Ruby, her mouth hanging open. "Ruby's hungry," she blurted out.

"There's a bottle in the refrigerator," I said, ignoring what it must've looked like to her.

"Thanks," she said and disappeared as quickly as she'd arrived.

I smiled after her. She was a gem, that was for sure. Most other people probably would have run for the hills after witnessing our little scene.

"So, that's two votes," I said to my other two husbands, still stroking Rex's head. "Who is going to make it three and have their own fantasy dealt with shortly?"

My sassy comment lit fires under both of them as they said, "Fine."

I chuckled. "I do expect you all to go out there and grill her to your own satisfaction."

"Good!" Lachlan exclaimed, and went off, rubbing his hands together.

I raised my eyebrow at Alex.

"Oh, I'm going," he said. "But this, right here, can't happen again," he added quietly. "It's not fair."

"Stay out of it," Rex growled at him.

"I don't mean just for you," he replied blandly, and then followed Lachlan out.

"Rise," I said to Rex, folding my arms across my chest.

He got to his feet and fixed me with a baleful glare.

"I know," I said, resigned. "I get that this was a bitch-move, but you weren't going to listen to me otherwise."

"Humph," he snorted and turned to leave. He stopped and turned back around, the war in his eyes clearly visible. "Don't do that again," he whispered. "Please."

I went to him immediately and took him in my arms. "I'm sorry," I murmured to him.

"Don't be sorry. But you have no idea how difficult this is going to be for me to not go back on my word. What you made me promise you."

"I do know," I replied, tears springing into my eyes. "But give her half a chance. I wouldn't let you down with something so important. Please trust me."

He kissed the top of my head and, with a nod, he left me alone.

I stayed in the nursery, giving my husbands all the time they needed to appease their worries over Aurora. I didn't hear her crying, so I assumed that Rex was behaving himself.

After about twenty minutes, Lachlan popped his head around the door and beckoned me out.

Aurora was smiling and cuddling Ruby. Rex and Alex were letting her, so I breathed out in relief.

"We have agreed that she can stay for a trial period of one week. Any fuckups and she's gone. If Ruby even so much as cries, she's out." He glared at Aurora, but she rolled her eyes at him.

I didn't bother to stifle my snort of amusement. Oh, she had him pegged, all right.

He glared back at me in annoyance, but he soon relaxed and smiled at me.

"Thank you," I said to my husbands. "I have a great feeling about this. You won't regret it."

Aurora gave me a big smile, then reluctantly handed Ruby back to me. "I should get going. I will see you Saturday."

I nodded. "Thanks," I said and led her to the door.

After seeing her out, I turned back to my husbands.

"Saturday?" Rex asked with a frown.

"I want her here during the party. If for no other reason than to keep my witch-mother away from my daughter," I growled at him.

His eyes went wide, and he raised his eyebrow at me. "Good call," he muttered.

"Now, about those fantasies," I said, placing Ruby back in her crib. She promptly fell asleep again. She was a wonder. "I'm still really sore, but I have a mouth and two hands. Take your pick."

"Mouth!" Alex shouted before either Rex or Lachlan could comment.

They both grumbled, pissed off, but dibs were dibs.

"Pants off," I said to my men as I sashayed into the bedroom, as best I could with my restriction, making sure to grab the baby monitor up off the sideboard on my way.

Chapter 7

~Rex~

I gritted my teeth. This was my worst nightmare. Well, okay, one of my worst nightmares. Being surrounded by all of these people invading our home, snooping around when they thought we weren't looking. It wasn't the way I wanted to spend my Saturday. I would much rather have been doing practically *anything* except this.

"You okay?" Cassie asked me quietly, slipping her hand into mine.

"I'll live," I replied gruffly, which made her purse her lips in that really sexy way that made me think only about her biting me, sinking her teeth into me, bruising me, bringing me the pain I craved, and, with it, the relief that followed.

"It won't be much longer," she murmured to me.

I nodded and went back to glowering at everyone who went near Ruby. It was taking everything that I had not to forcibly remove them from her vicinity. I needed to protect her, but how was I supposed to do that from my naughty corner?

Yes, Cassie — *my wife* — had told me to stand out of the way, because I was scaring the guests.

I did it because Cassie — *my Mistress* — was never far from the surface these days and as much as I wanted her to order me to do it, I knew she wouldn't abuse her role again, like she had the other day, even if she wanted to.

I knew she wanted to. She wanted to feel that power and that was fine. More than fine. I needed it for her. I needed for it to be *me* that gave it to her, as much as I needed to grovel at her pretty feet and have her treat me like her pet.

So, I'd removed myself from the group of well-wishers and stood in the corner.

"Just do me a favor when we are alone again," I murmured to her.

Her eyes lit up.

"Playtime?" she breathed.

"Yes," I croaked. I was so desperate for it. It was clawing at me. I knew she still couldn't have sex, but that mouth was more than enough to bring me relief, *if* she was willing to use it.

"Definitely," she murmured, her eyes on my mouth. She dug her nails into my palm. I narrowed my eyes at her. Yesterday, she'd had them shaped into sharp points like claws. I'd been furious, because I hadn't wanted them anywhere near Ruby. But, as usual, Cassie had shown me that she was more than capable of handling our daughter expertly and she'd satisfied me that she wouldn't hurt our baby with them. How women worked around those things was a mystery to me. I wasn't a clumsy guy. I had to have stealth, fluidity and a steady hand. I used to *need* it. But I couldn't do what Cassie did. She had risen to the occasion of being the perfect mother and excelled as only she could.

She was glaring at me, daring me to comment, but I kept quiet. I knew that she had done her nails for me. To use them on *me*.

It made my dick so hard, it was becoming a problem. I was sure everyone could see it bulging in my pants. The fact that Cassie was now leaning in close to me and brushing her other hand over my cock was about to make me burst into my jeans.

"Hold that thought," she whispered viciously. She turned from me, pulling her hand from mine and walked back over to where Ruby was nestled in her crib, being gawked at by all of those people. At least Aurora was proving to be an asset. She was hovering protectively and that had my seal of approval. As did she.

For now.

I had done a thorough background check on her. A deeper dive that Cassie wouldn't have the know-how to do. There were no red flags, but she wasn't squeaky clean either, which always threw up questions as well.

I looked over as the front door burst open. "For God's sake, this is like being the help!" Suzanne exclaimed, more than pissed off that I had shut out her elevator access and she had to enter the penthouse as a guest would. It made me smile.

It was caught by Derek, the ever-present henchman, and he glared at me. I glared back at him.

His gaze never wavered.

It pissed me off.

They always looked away. But not him. It made me think he was just like me. All I'd managed to find out about him was that he was ex-Special Forces. Retired and currently in private security. It was honorable enough for some, but he didn't strike me as the type to do this because he cared about protecting people. It was the money.

Why else would he put up with Suzanne and her bitchiness? I watched her shove her coat at him and demand that he get her a drink.

His eyes reluctantly left mine and went to hers and softened considerably.

I couldn't help the eye roll. It was such a cliché. Suzanne was banging her bodyguard. For fuck's sake.

I stifled my snort of amusement as I mentally pictured that. He was a large man, bigger than me, and Suzanne was a slight woman. She must definitely have the upper hand in the sack, or he would crush her.

Cassie was blatantly ignoring her.

It came as no surprise that Damien was a no-show. It was a shame that Suzanne hadn't stayed away.

"It's time," the Pagan priestess woman, who'd officiated our hand-fasting, called out now that Suzanne had decided to arrive an hour late.

I stepped forward out of my naughty corner, while Alex scooped up Ruby. He held her close, breathing in her sweet scent. I smiled at them, happy for Alex to hold the baby for the ceremony. Lachlan was looking a little put out, but he should've been quicker on the draw. It always came down to that with those two. I was slower to step in. I knew it. The men knew it. Cassie knew it. But none of them made a big deal over it. I was getting used to having this tiny person in my life and I needed to do it in my own way.

Cassie stood next to Alex with a big smile on her face, as Lachlan stood next to Alex. This left me to move in next to Cassie.

All eyes were on us as the room fell silent.

"Wait," Suzanne called out and all eyes then went to her. Including mine. She was up to something, that much was clear. "I, personally, think it would be better if Rex held the baby. He is, after-all, her real father."

I blinked as Cassie gasped next to me.

Alex and Lachlan turned to me and then back to Suzanne, as Cassie stormed forward and gripped her mother by her arm.

"What?" she spat out. "How do you know that?" She was flaming mad.

Suzanne gave her a callous smile as Derek stepped forward and removed Cassie's hand from his employer.

"Hey," Cassie snapped at him.

I was in front of him in two strides, shoving him on his chest to get him away from my wife.

"Touch her again and I will end you," I snarled at him. How dare he touch my angel! I had never been so angry before. I was seething. The darkness was shrouding me, enveloping me, making me see only one thing: Smashing the fuck out of this asshole who'd hurt my wife. I bunched my fist, ready to draw back and strike, but Cassie caught my hand and pulled on me.

"Don't," she whispered. "I'm fine."

I took in a deep breath, trying to control the rage inside me. It was ripping at me, begging me to do it justice. It had been locked away for too long and it needed to be let out now that it had found an opening.

Cassie must've seen it, because, in the next second, I felt her nails dig into my arm, so hard, she drew blood. It was the sting I needed to focus.

Derek was smirking at me, squared off, ready to go.

"Now-now," Suzanne drawled, the amusement in her voice clear. "There's no need for this. It was simply an idea..."

Cassie spun back to her mother, while the news she'd imparted finally sunk in.

I was Ruby's father.

"HOW DO YOU KNOW THIS?" Cassie roared at Suzanne, grabbing her arm again.

Derek put his hand up to remove her again, but that time I smacked it out of the way before he could touch her.

"Don't test me," I growled at him.

His bland look only served to ignite my fury again.

Out of the corner of my eye, I saw Alex hand Ruby off to Lachlan and approach us, dead set on doing something about this situation. I could see it in his eyes.

I shook my head at him, but it didn't stop him.

I put my hand up to stop him from getting anywhere near Derek.

Alex was a well-toned guy. We went to the gym most days to work out and I was confident he could win a fist fight with his peers. Derek, however, was *not* in the same weight class as the slighter-framed man. He was more on *my* level. There was no way I would allow Alex to take a beating from the prick, even if it meant me getting my ass half kicked to stop it.

The fucker was itching for a fight, I could tell. He had the same cold look in his eye that I knew was in mine when I forced myself to look in the mirror.

"He touches her again, I will kill him," Alex spat out, bunching his fists.

I looked over at Lachlan. He was a lover, not a fighter, despite his ability to throw down with the best of them. I gestured to him to come and get Alex before he did something he was going to regret.

He handed Ruby off to Aurora and strode over to grab Alex by the elbow and steered him over to the opposite side of the gawking crowd.

I re-focused on Cassie and her mother, my brain swimming in the mire of the casually thrown out information.

"...someone had to find out," Suzanne was saying. "You all were just standing around, happy to overlook it. It was ridiculous. One of them had to step up. Now you know."

"Mother!" Cassie snarled at her like a rabid dog. It was only my hand around her arm that stopped her from attacking her own mother. "This wasn't your business. It *isn't* any of your fucking business! We are in a relationship. We are *married*. We all love this child the same. It makes no difference to any of us who the real father is. They are *all* real fathers. You had no right! No right at all!"

I swallowed, completely motionless.

The baby was mine.

Ruby was mine.

I had a daughter that was *mine*.

I choked back the bile that rose in my throat.

I couldn't do it.

I couldn't stand here and pretend that it was *good* news.

Lachlan was at my back in an instant.

He had figured out my thoughts from my shitty reaction.

He grabbed my hand, but I pulled away from him and from the argument that was still raging between Cassie and her mother.

I headed for the door, dragging it open and then slamming it closed behind me, trying to close the door on the dread that had welled up inside me.

~Cassie~

I WATCHED AS REX LEFT the penthouse with Lachlan hot on his heels.

"We'll get him back," Alex said, stopping to kiss my forehead, before he ducked out as well, leaving me alone with the rest of my family, Lachlan's family, some family friends and my detested mother.

"I cannot believe that you went behind our backs and *stole* all three of my husbands' DNA. It's disgusting! It's vile! You are an awful creature and an even worse mother. Get out," I snarled at her. "I never want to see you again."

I folded my arms across my chest, mostly in an effort not to slap her across her smug face.

Her eyes narrowed. "I was looking out for you, Cassandra. I mean, come on. You can't seriously expect this disaster-waiting-to-happen to last, do you?" She gestured around my penthouse. "These men are all thinking with their dicks right now, but one day they will realize that they don't want to share you in this way, that they don't want their wife being a shameless whore right in front of them. One day, they will want to know who that child belongs to, so that they can step up and remove the other men from your life. The sooner everyone comes to this realization, the better. You are an embarrassment to me and your father. And don't get me started on your poor grandparents...."

"Suzanne!" Granddaddy snapped at her. "You don't speak for me."

"Daddy, please. You're indulging this lifestyle, encouraging her. You should be telling her it's unacceptable."

"It's her life," he said. "You have interfered and, with it, embarrassed this entire family with your revelations. I suggest you do as Cassandra says and get out."

I threw him a tight smile. I knew he would have my back. I knew he didn't think we were an embarrassment to this family.

Mother sniffed and held her hand out for Derek to hand her coat to her. I gave him a death stare, which didn't even faze him. I turned it on my mother, hoping for more of a response, but I got nothing. It deflated me. It made me feel silly about dominating Rex the way that I did. Were my men just indulging me in that area of my life?

"Gladly," she said and turned on her heel, stalking over to the door where Derek was already holding it open for her. She spun back around and added, "But, mark my words, Cassandra. This house of cards will come crashing down around you. Soon."

Then she was gone.

I choked back a sob as my grandmother finished ushering out the rest of the guests who had, unashamedly, hung around to witness the fallout from my mother's nastiness.

"We'll leave you to your business," Granddaddy said briskly. "Your men will have to come to terms with this in their own way."

I nodded at him and leaned into him as he took me in his arms and kissed the top of my head.

Grandmother hugged me as well and then they were gone, leaving me and Aurora, who was still clutching Ruby.

I sighed. "If you want to bail, I will fully understand," I told her as I held my arms out for my daughter.

"What? No way!" she said, handing me Ruby. "If nothing else, I can give up watching telenovelas." She chuckled at me and I laughed.

"No kidding," I agreed. "Thank you. I will see you Monday."

"Sure will," she chirped, and off she went, leaving me completely alone to contemplate what my mother had said.

Rex was Ruby's father.

He was her father and he'd run out on us.

I bit my lip.

"He'll come back," I whispered to her, as I rocked her gently. "He will come back and I will find out, once and for all, what is truly going on in his head."

She blinked sleepily at me and then her eyes closed. I kissed her gently and took her to the nursery. I was reluctant to put her down just yet. I wanted to stare at her and see if

I could see any of Rex in her. I knew the others would do it too. How could we not now that we knew?

"Your daddy is a stubborn man," I whispered to her. "But he will come back."

I put her down in her crib and then turned to the door as I heard a soft noise.

I smiled at Rex standing there, staring at us with a pained look on his face.

I moved closer to him, but he stopped me dead with his words.

"I have to go," he blurted out before I could reach him.

"What?" I asked, shaking my head. "Go where?" The cold hit my stomach and wormed its way up to my heart, as he continued to look at me in that way. I knew what he meant, but I couldn't believe it. I just couldn't.

"I can't stay here and be a father to that baby," he said. "I'm no good, Cassie. I am a dark, desperate soul, not a role model. I'm not someone a child should look up to. I am not a father. I am not good enough to be called her father. I need to leave you alone. You can build your life with Alex and Lachlan. They will take good care of you and your baby."

Your baby.

Not *our* baby, but *your* baby.

He might as well have punched me in the face.

I felt it crumple as tears threatened to flow.

Rex's father had abandoned him. For him to even be thinking about doing the same was unfathomable to me.

"No!" I hissed at him. "I love you. You love me and this baby. *Our* baby. If you walk out on us now, then *that* is what will make you a terrible person."

I stopped speaking as Alex and Lachlan arrived in the doorway, shell-shocked as they heard my words.

"How dare you?" Lachlan spat out, before I could say anything else.

I put my hand on my stomach to try to stop the retch I felt coming.

I looked from Rex to him. He was fuming.

"I have known you for a long time, Rex. I have seen the worst part of you. I know all about your darkness, but, if you do this, then you are truly not the man that I hoped you could be."

I gulped and looked back at Rex. He was glaring at Lachlan like he was ready to hit him. Their gaze simmered as I just stood there like a spare part. Something was going on between them that had nothing to do with me. I had never felt so left out, so alone, in all of the time that we'd been together.

"Excuse us," Lachlan said and grabbed Rex by the scruff of his neck and shoved him roughly out of the nursery.

I looked at Alex. His face was pale. He, too, had grown up without a father and this had to be bringing back those memories for him.

He swiftly took me in his arms, and I sobbed into his shirt.

"He doesn't get to leave," Alex said to me, drawing back so he could look me in the eye.

I sniffled and nodded at him, incapable of words.

How could Rex do this to me? To us? I should've been quicker to demand he stay. My insecurities had gotten the better of me. I could've used my role as his Mistress to get him to stay. I'd promised him I wouldn't use it again in that way, but this wasn't a normal situation.

I turned and paced and then walked out of the nursery. I didn't want to disturb Ruby.

I went into the bedroom and broke down. All of my fears, all of my worries over what he was still hiding from me, came out as I dropped to my knees and wept as my heart broke. I knew he was damaged. It was what I'd first fallen in love with. That wounded bird that I could help heal. But, clearly, I hadn't done that at all. For him to decide to leave me and our baby, because he'd found out she was his by blood was truly the worst part of him. Or, maybe, it wasn't. Maybe I didn't know him at all. Maybe he had only shown me a fraction of himself and the rest of his soul was beyond repair.

Lachlan's words bounced around in my head.

I know all about your darkness.

What weren't they telling me?

Did Alex know as well? Was that why I'd sometimes caught them whispering in corners? I hadn't thought anything of it until now. It'd never bothered me. In fact, I'd been glad that they'd been getting along great, becoming best friends. More, even. But this situation had now shone a light into that shadowed corner.

They'd been keeping something about Rex from me.

It was obvious.

I felt like such a fool for being so blind to it.

Whatever Rex didn't want to tell me about his past, whatever it was that he kept so close to himself, Lachlan and Alex knew.

And they hadn't told me.

I didn't know which hurt worse.

The fact that Rex didn't tell me, or that Lachlan — my *best* friend — had kept me in the dark about one of my husbands.

I quit sobbing as I found anger. I stood up and shook out my pretty white dress with the red roses on it that Alex loved so much. I always liked to dress to please him. The other two weren't that concerned, but Alex always made mention of my chosen outfit. It delighted me, so I indulged him. I stalked back into the living room, brushing my tears away. When they returned, with or without Rex, they were in for a world of hurt.

I wanted answers and I wanted them tonight.

Chapter 8

~Lachlan~

I'd dragged Rex to Finn's bar. Alex had joined us, and we were sitting in a booth staring into our beers. I was opposite Rex, while Alex had boxed him into the corner so he couldn't escape. He had some serious explaining to do.

I had no idea where to start. I knew the news had hit him hard, but I'd never expected this from him. I'd never thought he would ever even *think* about leaving Cassie, never mind our baby.

His baby.

I had to admit that it stung just a little.

I huffed out a breath, still totally fuming at Rex and his despicable behavior. I couldn't even speak to him yet, or I would rip his fucking head off.

We all brooded for a bit longer and then Alex looked up. "We need to tell Cassie everything. It's the only way she will understand this."

I shook my head at him, then Rex grabbed him by his tie and wrapped it around his fist.

"Never," he hissed into Alex's face. "*You* were never supposed to know this. Either of you," he glanced at me. "This is *my* life and you won't interfere with it."

Alex was now millimeters from a snarling Rex.

I leaned over the table and gripped the tie between Alex's chin and Rex's fist. "Down boy," I said to Rex.

He growled at me but loosened his hold.

I blinked at him. Interesting. I had expected that to go *a lot* differently than that. Seemed he was into taking orders and not just from Cassie.

That made my dick bust against my zipper.

So inappropriate — again.

I was going to have to fuck my wife the second she was healed up.

I let go of Alex's tie and sat back down. "We agreed that Cassie wouldn't know. She would fret and worry and worst-case scenario..."

"Turn from him?" Alex barked at me. "Like he just did to her?"

Rex pushed himself further into the corner of the booth, glowering into his beer.

"We need to stay calm," I pointed out, even though I was seething inside. We would get nowhere fast if we attacked him. He would close up even more and that actually *was* possible with him. "We made a promise to keep this between us and that is what we are going to do. Rex," I glared at him, "is going to drag his sorry ass back to our wife, grovel at her feet for being a fucking dick, beg her forgiveness and plead that she take him back or his life isn't worth living. Got it?" I snarled at him, forgetting to remain calm.

He didn't answer me. He didn't even look up.

I was about to lean over and whack him around the back of his head, when he looked up at me, the torment in his eyes stopping me mid-rise.

"I can't," he whispered. "I can't go back to her and pretend that I am good enough. I can't do it anymore. She deserves better than me. Ruby deserves better than to have me as her father."

"Don't be fucking ridiculous," Alex snapped at him. "She is lucky to have you as her father. No one will protect her and keep her safe better than you will. No one will love her as you can love her. You just have to man up and get over your fucking self."

Rex's eyes slowly shifted back to Alex. I knew what he was going to do a second before he did it.

He leaned over and gripped Alex around the neck and got right in his face. They were nose to nose.

"Get over my fucking self?" he roared. "You don't know the *demons* that live inside my head. You don't know how black my soul is. You don't know what I have had to do to survive."

"I do know!" Alex shouted back. "I *do* know. But I also know that you have people who love you now, who can help you, but you refuse to let us in. Refuse to let Cassie in. You will *never* move forward if you keep up this tormented loner bullshit routine!"

"Fuck you!" Rex yelled into his face.

The bar had gone completely quiet and everyone was staring at the spectacle we were making in our booth.

Rex let out a frustrated noise and let go of Alex again. Good thing, too, because Finn, the owner, was seconds away from kicking our asses out, never to return.

"Rex," I said to him, taking his hand gently in mine. He tried to pull it away, but I gripped it tighter. "Alex is right.

You have us. You don't need to carry this burden that you think you have all by yourself."

He looked at me. "*Think* I have? The guilt..." Tears welled up in his eyes.

Oh shit.

I heard Alex gulp.

I crushed Rex's hand in mine.

"They were all bad in some way," I murmured, just loud enough for the three of us to hear.

The bar had gone back to the normal hum, so we had little chance of being overheard.

"I know all about it, remember?" I pressed.

He dropped his eyes back to his drink. "Doesn't take away these feelings. Ever since Cassie agreed to be with me, it is all I can think about. I have tried to be a better man, one that she can be proud of, but how can I move forward with this weighing on me?"

I breathed in deeply. He was in serious pain and I didn't think there was much I could do to take it away. There was only one person in this world that could even try, but I wasn't letting him anywhere near Cassie right now. Not until he was ready to face her and apologize.

That left only one thing for it.

"Get up," I said, letting go of his hand and standing up.

I caught Alex's eye and gestured he should do the same. He did without question. Good, I needed him to follow my lead and not ask what I was doing.

"No," Rex said mutinously. "I'm not going anywhere with you."

"Oh, yes, you are," Alex said, leaning over, grabbing Rex's t-shirt and hauling him out of the booth.

I was impressed. Rex was not a small guy.

That was also good. He would need that strength in a few minutes.

I gripped Rex by his elbow. He didn't struggle. He looked completely lost and forlorn as I led him out of the bar. Alex trailed in our wake, taking off his suit jacket and tie as we left.

Oh, he knew exactly what I was up to.

I knew he was a smart guy, but he just went up in my estimations by several notches.

I shoved Rex into a nearby alley and watched with an eye roll as Alex carefully placed his jacket and tie on a dumpster and then started to roll up his sleeves.

"You want justice for what you did?" I asked Rex. "You want absolution?"

Rex looked at me, his eyes swimming with pain, looking so tortured in that dark alley that it broke my heart. But I had to follow this through. It would help him. "Yes," he said, having also caught on to my plan.

He wanted it. He *needed* it.

"Are you going to fight back?" I asked him with an arched eyebrow.

"No," he whimpered and dropped to his knees.

"You deserve this for abandoning your wife and daughter," I clipped out, looming over him as I moved closer.

I knew what I was doing. I was no stranger to dominating people. I knew Cassie wanted it from me. She was probably the only one that I would have trouble with. But I had absolutely *no* issues with doing this to Rex. He *did* deserve it for what he'd just done to Cassie and Ruby. But he *needed* it for what he had done to his victims. He felt, rightly or wrongly, guilt for his actions. I wasn't here to judge him, only to punish him as he thought he deserved.

He bowed his head and I placed my hand on the back of his neck. I shoved him even further down, getting him onto his hands and knees.

I glanced up at Alex. He was grim-faced, but ready. He wanted to dole out his own form of justice and I would let him. Within reason. Rex needed to be disciplined for his actions, without a doubt in my mind. Cassie would be suffering right now, thinking that she had lost her husband and a father for her daughter.

"Yes," Rex whispered eventually, knowing that I needed his consent to do what needed to be done.

I didn't let my feelings for him get in the way of the swift kick I gave him to his ribs.

He grunted in pain, but he took it, as I knew he would.

I did it again and again, gritting my teeth against the stomach-clenching action. I didn't want to hurt him like this, but I knew that it would help him, in his own way, to get over his demons. At least enough to get back to the one person who could help him for real. This was a band-aid to get him there, nothing more.

I leaned down and gripped his chin, forcing his face upwards. Then I punched him so hard, I flattened his nose. Again.

The blood went everywhere, all over me, all over him, but he still didn't utter a sound.

I hauled him to his feet and watched as he staggered, but steadied himself, ready for the next blow.

It came from Alex.

A blow so hard, it knocked Rex on his ass.

Whoa. Suits had game.

It was turning me on in all sorts of ways.

He caught me eyeing him up and grimaced at me. Then he leaned down and, with a fist bunched in Rex's t-shirt, he hit him a second time, and then a third.

He was panting as he said, "I have been wanting to kick your ass since I first laid eyes on you in Cassie's penthouse," he rasped. "You have no idea how good this feels." He hit him again.

Rex gurgled up a mouthful of blood, his lip split completely and gushing blood down his chin.

I was about to step in, when Alex stepped back, rubbing his fist. But he wasn't done. He dragged Rex to his feet by his t-shirt.

"You think that Cassie doesn't deserve you?" he asked Rex. "She doesn't. She deserves better than your darkness. But she loves you. Our daughter loves you. Lachlan, God knows why, loves you."

I stifled my amusement as a badly disguised cough.

"I care about you, man. You have all of these people ready to help you. We have told you this time and again. But you won't accept it. You'd rather be the brooding, sexy, dangerous man in the corner, glowering at everyone and threatening to end them if they slight you in any way."

"You think he's sexy?" I asked, choking back my guffaw.

"Yeah, 'course," Alex said with a shrug. "Look at him, for fuck's sake."

"Oh, you don't need to tell me," I murmured, giving him a raking once-over. Christ, if it was possible, he looked even sexier all beat up.

Alex balled his fist and hit Rex in the solar plexus, winding him and making him double over.

"Get. Over. Your. Fucking. Self," he said, leaning over to whisper into Rex's ear.

Alex stepped back. Done.

I snapped my fingers at Rex, and he looked up at me. I pointed to the ground and he dropped to his knees, head lowered, gasping for breath.

"You hit like a lightweight," he panted to Alex.

Alex choked back his indignation and stepped forward, hands clenched again. "You looking for another ass-kicking?"

"Another?" Rex scoffed, looking up.

"Quiet!" I demanded and he shut it.

Oh, this was too good, and so, *so* bad at the same time.

I didn't care what Cassie would have to say about it when we got home. When we dragged Rex back by his balls, I was fucking him in his ass so hard he would feel it for a week. Cassie could watch, but she wasn't having anything else to do with it. This was between him and me.

"Are you ready to face your wife and daughter?" I asked him quietly.

Silence.

I backhanded him across his face.

"Are you ready to go home and face your wife and daughter?"

"I-I can't," he sobbed, startling me.

I had never seen him actually cry before. I didn't think he could.

"Get up!" I commanded him.

He struggled to his feet.

Alex was white-faced as Rex sniffled.

"How can I ask her to take me back?" Rex whispered.

"You just do," I said shortly.

"How can I be a father to Ruby?" he asked, seemingly ignoring me.

"The same way you have been for the past couple of weeks," Alex said, approaching us with caution. "Nothing has changed, except that you are lucky enough to have a baby with the woman that you love. Why would you ever want to walk away from that?" He looked utterly perplexed.

"Are you ready?" I asked Rex again.

After a long pause, he nodded, his head bowed, blood and tears mingling and dripping onto his t-shirt.

"Say it," I barked out.

"Yes," he whispered. "I'm sorry."

"Don't apologize to us," Alex said stiffly. "Save it for your wife. You're gonna need it."

I didn't disagree.

I grabbed Rex by the elbow and helped him hobble out of the alley.

Cassie was going to be flaming mad with us when we all arrived home looking like something the cat had dragged in. Especially Rex. I was fairly certain that his punishment wasn't over yet.

Cassie was going to have his balls for dinner.

Along with ours.

Chapter 9

~Cassie~

An hour had dragged by and I still hadn't heard anything from my men. I hadn't wanted to call them as it would've made me look weak and I wouldn't give Rex the satisfaction of inquiring as to his whereabouts. If he truly decided not to come back, then I would have to accept that. I wasn't going to beg him to return.

Not yet, anyway.

If he needed a bit of time, then I would give it to him.

But that was *all* he was getting.

There was no way on this earth that he was going to walk out for good. He could forget that idea straight away.

I heard the elevator and my stomach clenched. Nerves shot through me, making me feel nauseous. My hands and feet felt like they were on fire.

The doors slid open, usually silent, but now sounding like gravel stuck in a blender, deafening me.

Boots clumped on the tiled floor, but I didn't move.

I stayed staring out of the window, not wanting to turn around and only see two men before me.

"We brought you something," Lachlan gritted out.

There was a soft thump, a snap of fingers and another thump.

"Do you want it?"

I took in a deep breath and, with my head held high, I turned around, my hands clasped in front of me.

I quickly took in the scene in front of me with a feeling of utter dread.

Rex was on his knees, holding his side gingerly, bloodied and bruised. Alex's hair was all spiked in agitation. He had his jacket and tie off, his sleeves were rolled up, and his hands were covered in blood.

Lachlan had blood sprayed all over his white t-shirt. He, too, had bloodied hands and looked mussed up.

"What is this?" I asked, trying to keep the waver out of my voice.

"Do you want it?" Lachlan asked me again, ignoring my question.

I tore my eyes away from Lachlan and gazed at Rex, my heart in my throat.

"Does *it* want to be here?" I emphasized 'it' to show my anger and hurt at him.

He flinched. His eyes lowered.

"Yes," he whispered.

I walked a few paces forward, the tension so thick you could hack away at it with a sword.

"I didn't hear you!" I snapped at him.

He whimpered and my anger dissolved in an instant. I wanted to bend down and kiss him, then tell him it was okay.

But it wasn't.

Plus, I was still struggling to bend over for long periods, so that forced me to just stand there, waiting for him to speak.

"Yes, Mistress," he said louder, his voice a rasp. He crawled forward and dropped his head onto the top of my feet. I wanted to tell him to get up, but the words didn't come out. "I am so sorry. I was an absolute dick. I panicked and I did what I always do and ran away. Please forgive me."

"What is there to panic over?" I asked him, expecting an answer.

He shook his head and kissed my feet. "Please, Cassie. Please forgive me and take me back."

I didn't answer him.

I let him wait.

I let him stew, just like the three of them had made me stew for over an hour, wondering if I had lost my husband and my daughter's father.

I looked over at Alex. He was ashen.

Lachlan was grim-faced and had an air about him that was pretty damn sexy. He was all dominant and he had Rex right where he wanted him.

In that instant, I wasn't sure how I felt about that.

I dropped my eyes back to Rex, giving myself time to process this new development.

Lachlan had taken Rex as his submissive and Rex had let him.

Where the fuck did that leave *me*? Was it just because this situation had warranted it, or was it something that both of them wanted? Was I going to be pushed into a corner to watch from the sidelines, because I couldn't give them exactly what they needed from me yet?

My own face went grim then. I looked back over at Lachlan with a filthy look that he took on the chin, but then shook his head slightly at me. He knew what I was thinking and gave me the answer I was seeking. It was temporary. To get Rex in line.

That, however, made it worse. Had he Dom'ed Rex into being here?

"I don't believe you," I snapped at Rex, breaking the eerie silence and startling the three men.

He sobbed onto my feet. "Please, Cassie. I love you. I love Ruby. I was an asshole. I don't deserve you, but I need you. Please don't throw me away."

"Like you made me believe you were doing to me and our daughter?" It just came out. I hadn't wanted to be so harsh with him, but the hurt was there, needing an outlet.

I felt his tears on my feet. I gulped. I had never seen him cry before. He was completely lost. I had *no* idea why.

"You need to tell me what is going on in your head," I said to him quietly. "I will give you a bit of time to sort your thoughts out, but I want to know, or we cannot move forward. Do you hear me?"

He nodded his head.

"Consent!" I barked at him, finally bending over and running my hand into his hair to grip it tightly and lift his head up.

"Yes," he croaked. "Mistress." The last word was a whisper, as if he couldn't bear to speak anymore. I let him go and then gave the evil eye to my other two husbands.

"You lay a hand on him again in this manner and you will have me to deal with. Are we clear?"

"Yes," they both said quietly, but not at all sorry for it.

In a way, I was thrilled that they had defended my honor and that of our daughter's. But, on the other hand, Rex looked like he had gone ten rounds with Mike Tyson.

I walked away, needing a minute to gather myself after this confrontation. I stopped in front of the kitchen island and glared at the food that Aurora had quickly piled up after the naming ceremony that hadn't happened.

I stared at the chocolate cake, wondering what I was going to do with all of the leftovers, when Rex spoke.

"Do you forgive me?" he asked.

I turned around in surprise. He was still on his knees. Lachlan was standing over him, his hand on the back of his neck, as if he was holding him down, making him submit.

I blinked a couple of times and then realized that I hadn't actually said it. I turned back to the cake, trying to figure out what to say to him. I didn't want to give him a straight out 'yes', but I didn't want to reiterate what I'd already said. He knew what he needed to do.

I picked up the cake as a wicked thought popped into my head. I had no idea where it'd come from. Suddenly, I felt a lot lighter than I had ten minutes ago. I walked back over to Rex with Alex and Lachlan's eyes on me.

"Do I forgive you?" I asked him, holding the cake up and then smashing it into his face, sending chocolate frosting flying all over me and Lachlan.

Rex grunted, his entire face covered in cake, then spluttered as it got into his mouth.

"Sure," I said breezily. "*Now,* I do."

Then I leaned down again and scooped up two handfuls of cake off Rex's face. One went into Lachlan's face and the other I threw at Alex, as he was still standing a bit further away. It hit him on his chin and slid down to land on his white shirt dotted with blood. The men all looked at me like I had lost my mind, but I was giggling uncontrollably. I scooted around Lachlan and back to the kitchen island to grab up a tray of tiny, triangular cut sandwiches and started to pelt my husbands with them. Bread, ham, lettuce, cucumber, salmon...it all went flying all over the living room.

The men ducked for cover behind the sofa, but that wasn't going to protect them.

Rex crawled to catch up to the swifter other two.

I threw a banana at him and it hit him on his ass, just before he disappeared behind the sofa.

Laughing, they held up their hands in surrender, but I had just gotten started. I grabbed a bottle of Champagne and shook it vigorously, stalking over to them behind their expensive leather shield. I popped the cork and let the Cristal shoot out of the bottle and all down the back of the sofa, drenching them in a pricey, bubbly shower.

"You are all forgiven," I panted in between giggles, before I sobered up. "But this *never* happens again without my consent. Now, will one of you call Dr. Greenwood, please. Rex looks like he needs medical attention."

I stalked off, leaving them to sort that out so that I could wash up and change my clothes.

Alex followed me.

It surprised me.

I thought, out of the three of them, he would be the last to come to me. I was madly curious as to what he was going to say as I washed my hands slowly and waited for him to speak.

~Alex~

I WATCHED CASSIE WASHING her hands slowly. She looked at me in the mirror and I knew I had to say something. I approached her and propped myself up against the His & Hers basins as she dried her hands.

"I really don't know where I fit into this," I said to her slowly, so that I could try to figure out what to say after that.

"What do you mean?" she asked.

I shrugged and ran my hand through my hair again, for what seemed like the millionth time that night.

"I'm not into bending people to do what I want them to, nor am I going to accept someone trying to bend me. So...where does that leave me?"

"Oh, I see," she said and bit her lip.

I wasn't sure if she was trying not to laugh at me. But it sure as shit looked like it.

I grimaced at her and she straightened her face.

"Alex," she sighed, after a beat. "You don't have to do anything. What happens between me and Rex and, apparently now Rex and Lachlan," she frowned fiercely with jealousy at that before she continued, "is between us. It's what he wants, and I want to give that to him. I also need to feel that power. It's hard to explain. If you don't have that desire, you can't learn it. It's in you, or it isn't."

I nodded, taking that in.

"So, I'm just supposed to sit there and watch, while you cuff him up and whip him?"

"You have so far and without complaint, I might add," she pointed out.

"Because I am trying to figure out what I want," I muttered, pursing my lips at her. "What do *you* want from me?" There, I'd asked the question. The ball was in her court.

"You ask me this now? After all these months? Why?" She neatly ducked the question.

Again, I shrugged. "I guess I was waiting for you to tell me."

"Like a Mistress would?" she asked, raising her eyebrow.

"No, like a wife would," I snapped at her. We were getting nowhere fast here.

"Alex, I can't tell you what I want you to be. *You* have to decide that."

"Well, I don't know. I like to watch it," I blurted out. "I just don't think I can get involved in it."

"And that's fine," she said, moving in closer.

I opened my arms up for her and she pressed herself against me covered in blood and cake as I was. I wanted nothing more than to lift her up onto the counter and fuck her until she screamed.

"Are you sure?" I mumbled into her hair.

"Of course," she replied. "I like you being a voyeur anyway. It turns me on to have you watch and not say anything, not get involved."

"A voyeur," I muttered. Was that what I was? Someone who got off on watching other people having sex? Yeah, I guessed I was, because it was fucking hot watching Cassie work her magic on Rex and then turn around and fuck Lachlan like it was the most natural thing in the world. "So, is that, like, my thing?" I asked her with a smirk.

"Well, *I* don't want to label you..." She smiled up at me.

"You want Lachlan to dominate you, don't you?" I asked her suddenly.

She frowned at me but then nodded her head. "Yes, if he will. I used to get it from Rex, but since we got married, he won't do it anymore. He always submits to me."

"I am not sure I can watch that," I whispered to her. "If he hurts you..."

"It's nothing that I don't want," she told me quickly, placing her hands on my chest and then running them up into my hair. "You look so fucking adorable with your hair standing up on end."

I grinned at her, but then went serious again. "What if he goes too far?" I had to ask, and I didn't care how it sounded.

"He won't. In fact, I think he will be hard-pressed to do it at all. However, if he actually hurts me, I have a safe word."

"Oh," I said and closed my eyes as she ran her new, sharp nails over my scalp. It felt good. Real good.

I breathed in her scent. Chocolate and Chanel No. 5 filled my senses. It was intoxicating.

She ever so slowly dragged her nails down the back of my neck, scraping them over my skin.

I breathed in deeply again, keeping my eyes closed. Lachlan had once told me that to blindfold yourself left it all to the imagination. What would happen next? Would it be pleasure or pain?

I couldn't deny that it was exciting.

I was rock hard, pressing against her, straining to get inside her.

Cassie's breathing also went heavier. She had taken control and I was going to let her, just to see what would happen.

She flicked open the buttons on my shirt and trailed a nail down my chest gently. It tickled as she swirled it down and down in an 's' shape, reaching the top of my pants and then stopping.

I waited and frowned as nothing else happened. I was about to open my eyes, thinking she was done playing with me, when I felt the tips of the pointy claws dig into my skin at the top of my chest. Then she dragged her nails down me excruciatingly slowly.

The burn hurt.

I grunted with the pain as she dug in even deeper.

I knew she would leave red welts down my chest and abs, but I didn't care. I wanted her to mark me. I understood now why Rex was so eager to strip off and show the bite marks and bruises he'd gotten from her at the gym. It was like she was marking her territory. I was hers and hers alone. No one else could ever come near me.

My cock twitched in my pants. I was ready to burst.

There were no words as she clawed her way down me. She stopped. Then her tongue was on my hot skin, licking all the way down over the welts, soothing them briefly before the sting returned.

"Fuck," I breathed out.

I was lost.

Completely lost in her touch. She gave me pain and pleasure. And I finally got it.

It was fucking amazing.

"Jesus," I whispered as she started to undo my pants. I was about to get real lucky here. All of us had tried to get her on her own, but she hadn't been having any of it. Seemed I was the one that was about to have her all to myself.

That was when I heard the shuffle in the doorway.

I smiled.

Nope, I should've known. Rex and Lachlan were here, watching, and probably getting as turned on as I was.

"Keep your eyes closed," Cassie murmured to me, even though I had no intention of opening them again.

Then she was kneeling in front of me, her mouth millimeters from my cock.

I could feel her hot breath on me. I twitched, eager for her.

It was only when she took me in her perfect mouth that my eyes flew open.

I stared down at Lachlan, my cock stuffed into his mouth, as he gave me a fucking great blowjob.

His brown eyes were full of a wicked mischief that made my heart thump.

"Fuck," I muttered, my nerves suddenly causing a fire in my veins.

He grazed his teeth gently down my length, before he circled his tongue around my tip.

I ran my hand over his head. His short hair wasn't long enough to grip and hold him there. I made do with a firm hold on the back of his head and then I moved my hips.

He muffled his moan of desire as I took over and fucked his mouth as Cassie and Rex stood in the doorway and watched me.

"Oh, that feels good," I whispered to him as I closed my eyes and let my head fall back.

I just went with it and it was fucking hot.

After a few moments, I stopped and gave him back control. He took it and, with both hands and his mouth, he brought me to a climax that made my knees weak.

"Oh, God," I groaned and shot my load into his mouth. I didn't know if that was what he'd wanted, but I hadn't been able to help it. I'd already been so riled up from Cassie's attention and on the verge, even before she'd undone my pants.

"Mm," Lachlan murmured to me. "You taste good, Suits."

I stared down at him wide-eyed. He had swallowed the lot and was licking his lips with a big grin.

"Good?" he asked, getting to his feet.

"Yes," I panted. I looked over at Cassie. She was enthralled. Her nipples were peaked against the fabric of her dress and I didn't have to touch her to know she was trembling. "Are you okay?" I asked her.

She gave me a curious look, but then giggled. "I'm fine. It won't be long until we can make love," she said with a sassy grin.

"I thought you didn't want this until then?" I said, bending down to pull my pants back up, suddenly self-conscious of standing there with my dick out while everyone else was fully clothed.

"The opportunity presented itself," she said with a shrug. "I am not going to stand in your way again. Just one rule. You don't do this without me." Then she spun on her heel and disappeared back into the bedroom.

"Dr. Greenwood is here," she called out and Rex trudged back out after her, still silent and covered in food.

Well, we all were.

But I think Cassie had forgiven Rex. She had also shown me what I was missing out on. I didn't want her to treat me like she did Rex, but I was willing for her to give me a bit of pain and, with it, a bit of that power she was seeking.

Chapter 10

~Rex~

"Get cleaned up," Lachlan said to me, guiding me back towards the bathroom, as he called over his shoulder, "We'll just be a minute!"

Cassie made a noise that sounded like, "Uh-huh," and disappeared with Alex to let the doctor in.

I shrugged Lachlan off me. I leaned into the shower and turned on the jets. The water shot out and started to heat up as I pulled away and attempted to remove my t-shirt. Lachlan had broken my ribs. I knew that without a doubt. I had been in more than one brawl in my younger days before I'd found the pseudo-peace that being a contract killer had provided.

Asshole.

He was standing there watching me, itching to help, but he could go and get fucked. He had flattened my nose *twice* in less than a month.

He let me get on with it, undoing my jeans and letting them drop around my ankles, so that I could awkwardly kick them off. I grunted as the pain got a little bit too much for me. My head swam, but I shook it off and stepped under the streaming water. I turned my face into it to wash it of blood and cake. It stung and I groaned.

"Need some help?" Lachlan asked, leaning back against the basins with his arms crossed.

"No," I gritted out. "Keep your hands off me."

"Suit yourself," he muttered, but didn't go anywhere.

I ignored him. I had some serious thinking to do. I had walked right back into the place I needed to get away from.

As I'd left the penthouse after Suzanne's shocking statement, I'd received a text. I'd finally learned what the blackmailer wanted from me. It hadn't come as a huge surprise, if I was being totally honest.

One last job and Cassandra never finds out.

One last job.

They wanted me to kill someone for them, wipe them off the face of the earth, to keep my secret.

I wasn't so sure it was Suzanne anymore as she and Derek had still been inside the penthouse with Cassie when it had come through. It was possible, but I had bigger issues to deal with than *who* was behind the text, like *what* they wanted me to do.

I was caught between a rock and a hard place, but, as far as I was concerned, there was only one answer.

I was going to do what they wanted me to do.

I would kill one last time to get rid of them and keep Cassie and our daughter—*my* daughter—safe from my horrific past. There was no way that Cassie could ever find out. She would hate me. She would cut me out of her life and Ruby's as well. I would rather die a thousand deaths than live in the world without either of them. I would rather *kill* a thousand more times than exist without them.

It was simple for me.

I just wanted, needed, the time away from them to do the job, clear my head of it, and come back to them as if it hadn't happened.

I couldn't even tell Lachlan or Alex about it. They, too, would turn from me. They were expecting me to be better than this. A better man, one that our daughter could look up to. I wanted that as well but keeping my past buried was more important than sharing the burden with the other men. I couldn't allow them the opportunity to know that I wasn't worth the time and effort that they were putting into me. I needed to feel that they cared about me. Also, if they turned from me, Cassie would know, and the whole sordid tale would come out eventually. So, it really was a simple decision, a necessary cross to bear on my own, to do the job and then try to move forward.

"You okay in there?" Lachlan asked.

"Yes," I snapped at him. "And by the way..." I opened the shower door to glare at him. I ignored his eyes roving over my body, ignored my stirring cock under his heated gaze, "...*you* are not my Master. Are we clear?"

"Very," Lachlan said, his eyes finding mine. "It's not a role I relish."

"Really?" I drawled. "You seemed to be getting quite into it." I shut the shower door again and clutched at my side. The pain in my ribs was getting more unbearable the longer I was on my feet.

I grabbed the soap and washed up as best I could. Then I turned the shower off and climbed out.

Lachlan was holding out a towel for me. "I'm helping you, Angelwings. You look like you're about to pass out."

"You didn't hurt me," I told him.

"Sure. Keep telling yourself that," he answered with a smirk.

I grimaced at him as he wrapped the towel around my hips. I hated to admit it, but he was one hell of a fighter. Alex as well. I had always assumed that he could at least hold his own in a brawl, but he had a fucking hard punch. I was impressed. Not that I would ever say that to him.

"Where's Cassie?" I asked. "She can help me get dressed. Not you."

"She is with Alex. He needed a bit of one-on-one with her after I sucked him off good and proper," he said with a laugh. "Did you get jealous?"

"I already told you, in your dreams," I barked out at him, but let him lead me back into the bedroom.

I sat gingerly on the edge of the bed as he rooted through my drawers for a t-shirt and then the closet for more jeans. Then he went back to the bathroom and came back out with another towel. I sat there as he silently dried me off, smirking at me as he patted at my dick with the towel. I growled and grabbed it off him and dried myself properly, flinging the towel back to him when I was done. Then he carefully held out the t-shirt as I maneuvered my head into it so that I didn't catch my busted nose.

"Fuck's sake," I muttered as I finally managed it, but then he had to help me get my arms in it as well. This was ridiculous.

"You're an asshole," I blurted out.

"So are you," he retorted, dropping to his knees and holding my jeans out for me to slide my feet into. "Don't make me ever have to do this again. Got it?"

"What? Get me dressed?" I asked sarcastically. "Thought that would be a turn on for you."

"Oh, it is," he said with a smile, "I meant, hurt you. Stand up."

I did as I was told only because I had given up. I couldn't do this on my own without passing out. He pulled my jeans up and lingered with doing them up.

"I love that you go commando," he murmured. "Cassie does too."

"Humph," I muttered.

"You know that she is still pissed with you, don't you?"

"She said she forgave me," I said slowly, the frown hurting my face.

"Oh, she did. But she hasn't forgotten, and she won't for a while. You really hurt her."

"I know," I muttered. "I was trying to do the right thing."

He shook his head at me but didn't say anything. I was glad. The more he pushed at it, the closer I would get to telling him everything. That was something that I couldn't do. Not now, not ever.

He held my deodorant out for me, shoving it up my t-shirt to apply.

I grunted as he jostled me. "Didn't think of that before you put my t-shirt on?"

"Sorry, not used to dressing other people. Go now and get patched up. Then go to Cassie, apologize again, and then leave her to attend to you, however she sees fit."

"I know my wife," I snarled at him, getting pissed off at his attitude.

"I have known her for over a decade," he replied with a shrug. "I know her better than she knows herself."

I turned from him. I hated it when that was thrown in my face. I was sure it pissed Alex off as well.

I held my side as I hobbled into the living room, pausing at Ruby's nursery door and putting my hand up to press against the wood. I wanted to see her, but I didn't want to disturb her.

I sighed and carried on through the living room, to see Cassie and Alex cuddling on the sofa.

"Dr. Greenwood is in the office," she said, eyeing me up with concern.

"Thanks," I said quietly and aimed for the office door, which was down the corridor that led to the playroom.

I pushed open the door and Dr. Greenwood looked up from his notes.

"Rex," he said.

I gave him a half-smile that was all I could summon up.

"Sit," he said and indicated that I perch on the edge of the desk. "Nose and ribs? Is that right?"

"Guess so."

He nodded and then silently set to work on my nose.

I studied his face. He was an attractive man in his early forties. I'd learned everything I could about him when I'd become aware that he was Cassie's private physician. There wasn't much to tell, really. His father had been the Bellingham physician for decades before *he'd* taken over. He was overqualified for a concierge doctor, but that meant he knew what he was doing and could take care of Cassie and our daughter.

"This hasn't healed properly from before," he said after a few minutes. "You may need surgery."

I shrugged. I really didn't care if I looked like a boxer that had lost one too many fights. I supposed Cassie might, though. Maybe Lachlan, as well.

"This is a safe space, Rex. Anything you tell me will remain confidential," he said quietly, pursing his lips.

I gave him a puzzled look, before the penny dropped. I let out a painful snort that half-choked me.

"I'm not being abused if that is what you are ass-backwards asking me, Doctor."

"Just know that you can tell me what happened, and I won't judge, or break confidentiality."

"A bar brawl. Nothing more," I stated. I wasn't going to go into our private business with this man. He wouldn't get it, for a start. He had probably never been tied up and whipped by his wife a day in his life.

He nodded and went back to work patching up my nose.

Then he started on my ribs.

I groaned as he poked and prodded and confirmed that it was, in fact, broken ribs. Three of them.

Lachlan was in for an ass-kicking, when I could gather up the strength to issue one.

He strapped me up and then handed me a prescription for painkillers.

"No thanks." I declined his offer.

"Don't be a hero," he chided me and shoved the script in the front pocket of my jeans. "I will follow up with Cassie, so I suggest you fill that. It will help you sleep."

"Don't need it," I said, shortly. All I needed to sleep was Cassie. It lengthened my sleep from half an hour a night to going on nearly three hours. It was more than enough. Besides, if that changed, and I slept more, we would struggle for bed space. This way, we all got into bed with Cassie at some point during the night.

I let the doctor leave first and then, after he had words with Cassie, I left the office and made my way into the living room.

My wife was wedged between her other two husbands, but they helped her up and Dr. Greenwood led her into our bedroom.

I growled at the other two men. "What is going on?"

Alex sighed. "Cassie is determined to follow through with that hare-brained scheme of hers to go back to work in two days' time. We thought it best if the doctor gave her a once-over before he left."

I glared him. "It doesn't bother you that the attractive doctor just took our wife into our bedroom?"

Alex looked over his shoulder. "You think he's attractive? I never even noticed."

"Me neither," Lachlan piped up. "But now that you mention it..." He frowned at the hallway as well.

"She wouldn't," Alex said confidently. "Besides, he could hardly examine her in the office."

"What's wrong with this sofa?" I snapped at him.

"Err," he stammered and looked down at it.

Then we all looked back to the hallway and, as one, scrambled to reach the door to the bedroom first.

~Cassie~

"HOW DO YOU FEEL?" DR. Greenwood asked me as I sat on the edge of the bed. He was looking at his notes and glanced up as my husbands came crashing through the bedroom door like a herd of elephants. Lachlan came to a dead halt, as Alex skidded in behind him, and, Rex, struggling to remain on his feet, by the looks of it, brought up the rear.

"What are you doing?" I asked them with a frown. "You'll wake Ruby."

"Uhm," Lachlan started and looked between me and Dr. Greenwood. "Rex needs to lie down," he added hurriedly.

Rex gave him a fierce glare, which turned bland again as I looked over at him. "Of course," I said quickly and stood up. "Come." I gestured to him. He looked awful.

Dr. Greenwood held his hand up and stopped me from taking Rex's hand. He leaned over and stuck his hand in my husband's front pocket, much to my amusement. He pulled out a piece of paper and thrust it at Alex. "Go and get this filled," he ordered.

I bit my lip to stop the laugh at Alex's thunderous face that he had just been commanded to do Rex's errand.

"Fine," he said, snatching it out of Dr. Greenwood's hand, giving him a filthy look that made me raise my eyebrow. He wasn't usually so rude. He made a big deal about leaving and then Lachlan led Rex over to the bed.

"We'll be in the living room, then, I guess," I said and walked out of the room, brushing my hand against Rex's as I went. I was still angry with him, but I wanted him to know that I had forgiven him. It would just take me a bit to get over the betrayal.

They watched as we left, Dr. Greenwood closing the door behind him as he trailed out after me.

Once seated on the sofa, Dr. Greenwood asked me again. "How do you feel?"

"Honestly, I feel fine," I said. "I'm still a bit sore when I've been on my feet, but I am fine to go back to work. I will be driven door-to-door, I'll take an elevator to my office, then I will be sitting all day."

He blinked at my over explanation. "Trying to convince yourself, or me, that you are ready?" he asked with a slight smirk.

I giggled and looked down. "You've got me," I admitted. "But I *am* ready to go back." I looked back up and gave him a stern glare.

He held my gaze for a long moment that bordered on uncomfortable, then he looked back at his notes. "Are you still bleeding?" he asked.

My cheeks went pink. Not usually shy about those things, I suddenly felt all hot and sweaty. His gaze came back to mine and it startled me. It was heated and sultry.

"I—I—err..." I stammered and tore my gaze away from his eyes and dropped them. Only *now* I was staring at his crotch, which was sporting a small bulge that was so obvious, I wanted to dive over the back of the sofa and hide.

My eyes shot back up to his. A glint of amusement played with the heat in their bright green depths. I licked my lips, because my mouth had gone so dry, but it was the wrong thing to do. His gaze dropped to my mouth and lingered there for a long moment.

"Uhm, uhm," I tried to speak, but I had no saliva flowing. My tongue was practically stuck to the roof of my mouth. "How is Beth?" I blurted out, hoping that the mention of his wife would stop this flirtation dead in its tracks. Clearly, my own husbands right down the hallway were not a deterrent to him.

He cleared his throat. "We are getting divorced," he said and looked back at his notes, scrawling something and then looking back up.

"Oh," I said flatly. This was so awkward. "Sorry to hear that," I added under my breath.

"Bleeding?" he prompted, ignoring my platitude.

"I—I—err," I stammered again and then mentally gave myself a kick up the ass. He was my *doctor*, for fuck's sake. I had known him since I was a child. Okay, yes, I'd had a bit of a crush on him when he'd been training with his father and he'd come to the Bellingham estate to see Granddaddy now and again. Good-looking, sure, but he was practically twice my age. I lifted my chin up and looked him dead in the eyes. "Actually, I stopped today."

"That's good," he said. "You are healing up nicely. May I take a look at your scar?"

Okay, he had thrown me off my game again. I was wearing a dress. That meant he would have to lift it and pull down my granny panties to have a look at it. I gulped.

"Sure," I croaked out.

He leaned over me and pulled a few cushions out from behind me and set them out for me to rest my head on as I lay down.

He helped me as I lowered myself to the sofa and then I slammed my eyes shut as he lifted my dress and, yep, pulled down my granny panties. I was so embarrassed, I wanted to die. I had to wear them so that they didn't sit on my scar. I knew that he probably knew that, but it didn't change the fact that they were the most unsexy things *ever*. Then I wondered why the fuck I cared about sexy underwear. I should be glad that I was sporting an unflattering pair of panties. Maybe it would put an end to this, whatever the hell it was.

He gently prodded me along the scar, making me wince. "It looks good," he said, leaning over me to look into my eyes again. "You are a quick healer." He grinned at me and then took me under my elbow and helped me to sit up.

"Uh, thanks?" I said with a frown. "Dr. Greenwood..." I needed to say something, anything, break this heat.

He brushed a stray lock of hair out of my face. "Call me Rob," he said and then sat down on the coffee table.

"Uh, okay," I said, because I had no idea what else I *could* say. "So, you agree that I am fit for work?"

"Hmm." He looked back at his notes again. "I see no reason, if what you said before is true. You will take it easy? Your Grandfather would have my balls if I cleared you and you ended up getting hurt."

I stared at him like a deer in headlights. Why was he mentioning his balls to me? Why was I picturing them now and that's it?

Fuck.

I needed to get my head back under control.

I was married to *three* men. I had enough balls to keep me going, thank you very much. I didn't need to be thinking about another pair.

"Cassie?" he said.

"Yes, balls," I blurted out and my cheeks went as hot as the fires of hell. "Uhm, *easy*," I added slowly. "Yes, easy."

He nodded, that smirk back on his face. It didn't make him look arrogant, just really fucking hot, all of a sudden.

Oh, Christ.

I closed my eyes.

I knew this appointment was coming to an end and I had something I had to ask him. Something, that if I didn't, my husbands would want to know why. I sure as shit didn't want to tell any of them about this situation that was getting me a bit flustered. Well, a lot flustered. They wouldn't take it well. Nor should they. I gulped and pulled my granny panties up even higher. Figuratively speaking, of course. They *literally* couldn't get much higher

"When can I have sex again?" I asked in a rush, opening my eyes, but avoiding his at all costs.

"As soon as you feel ready," he breathed at me.

I had to look back at him. Yes, sure enough, the heat was simmering in his eyes again. I definitely was not imagining this entire flirtation. It was happening and I had completely lost my cool.

"You are no longer bleeding and your scar is healing up nicely. I wouldn't engage in anything too...*vigorous* for a while yet and, of course, you should ensure you are suitably protected."

"Okay," I croaked out. At least that was good news for my husbands.

"I will write you a prescription for your birth control pills. Start taking them again right away, if you wish to have sex soon." His eyes bored into mine, but I couldn't look away. I gazed back into them, then at his mouth, before I looked back up.

His own gaze was on my mouth and he was inches from me. I stood up quickly and he did the same, only he was so close to me that he brushed against my boobs.

I had nowhere to go. I was wedged between his hard body and the sofa. My heart was hammering in my chest. I looked up at him, standing a good few inches taller than me, and he looked down.

We were in the perfect pose to kiss and it freaked me out.

Luckily, we were interrupted by Alex storming back into the penthouse like a snake had bit his ass.

He stopped dead as he took in the situation before him, his eyes narrowing into two thin slits.

"Cassie is healing well," Dr. Greenwood, *Rob*, said to Alex, stepping back a fraction and allowing me to breathe again. "I see no reason why she can't return to work so long as she takes it..." his mischievous eyes landed on mine again, "*easy.*"

"Humph," Alex muttered, clearly not happy with this diagnosis, but he no longer looked suspicious about the close quarters in which he'd found me and the good doctor. He threw Rex's prescription on the side table, along with his keys and phone. "Are you absolutely sure about this?" he asked me, full of concern.

I nodded. I knew he was also concerned about me leaving Ruby, but she was in good hands. Lachlan had already decided to go part-time, having hired someone to oversee Corsets & Collars for him when he wasn't there, and Rex's job was flexible. Aurora would have them around, probably more than she would care to, if I was honest. I would miss my baby girl, but I had to ensure her legacy. "It'll just be for a few hours a day, I promise."

"Fine," he grumbled. "I'll see you out," he added to Dr. Greenwood.

Rob nodded and gathered up his things. He straightened up and said to me, "Come and see me at the end of the week, so that I can make sure you aren't overdoing it."

"Can't *you* come *here*?" Alex barked at him.

"My office is only a block away from Cassie's," he said, almost smugly. "It's on her way home."

I gulped.

I knew why he wanted me to go there. It was so we would be alone and not surrounded by my husbands.

I didn't quite know what to do about that.

Chapter 11

~Lachlan~

I was propped up in bed on Sunday morning watching Cassie feed Ruby. She was sitting in the white leather armchair in the corner of the darkened room, a short white cotton nightgown covering up her gorgeous body. Rex had only just fallen asleep about forty minutes ago and Alex was out for the count.

Cassie looked up and gave me a small, secretive smile.

I narrowed my eyes at her. What was she up to?

Alex stirred and groaned softly, before he sat up and rubbed his forehead.

"Shh," I murmured to him and indicated Rex.

He glanced over and then slid off the bed without his usual buoyancy and sloped off to the bathroom. I frowned after him. He was the biggest morning person I had ever known. Something wasn't right.

Cassie was concerned as well, as her face had turned into a frown as she stared at the bathroom door.

I was about to follow Alex, when he came back out of the bathroom, his hair all mussed and his glasses on. He *never* wore his glasses. He got up with a smile and put his contacts in. It was his routine and he stuck to it.

"What's up?" I whispered to him.

He glanced at Rex and shook his head. He leaned over to give Cassie a soft kiss on the top of her head and then he disappeared out of the room.

"Go," Cassie mouthed to me, indicating with her head, and then made me chuckle as she made a rude gesture, thrusting her tongue into her cheek

I climbed carefully out of bed and pulled on a pair of sweats. Alex hadn't even bothered to cover up, so I wondered why I was.

I found him in the kitchen staring at the coffee machine.

"Alex?" I asked him in normal tones.

"Hmm?" he mumbled.

"Everything okay?"

"Headache," he said shortly.

"Come," I said and guided him by his elbow to the sofa. I sat him down and went around the back. I started to massage his shoulders and neck, digging my fingers in at the base of his skull. He groaned, but, this time, with relief.

"Speak to me," I ordered him. He was on the verge of a migraine. He didn't get them often, but I'd learned when he did, it wasn't pretty. He hated admitting it, as well. Stubborn asshole.

"It's nothing," he said.

"You are tense as fuck. Something is wrong. You've been in a mood since the doctor sent you out to get Rex's meds. What bit you on the ass while you were out?"

He huffed out a breath and tensed up even more, if that was possible. "It wasn't while I was out, but when I returned," he muttered.

I thought back to that time. "And?" I prompted. I couldn't think of anything that had happened to stress him out so badly.

He abruptly stood up and stalked over to the windows. I followed him and stood next to him with my arms crossed.

"When I got back, Cassie and that doctor were standing close together. Real close. He looked smug. Like he was up to something and had gotten what he was looking for."

I frowned hard at him. "What do you mean by 'close'?" I asked.

He turned to me, so I faced him. He came in very close to me. We were touching, skin-to-skin.

I was slightly taller than him, so I looked down and he looked up at me. We could have kissed quite easily by just me leaning down to press my lips to his.

"Are you sure?" I growled at him.

"Obviously," he growled as well, stepping back. He was aware of his nudity and, while not shy about it, he also didn't want his dick within touching distance of me. Shame. Cassie had given us her blessing and he looked like he needed a good seeing to.

"So, what are you saying?"

"Rex called it last night. I defended her, but I don't know about *him*," Alex snapped at me. "He wants to see her at his office at the end of the week. Alone, by the sounds of it."

"Well, that isn't going to happen," I snapped back at him.

He grimaced at me, the tension in his head getting too much for him.

"Besides, he is old enough to be her father," I pointed out.

"What has that got to do with anything? Her own father abandoned her. Maybe she is looking for a... I dunno...maybe she's looking for a bit of daddy kink."

I snorted into my hand. "You been looking on the internet again?" I asked him, amused.

"I have to, to keep up with the three of you," he snarled at me, clearly irate.

"I have known her for a long time." I did so enjoy pointing that out to him and Rex. It pissed them off and it amused me to see their jealousy. Alex glared at me, giving me what I wanted. "I have never known her to be into daddy kink."

"Maybe things have changed, or maybe you don't know her as well as you think you do."

"Ouch," I drawled. "I'll let that go, because you are clearly in pain. Turn around," I ordered him. He did and I started to massage his shoulders and neck again.

We stood in silence for a few minutes.

"You like that?" I murmured to him.

"Mm," he replied.

"Everything okay in here?" Cassie asked, walking into the room, causing Alex to tense up again.

"Yeah, fine. Alex has a headache. Where's Ruby?"

"I put her in the bassinet next to Rex. Oh no," she said, full of concern. "It's not a migraine is it?" She came over to us and rested her hand on his chest.

He looked down at her and pulled away from me, just as I was expecting him to. It hurt, but whatever. She took him in her arms, and he kissed her, passionately, almost desperately. I turned away and stared out of the windows, contemplating what he'd said.

Daddy kink?

No, I would know if she was into that. She would've said.

But the doubt lurked now. Alex wasn't into fabricating evidence to suit his mood, unlike a dark, brooding psychopath I knew. He knew what he'd seen, and he'd known what it looked like. I completely believed him about Dr. Greenwood having ulterior motives.

Alex pulled away from Cassie and, to my surprise, slipped his hand into mine.

He pulled us both over to the sofa with an inquiring look at Cassie. "Are you ready yet?" he murmured to her.

She shook her head, to my crushing disappointment. I hadn't gone this long without sex...ever. I was dying over here. So was Alex, by the looks of it.

"I have to get back on my birth control pills first," she said. "I'm getting them today. Give me another week, okay?"

"Okay," we both whined.

"Don't suppose I can convince you to give him a blowjob while I watch you?" Alex piped up hopefully, after a brief pause.

She grinned. "Well, *that* I can do," she said to my delight. I was going to give us both something we wanted.

"On your knees," I whispered to her, fisting my hand into her raven hair and pulling just a little bit.

Her eyes lit up and went all sultry and sexy as she licked her lips. "Yes, sir," she murmured.

"Wait," Alex said, putting his hand up. "She's..."

"It's okay," Cassie said, her eyes dropping to her feet and grabbing hold of Alex's outstretched hand to help lower herself to her knees.

I felt like a dick now. I'd totally forgotten in the moment that she was still in pain.

"Wait," I said, but she shook her head.

"I'm fine," she said, and let go of Alex's hand.

She reached up and pulled my sweats down. My dick sprang free, right against her lips.

"Oh," I moaned as I twitched against her mouth.

She opened up and slowly took me in, sliding her tongue all the way down my length, before she worked her way back up to the tip, wrapping it expertly around me, before she sucked me so hard, I cried out.

As much as I was enjoying this and so was Alex, apparently, as he had taken up residence on the sofa, and was gently stroking himself as he watched us with hooded eyes, it wasn't what I'd been going for.

I grabbed a handful of her hair and wrapped it tightly around my fist. She gasped but stopped what she was doing immediately.

"That's better," I said to her in a low tone.

I started to jerk my hips roughly, fucking her mouth, forcing her to deep throat me.

She took it and reveled in it.

Her eyes were shining, and she was in sheer rapture as I used her mouth to pleasure myself. She sat back on her heels, her hands at her sides.

"Take her hands and hold them behind her," I demanded Alex.

His eyes went wide, but he leapt off the sofa and knelt behind her, holding her hands behind her like I'd ordered.

"Much better," I said, keeping up the low, dark tone that made her shiver.

I had never dominated her before. Not like this. I hadn't thought I would be able to, but it was intoxicating. She was enthralling.

I pumped my hips a few more times and then stopped, keeping my dick in her mouth as I stared down at her. She was beautiful.

"Alex," I said, keeping my eyes on Cassie. "Let go of her and kneel next to her."

He gave me a furious look, but he did exactly as he was told.

I gave him a smug smile that was wiped off my face when I remembered what he'd said about Dr. Greenwood.

I scowled at him and said, "Open up, you owe me."

His eyes flashed, but when I pulled my dick out of Cassie's mouth and shoved it in his, he didn't complain. I knew it was very different going from having your cock sucked to sucking a cock, but he took it and did a damn fine job. Not as skilled as Cassie, but it was his first time. He would get there.

I pulled my cock out of Alex's mouth and thrust into Cassie's, then I dragged out and thrust back into Alex's. I did this several times and seeing them both on their knees, servicing me with their mouths, got too much. I drew back and came all over their faces with a loud groan as my cum spurted out to cover them.

"Fuck, yes," I moaned, and then I did something so profoundly stupid, I would live to regret it until the end of my days.

I looked down at Cassie and asked quietly, "Who's your Daddy?"

Alex's eyes shot straight to my face in horror.

Cassie breathed in deeply, her green eyes swimming with unbridled lust. She licked her lips and then lowered her gaze as she answered.

"You are."

~Cassie~

I WAITED AS LACHLAN went silent.

I felt Alex's eyes on me, boring into me, probably confused and surprised.

I had only ever done this once before, with an older man at Corsets & Collars, before I'd found Rex. He'd tried to make me his princess, but I just hadn't felt it with him. Not that I was averse to the idea, quite the opposite. I found it quite hot. I had *not* known that Lachlan was into it. Did *he* want to make me his princess? I'd wanted him to dominate me as his sub, but I could fully get on board with calling him 'Daddy'.

"On your feet," Lachlan said curtly and held a hand out for me to take so he could help me up.

I took it, suddenly confused as well. Did he not want this, after all?

He gently helped me to my feet and Alex shot up as well, naked and covered in cum, looking really hot. His face was pinched. He was still fighting off that migraine. I gave him a smile and slipped my hand into his. I drew him down and kissed him, swirling my tongue around his. I felt he needed it after having Lachlan's cock in his mouth. He fell into it, so I guessed I was right.

Then, I pulled back and looked at Lachlan. He was frowning at me, his eyes full of something that I hadn't ever seen there before and couldn't quite place. Was it jealousy? Not of Alex, surely. No, I had to have that wrong. Lachlan didn't get jealous. It wasn't his style. He was so laid back. It was why he bounced so well off Rex, who made uptight seem like a casual day at the beach.

"Everything okay?" I ventured.

"Yeah," he said and then with a hard look at Alex, he stalked off.

"Know what that was about?" I asked Alex.

He shook his head.

"Let's get you cleaned up, although I could lick it off you, if you'd prefer?" I trailed a sharp nail down his bare chest.

"I wouldn't normally say no to that, but if you do that, then I will want to ravage you and you aren't ready yet," he said and he, too, stalked off, leaving me staring after him, alone and suddenly feeling more insecure than I had been when I was pregnant.

"What the hell is going on?" I said out loud, stamping my foot and putting my hands on my hips. First, Lachlan was acting all weird and now Alex. I couldn't cope with it on top of Rex being so secretive and broody.

Things were going to have to change around here. Soon. *I* ruled this roost, not them. They were supposed to be the ones left alone in rooms wondering what the fuck? Not me. Oh no. Not. Me.

Well, the only thing left for me to do was shower and then ignore them until they apologized for being...whatever they were being. I still didn't know. I didn't like being confused.

I heard Ruby cry and I rushed to her, but Rex was up and holding her gently, white-faced against the pain it was causing him.

"I'll take her," I said briskly. I was still pissed with him as well.

"No," he said, standing up to me by actually standing up and moving out of my way. "I want her."

I gritted my teeth. I couldn't deny him. It was kind of the first time he had been so determined to hold her, instead of being the only one left to do it.

"Fine. I'm showering," I said. Knowing that Alex and Lachlan were both in the bathroom, doing who knew what, I stalked off to the guest bathroom, which contained a small, simple shower, as opposed to the huge power-shower in the en-suite.

I was *not* amused.

As I stood there under the torrent of water, I felt around my scar. It definitely felt better, and Dr. Greenwood had said it was healing nicely.

Dr. Greenwood.

Rob.

I mean, what the fuck was all that about?

He'd never flirted with me before, so why now? Because he was getting divorced? Was I a trial run for him getting back out there? Making sure he hadn't lost his mojo?

Well, I huffed out a breath. He definitely hadn't lost anything.

I narrowed my eyes. Had Alex told Lachlan about what he'd walked into last night? Was that why he was being weird all of a sudden? Although, what he'd walked into had been an unknown. It hadn't been *anything,* really. But it might have looked like *something* to one of my husbands.

Shit.

Fuck.

They must've discussed it and come down on the side that I'm to blame.

But why go through with the sexy times if that was the case? And *why* had Lachlan said what he had and then backtracked?

I let out a noise of frustration as I was going around and around in circles. The easiest thing to do would be to confront them, but then that would give them the satisfaction of an easy resolution. I wanted them to suffer a bit with my cold shoulder first.

I left the bathroom in a foul mood and they all knew it as I entered the bedroom. Even Ruby must've sensed the growing atmosphere as she started to scream, and Rex got way out of his depth. His panicked look would've made me laugh had I not been trying to act stern and pissed off. He quickly gave her to me, and I was happy to disappear, clad only in my towel, into her nursery to settle her.

I sensed my men hovering outside, as I sat in the rocker, but none of them had the balls to come in. I chewed my lip. The thought of balls only made me think about Rob again. Aw, shit. Rob. It was becoming way too easy to think of him that way. I was going to have to nip the infatuation in the bud. From both sides. His, especially. *I* would never do anything with him. I was thrice married, and I had no intention of adding a fourth husband to my little harem. As it stood now, everyone had a hole. Add in another and what would happen then? Double vag penetration? Double anal?

Hmm.

On second thoughts, it sounded kinda fun.

I shook my head. "No," I whispered to Ruby. "I have more than enough on my plate with your daddies."

A soft knock scattered my sinful thoughts.

"What?" I snapped.

Rex popped his head around the door and, with a sheepish look, came into the room, closing the door behind him.

"She okay?" he asked.

"Fine."

He nodded.

An awkward pause.

"I know you are still angry with me and you should be, but I am so sorry, Cassie. Please, you have to forgive me."

"I have," I replied. "But I am still angry, disappointed and hurt, really. You didn't trust me to help you through it. You just decided to bail. What will happen next time something gets too much for you?"

"It won't," he said, coming over to me and kneeling down painfully, but pretending it wasn't. "I will *never* leave you again, Cassie. I love you. I *cannot* live without you, or Ruby."

"I believe you," I sighed after a minute. "I know that I bring you some sort of peace, I just wish you would trust me with everything. I could help you so much more than you let me."

"I know," he muttered, looking at Ruby. "One day, Cassie, I promise you. I just need to find the words."

"Lachlan knows," I accused him without thinking.

His black eyes searched mine. "Not really," he said slowly. "He knows...more...only because of the way I was before I met you when I went to his club to seek...something. It's not because I sought him out to tell him."

"I don't want him to know more about you than I do," I pouted at him, running my hand through his hair and scraping my nails across his scalp.

He sighed. "I don't want that either. I—I have a job. It'll require me to go away for a day or two. I swear to you I will tell you whatever you want to know when I get back."

His words gripped my heart. "Will you come back?" I asked tightly. "Or, is this an excuse to leave, an easy way out?"

"No," he said forcefully. "I *will* come back. This is work, nothing more."

"Can't you refuse the job? It's not like you need to do it." I was still in full sulk mode.

I saw him take that in, but then he shook his head. "I am not relying on your money to make a life for my daughter," he said, almost angrily. "*I* will provide for her." He stood up to make his point.

I had two choices. Either let him go away and trust that he would come back. Or, emasculate him completely by telling him he had to quit his job and tie himself to the penthouse because I didn't trust him.

"Fine," I groused, not looking at him, knowing it really was the only choice. Besides, if he was away, it was one less husband on my tail when I went to see Rob to figure out what he wanted from me before I told him to get lost.

He nodded and dropped a kiss on my head and one for Ruby, before he left me alone again as she had started to cry. She was tired. So was I. I'd been up most of last night with her, because the whole night had been restless with Rex struggling to get comfortable enough to sleep and disturbing me and Lachlan. The only one who'd had any real sleep was Alex, but he was also in a mood today. Not to mention, I had a case of nerves about going back to work tomorrow and leaving Ruby for the first time, as well as the knowledge that I had to go to see Rob.

I sat back with a sigh and rocked Ruby to sleep.

Today was going to be great. Just great.

Chapter 12

~Alex~

"You really are a dick," I told Lachlan for about the tenth time. "What exactly were you hoping to achieve?"

He shrugged. "I was testing your theory."

"On *yourself*?" My incredulity made him roll his eyes at me. "Or is that something that you want with her? You want to make her your..." I snapped my fingers trying to remember the word, "...your, like, kitten. Or whatever?"

He shook his head at me. "You really need to stop looking at stuff on the internet. I've told you that before. If you want to learn stuff, ask me. Or, better yet, come to CoCo and learn first-hand."

"Yes, we've had this discussion," I said haughtily. "I'm *not* going to your club."

"Well, tough, because the Mistresses Ball is coming up soon and I'm holding it there because of the delay I had to put on it for Cassie to attend. She will want you there, whether you like it, or not."

I grimaced. I'd heard of the Ball. It was where Cassie had flitted off to with Rex the night I'd told her I'd wanted to date her.

We stopped talking as Cassie made her way into the living room and gave us the stink-eye before she turned into the kitchen. It was all open plan so we could still see her, but she wasn't looking at us. She was pissed. I didn't blame her. Lachlan had played a dangerous game with her and then bailed, while I'd rejected her and made her feel like shit, because of her surgery.

We were both a pair of assholes who didn't deserve her.

Don't even get me started on Rex.

"I'm going out," she said, coming back into the living room and glaring at us huddled on the sofa. "Ruby is asleep. She's exhausted. I'll be about an hour. If she wakes before then, feed her, please."

Then, she turned on her heel and walked over to the elevator and punched the button.

"Where are you going?" Lachlan asked her, a braver soul than me.

"Out," she snapped at him and stepped into the elevator, smashing the button on the inside to get the doors to close.

"Fuck," he muttered.

"I think you have driven her straight to him," I growled into his ear and stood up.

"Where are *you* going?" he asked. "And, this isn't my fault. I honestly thought she would tell me to get fucked. I didn't know she would be into it."

"Into what?" Rex asked, coming into the room, freshly showered.

"Nothing," Lachlan said as I said, "Daddy kink," at the same time.

To say Rex's eyes nearly popped out of his head was an understatement, before they hooded so fiercely, his face practically folded in half.

"What?" he asked, deathly quiet.

"It was a test," Lachlan said, putting his hands up defensively. "It was Alex's theory."

"Not really," I barked at him, coming to my own defense before Rex tore my head from my shoulders. "I was talking about the doctor being into her and things got..."

I didn't get to finish my sentence as Rex's hand closed around my throat. "Say that again," he growled.

"You have got to stop doing that," Lachlan chided Rex and removed his hand from me. "We are wasting time. Someone needs to follow her, find out where she's gone."

"I don't think that's a good idea," I started, but Rex was already at the front door, dragging it open.

"If he so much as touches her, I will kill him," he said on his way out.

"Now look what you've done!" I blamed Lachlan.

"I'd better..." He pointed to where Rex had stormed out.

"You think?" I responded and put my hand to my eyes as he left. My head was killing me. This migraine was about to hit me full force, but I couldn't succumb to it. I had been left alone with Ruby and that took precedence over my own need to crawl into a dark hole and puke until my stomach lining came up.

If Cassie had decided to pursue the doctor, it would devastate me. I already felt woefully inadequate around her and the other two men. They each gave her something she craved, but not me. My own stupid insecurities and inhibitions got in the way of that.

A phone buzzed on the side and it caught my attention. It was Rex's. He'd been so hell-bent on getting to Cassie that he'd forgotten it. I snatched it up and glanced at the screen. All I got was a notification of a text message. He wasn't dumb enough to have previews like the rest of us. The number was unknown, so it had to be from the dick who was threatening him.

I had no way of getting into his phone, so I threw it back on the sideboard and went to sit down, dropping my head into my hands.

"Who's your Daddy?" I scoffed. "What a fucking prick."

My vision went blurry, so I stood up and stumbled into the nursery as quietly as I could.

Ruby was fast asleep, looking so sweet and beautiful. I couldn't let her down, but I was failing. Fast.

I laid down next to her crib and closed my eyes. If she needed anything, I was right here. I just needed to shut out the light for a moment and gather the strength to push it away until Cassie or the other men returned.

"WAKE UP," CASSIE CALLED to me softly, her hand on my shoulder.

I cracked my eyes open, but all I could see was a swirl of dots and lights. I squinted at her.

"Alex, can you get up?" she murmured to me.

"Yeah," I said and hauled myself to my feet.

She grabbed my hand and led me out of the room and down the hall. She pushed me gently down and left me to go and close the drapes. The scrape of the metal rings on the metal pole made me feel nauseous.

I flopped back to the bed and curled up in a ball.

"Rest," she whispered to me, stroking my hair and giving me a light kiss. "I will kill the other two for leaving you like this with Ruby."

I wasn't sure if she was pissed because they'd left me. Or left me with Ruby. Or both. Probably the latter. She was in a mood with us and I didn't think she was feeling very generous where we were concerned.

"I'm sorry," I muttered.

"What for?" she asked softly, sitting on the bed.

"Rejecting you earlier. I was weirded out." It was as good an excuse as any.

"Oh," she said. "Yeah, I get that. You've had an adventurous morning."

I snorted and then winced as it felt like a rocket had launched in my head. "What Lachlan said to you? Do you want that from him?" I ventured cautiously, seizing the opportunity.

I felt her shrug. "Maybe. I was surprised that you allowed him to treat you that way."

"I went with it," I slurred, drooling onto the pillow. This conversation was taking its toll on me.

She knew it and kissed me again, leaving me alone to sleep it off, wondering why the other two men hadn't found her.

~Cassie~

I WAS DREADING TODAY. Monday had come around far too quickly and now it was the day that I had to leave my baby girl. I had to keep these concerns to myself, or my husbands would jump on it, making me stay at home instead of going to work.

I also had to go to see Rob. I'd wanted to go yesterday when I'd stormed out, but I'd been pretty sure that one, or more of them, would've followed me. Normally, it wouldn't really bother me, but yesterday I had wanted to be alone just for a little bit. So, I'd gone to the 24-hour pharmacy and then I'd doubled back to find Alex on the floor next to Ruby's crib, completely out of it and no Lachlan or Rex in sight. I was positive that Rex had followed me, and Lachlan had followed Rex. To say I'd been furious was an understatement, but I'd become sick to death of everything being weird and tense and the atmosphere wasn't good for Ruby, so I'd forgiven them for being idiots. Plus, they had made it up to me by attending to my every whim for the rest of the evening. Alex had remained in bed and only surfaced this morning with his usual bright smile and go get 'em attitude.

Aurora had arrived at 7am sharp and she was settling in nicely as Rex and Lachlan watched from the sidelines.

"Be nice," I murmured to them, as I bustled about getting ready with way less enthusiasm than I was showing them. "I will be ready to leave the office just after lunch, okay? It's only a few hours."

Rex nodded at me and picked up his keys. I gave Lachlan a deep kiss and then Alex, who was already on his way out. Then, I bent to snuggle into Ruby, fighting back the tears. Maybe this was a bad idea. Maybe I was being foolish to think I could run an empire *and* have a baby. Feminists everywhere would be shaking their fists at me and throwing burning bras my way, but I couldn't help how desolate I felt when I stepped into the elevator with Rex.

The drive was silent without Lachlan accompanying us to break Rex's natural terseness.

"When are you leaving?" I blurted out when I couldn't stand it any longer.

He gave me such a filthy look, I gulped. What had I said?

"I am *not* leaving," he replied coldly. "I'm going away for work."

I failed to see the difference, but clearly, he had an issue with the word 'leaving'.

"Okay," I squeaked, a world away from his Mistress.

"I'm not sure," he said, after shooting me an apologetic look.

"Oh."

We went back to silence, so when my phone beeped, I snatched it up quickly with relief, which quickly turned to dread.

It was Rob.

Come and see me today, Cassandra.

I can't.

I need to know you are okay after your first day back.

I glanced at Rex. If he was suspicious about the messages, he didn't show it.

Fine. My office. Lunch.

I didn't see why I should go to *him* when I was the one who'd just had surgery.

See you then.

I stuffed my phone back into my briefcase and clutched it to me, lest Rex grab it off me and search through my messages.

He didn't, though. He pulled up outside my office and leaned over to kiss me.

I returned it deeply, needing things to be right with us again after his breach of trust on Saturday.

"I love you," he whispered to me.

"I love you," I answered with a soft smile.

He returned it and then he climbed out of the SUV to come around to my side to help me out.

He kissed me again before he led me to the door.

Then I went it alone from there, heading up to my office where a pile of paperwork was waiting for me to go through.

I'D HAD ENOUGH BY 11AM.

I'd video called Aurora three times already to see my darling Ruby and was on the verge of making it four. I knew that Lachlan and Rex would have something to say about it when I got home, but I didn't care. I was uncomfortable in my office chair, tired, frustrated and in need of some good sex before I exploded.

I moved over to the sofa and sighed in relief as the pressure eased up on my scar a bit as I took off my shoes and propped my feet up. I uncurled my hair from its hairband and took my phone to make my video call home when there was a knock at the door. I frowned at it. No one ever knocked. They were buzzed in by my assistant, Marjorie.

"Yes?" I called out.

The door opened and Rob stuck his head in. "Hi," he said. "Marjorie wasn't at her desk, so I knocked."

"Oh," I said and gave him a tight smile. He was an hour early and I wasn't prepared.

He came all the way in and shut the door. "I know I'm early, but I couldn't wait to see you," he said, approaching me slowly, almost stalking towards me, his eyes raking over me in my white business suit and bare feet.

He ran his hand through his short, dark hair and gave me a sexy smile as he sat in the armchair adjacent to the sofa.

"How are you?" he asked.

"I'm fine," I replied, my heart hammering in my chest. "A little tired." He would see that, just by looking at me, so there was no point in denying it.

He nodded slowly as he took in every inch of my face.

I had to get to the bottom of this, but I took a few seconds to take him in as well. He was very good-looking, and he had a hard body. He kept himself in shape. He had that distinguished look about him that I knew Alex would get when he got older. I couldn't deny that it was having an effect on me.

"What do you want from me?" I asked him bluntly.

He tilted his head and gave me a questioning look but didn't say anything. It unnerved me and made me start to babble like an idiot.

"I mean, you have never flirted with me before. Why now? All of a sudden? What are you expecting from me?" I stood up and started to pace, my eyes never leaving his.

"I have always found you attractive, Cassandra, but I was married. Now that I'm not, I have decided to do something about it," he said matter-of-factly.

I gaped at him. "*I* am married!" I exclaimed, jabbing myself in the chest to emphasize this point he seemed to have completely overlooked. "To three men!"

"Yes. It's interesting that you sleep with all of those men, but they don't seem to mind," he said now standing up as well.

"What?" I practically yelled at him. What was he trying to say?

"I don't see an issue in pursuing you, Cassandra. Fidelity obviously isn't something that bothers you."

My mouth dropped open in shock. "How dare you!" I spat out at him. "I am completely faithful to them."

"Yes, *them*," he said. "Multiple men. Why not consider one more?"

"For starters, I am in love with my husbands and we are in a *committed* relationship with one another. Secondly, you are *my doctor*, for fuck's sake."

He shrugged. "I can recommend someone. That's not a problem."

I stared at him wide-eyed in utter disbelief. "This isn't going to happen."

"Why not?" he asked, coming closer to me. I backed up, only to hit the wall behind me.

I was boxed in between him and the wall. He had a habit of doing that.

"I know all about you, Cassie. I know what you're into. I've seen you in Corsets & Collars. I go, too. I like...certain things and I know you can give me what I'm looking for," he said in a deliciously low tone that made me shiver.

"You don't know anything about me," I insisted, highly pissed off with Lachlan for never telling me that my doctor frequented his club. I got the whole confidentiality thing, but this should've been mentioned, as far as I was concerned.

"I know you will be open to what I want from you," he said, curling a lock of my loose hair around his finger.

I swallowed. "What is that then?"

He sighed, his eyes on my mouth. "I have searched for someone who I could take care of. Someone I could make my princess, but I have never found the right girl. They always ruined it by wanting more from me than I was able to give because of Beth. Now, I'm searching, but all I can find are subpar versions of you. I want the real thing, Cassie. I want *you*. If you agree to be my princess, I will treat you like a queen," he smiled at that, knowing how corny it was. He leaned in closer, encouraged by me not telling him to shut the fuck up and get away from me. Why wasn't I? I didn't know. My body was betraying me. I was so turned on by his words that I was close to agreeing to everything, regardless of what my husbands would have to say.

"I know you seek approval from your father, Cassie, deep down. Who doesn't? He doesn't deserve to have that kind of devotion from you. I can give you everything you want from him, and more. I can love you, shower you with affection and give you the acceptance, praise and admiration that you desperately need."

I licked my lips.

Holy fuck.

He had hit my sore spot dead on.

My father was a cold, distant, awful man who had never given me the time of day. All he cared about was my mother's money and the lifestyle in which she kept him. He'd never once hugged me, or told me that he'd loved me, or even cared about me. I didn't think he had ever even looked me in the eye, choosing to ignore me, no matter what I'd done to try to get his attention. But I still wanted him to love me.

My breathing was getting heavier by the second. I stared into the green eyes of Rob Greenwood and wanted what he was prepared to give me. Whatever game Lachlan had played with me yesterday had everything to do with this. He must've known this was coming and he'd been testing me. It hadn't been real. He'd played with my emotions and it had stung. Especially coming from him.

But, as much as I wanted this, I couldn't do that to my husbands. I *was* faithful to them. I didn't want to add another man into my life, even one who was offering me everything I wanted, but in a different form. A form that would give me so much more satisfaction than I'd ever known possible. It was hard to turn down, but I had to. My husbands would never agree to me becoming Rob's princess. They wouldn't stand there and allow me to call him, 'Daddy' and have him take care of me and punish me when I was naughty.

I was about to open my mouth and tell him that it wasn't going to happen, when the door burst open and Alex strode in with a face of thunder.

"I fucking knew it!" he yelled.

Chapter 13

~Cassie~

"This isn't what it looks like!" I blurted out, pushing Rob away from me quickly. His finger was still curled in my hair and it *so* looked exactly like what my husband was thinking. But I was glad that it was just Alex. I could sway him around to my way of thinking. If it had been Rex, then shit would've been way worse.

I groaned as I totally jinxed myself.

Rex stormed in behind Alex with a matching look of thunder, followed by Lachlan, looking less surprised, more resigned.

Rob's eyes were on me, daring me to come clean about our entire conversation.

What the hell was I supposed to say?

Oh, guys, by the way, Rob, here, has decided he wants me to engage in daddy kink with him and I'm totally into it?

Somehow, I knew it would go down like a lead balloon.

"What are you doing here?" Alex asked Rex and Lachlan.

"Probably the same as you," Lachlan replied, because Rex was too busy giving Rob a death stare and clenching his fists like he was ready to throw a punch.

"How did you know?" Alex asked.

"How did you?" I asked Alex. "What are you all doing here?"

"I knew something was going on Saturday night," he replied. "I knew you would meet up with him today."

I blinked at him. That was unexpected. He'd really known that? Was I that transparent?

"You don't want to know how we ended up here," Lachlan muttered under his breath, but I didn't get to ask what *that* meant, because Rex had reached out and grabbed Rob by the throat.

"Let him go!" I ordered my husband.

He did as I asked, but with a rough shove, which had Rob stumbling backward.

"Explain," Rex said, shortly, his eyes landing on me.

"Yes, Cassie," Rob piped up. "Tell them what I asked of you."

I sighed. For the love of God. There was no way I could get out of this now. "Rob asked me to enter into an arrangement with him."

"Oh, did he now?" Lachlan asked, edging closer with the evil eye on my doctor. "And what was that then?"

"I want to take her as my princess," Rob said, not giving a rat's ass that he had the scariest looking man on the planet glaring at him.

Before Rex could even comment on that, though, Lachlan came even closer, elbowing Rex out of the way.

"Well, I hope that you aren't too disappointed to learn that she has already been claimed in that respect," he said, making my heart pound.

"Oh? By whom? She never said."

Lachlan's eyes flicked to mine and then back to Rob's. "By me," he said in a tone so deliciously, downright danger-ous, I caught my breath.

"You did *what*?" Rex growled at him, but Lachlan ig-nored him as he focused completely on Rob.

"She is *my* Little Girl and I don't take kindly to her being poached."

I had stopped breathing. Lachlan had been serious about the role he'd wanted to play with me? The shiver that went over me was one of sheer pleasure at the thought.

"I've known you a long time, Clarke. Didn't think that was your thing," Rob scoffed.

"You don't know anything about me," Lachlan replied, still in that dark tone that had made even Rex stay silent.

Rob looked at me. "Is this true?"

I leapt into action. "Yes. You didn't give me a chance to tell you before my husbands stormed in. But now that I have your undivided attention you will listen to me. You are a fucking dick!" I spat out. "How dare you insinuate that I am some sort of whore sleeping around and thinking you can be another notch on my bedpost." I was furious as the bubble of the last few minutes had been burst by reality.

"He said that?" Rex asked me, coming forward again.

I nodded my confirmation, expecting there to be words, but what happened next caught me by surprise.

Rex bunched his fist up and smashed it into Rob's face so hard, I heard bones shatter. Blood splashed out everywhere and Rob's cries of agony alerted Marjorie — who had appar-ently returned to her desk sometime in the last five minutes

— who came rushing through the door to see what was going on.

"Holy fucking shit balls!" I cried at Rex, but he was like a raging bull.

He pulled back and threw another punch and then another and then grabbed Rob by the throat. "If you ever even *look* at her again, I will kill you," he threatened. I gulped. He was deadly serious. He was like a raving lunatic.

Then he hit Rob in the solar plexus so hard, I was sure he must've done permanent damage. He dropped like a stone, completely winded.

"Jesus!" I screeched, staring down at the heap on the floor and then up at Rex in utter shock. He was glowering down at me, his face turning from pure rage to a blank, dead look that I had never seen before. It scared me. But somewhere deep inside, it also excited me. I knew that he was over-protective, but I had never witnessed first-hand just how much. He had defended my honor in the old-fashioned way, and it had desire coursing through me for him. However, this was completely unacceptable. What had he been thinking? Marjorie was wailing about calling the cops and worse, my *grandfather*. There was no way I could let my husband go to jail, or have Granddaddy ever find out about this. He would skin us all alive for bringing this mess into the workplace. I stepped forward with a look at Alex that he understood immediately. He knew Marjorie and he knew she was still close with my grandfather after working for him for thirty years. He grabbed her by the arm and with a soothing tone, he said, "Let's get you a cup of tea and a sit down, love." He steered her out of my office as I started to shake. Lachlan was just standing there looking at Rex, expecting some kind of backlash.

He got it.

Rex advanced on him, but didn't lay a hand on him as he snarled, "When did you decide this?"

"Yesterday morning," Lachlan said. "I was going to mention it when we had worked out the details." He cast a curious gaze at me.

I tuned them out as I reached for my phone. There was only one person I could call in a situation like this, my Uncle Teddy. He would know what to do. He had connections in the police department, and he could...well...I didn't know what he could do, but I knew I had to call him.

As I waited for the call to connect, Rex finished his conversation with Lachlan. He was pissed. He threw me a look that showed me his hurt and anger that I had decided to become Lachlan's princess.

"This really isn't anything to do with you," Lachlan said to him quietly. "I don't get in the middle of what you have with her."

"You still should have discussed this with me first. She is my Mistress. You owed me that." With that, he stormed out of the office.

"Wait!" I shouted at him. "You can't leave!" But I was talking to myself. He was gone.

"Fuck!" I yelled at Lachlan with a desperate look.

"Not this time," he said calmly, taking the phone from me. "You need me. This time, he will have to deal with his shit on his own."

"I—I..." I choked back a sob that threatened to come out. This had all gotten way out of hand.

"Teddy?" Lachlan said into the phone and then he turned and had a hushed conversation with my uncle.

I turned back to Rob. He was hauling himself to his feet and then he slumped on the sofa.

"An ambulance is on the way," Lachlan called over and then went back to his conversation.

"You shouldn't have done this," I chided Rob. "You don't know Rex."

"If you think this is going to stop me from getting what I want, then you don't know *me*," he responded, wiping his bloodied nose on his shirt sleeve and cursing as the pain shot through his face. "Fucker," he muttered.

"You have to give this up. Lachlan has claimed me. You can't interfere with that," I said.

"Like hell," he rasped back at me. "This is new between you two. I am pretty clear on his motivations, as well. I want this for the right reasons."

"What does that mean?" I asked, turning to him and giving him a filthy look.

Lachlan had finished his call and handed me back my phone. "Don't worry. Teddy's got it covered."

"Fuck that," Rob spat out. "If you think you can cover this up, you are dead wrong. That bastard is serving time for this."

"No, he won't," I said, "because if you press charges against him, then any chance you had of me changing my mind about you, will vanish without a trace."

Lachlan cleared his throat and gave me a penetrating look.

"So, you are saying, if I let this go, you will consider my offer?" Rob asked, sitting as upright as he could under the circumstances.

"Yes," I said and ignored Lachlan as best I could under the circumstances. "I can be a princess to you both, but you need to drop this," I added.

"Done," Rob said.

Ha, who needed help in dealing with this? I just needed to trust I could handle this on my own.

"This is just me considering it," I made clear.

Rob nodded slowly.

"May I have a word?" Lachlan asked me, absolutely furious, with good reason.

I nodded and left Rob prodding his nose and face to assess the damage.

"What do you think you are doing?" he hissed at me.

"Trying to smooth things over. If he presses charges, Rex is going to jail," I hissed back. "I'm using what he wants as leverage."

"He's hardly going to prison," he scoffed. "He's got Bellingham protection."

I scowled at him, but his face was ashen. He wasn't confident of his words and it scared him.

"That aside, I thought *we* had an arrangement," he said in a stilted tone that was rare coming from him.

"Do we?" I asked, folding my arms across my chest and looking up at him. "We have never discussed this as something that you want from me. It was sudden and then you sort of bailed on it."

"Do *you* want it?"

"Yes," I said. I'd been game before, but Rob had awoken the beast inside me that wanted this with every fiber of its being. "Can you be that for me?" I looked back at Rob quickly, before finding his eyes again. "Fully. Truly. Or, was it because you knew Rob wanted it and you were attempting to stake a claim, so he couldn't?"

He didn't answer me a long time.

~Lachlan~

I LOOKED AT MY WIFE, my best friend, and knew that I had to lie to her. If she knew I'd been testing her, to see if it was something she'd really wanted, she would be hurt, and she would have every right to be pissed with me.

"Yes, fully and truly," I replied, after searching her eyes and seeing that she needed this from me. If *I* didn't do it, then Rob would be lined up to give her what she was after. I should've known this about her all along. I should have seen the signs. It was my fucking *job* to get to the bottom of people's kinks and give them what their heart's desired. Why hadn't I seen this about the woman that I loved?

The relief in her eyes made me realize that I had made the right decision. I could do this. It wasn't like I hadn't done it before. I had done *everything* before. I couldn't run a sex club and not have tried everything that I had to offer the good people of New York.

I pulled her to me and kissed her, not caring that Rob was still in the room. I ravaged her mouth, wishing it could go so much further. I drew back and murmured against her lips, "I want you to be my princess, Cassie. I will give you everything you want. You will get everything you need from me."

Her eyes filled with love and it solidified it for me.

"Now, go and see Alex and Marjorie and tell them everything is going to be okay," I said, giving her a light pat on the rear. "I'll stay with him until the paramedics arrive."

She looked back at Rob and bit her lip.

"I won't touch him, I swear," I told her with a smile.

She chuckled and then she grabbed her shoes and disappeared out of the office.

I fixed my gaze on Rob and crossed my arms across my chest. "You will never have her," I said. "If you think Rex is dangerous, you have never seen me protect someone I love. She is half your age, you filthy pervert. If you think for a second, I will let you get your hands on her in *any* way, you are deluded." I hated to judge anyone, but this was different. This was about Cassie.

"She does this, or that bastard goes down for assault. It's a simple decision for her. She will do this," he stated.

"No, she won't. You will not interfere with our relationship. You are fired as her doctor, you are banned from Corsets & Collars, and if I so much as even *hear* your name again, I will make what Rex did to you today seem like a playground tussle. Are we clear?"

He licked his split lip and winced. The fear was in his eyes. He knew I was serious, and he knew I was capable, because he knew I would do anything for Cassie.

"You don't get to decide that," he tried again.

"Cassandra is *my* Little Girl now. If I order her to never see you again, she will obey me or face punishment."

"You'll use your role to dictate to her?" Rob scoffed. "She will never stand for that. She is stronger than that."

"She takes her play seriously. If you knew that, you wouldn't think you are right about what I can, or can't, make her do."

I saw the realization hit him, but he wasn't backing down. He was a sucker for punishment.

"If she ever comes to me and says she wants what I can give her, all the threats in the world won't stop me from taking her. She is everything that I have wanted for a very long time and despite what you think, I *know* her. I have been around her family a lot longer than you have. I have seen first-hand how her parents treat her. How *Damien* treats her. I have waited for the right time to seize this opportunity and I am serious about what I can give her. *You* are doing this to stop me. She will realize that what you are offering her isn't true and she will come seeking what she needs from *me* and there isn't a damn thing you can do to stop it."

I leaned down and got right in his face. "You will have to go through me first. Mark my words, when I am done with you, there won't be much left over for Rex to pick off. If he doesn't kill you, I am pretty sure that Alex has it in him somewhere to keep your disgusting hands off his wife. Stay the fuck away from her."

With that, I straightened up and left him alone to con-template my words, passing the paramedics on my way out of Cassie's office.

Alex looked up from where he was sitting with Marjorie and Cassie. His gaze was questioning, and I gave him a de-termined nod back.

He grimaced, but he knew what page we were on. "Cassie? Can we have a word please?" he said.

She patted Marjorie's hand and stood up, leading us to the outer foyer that separated her offices from the rest of the executives.

"Before you say anything, let me explain," she started.

"There is nothing to explain," I said. It was clear that Alex didn't agree with me, but I would take him aside later and fill him in. "He tapped into your desires, Cassie, and used it against you. You don't have to feel bad, or like you did some-thing wrong, because he offered you what you wanted. But, know that you don't need him, or anyone else. If you ever need *anything* from us, any of us, whatever it is, you must never feel ashamed, or worried about what we might think. We love you and accept you and we will *always* support you, no matter what. You can count on us to give you your deep-est, darkest desires without judgment, as I know you will do the same for us."

Her eyes filled with tears and she fell into my arms. "You have no idea how much I needed to hear that," she sobbed. "But, please, you need to go after Rex. What he did in there...I have never seen him so out of control. Please go to him and we will talk more later." She turned to Alex and held him for a moment, before she pulled away and headed back to Marjorie and also Rob, who was still in her office. I could only hope that Teddy turned up soon now to protect her, because I knew, without a doubt, that Rob wasn't going to give up pursuing her unless we did something permanent about it.

Chapter 14

~Rex~

I was shaking. I was so furious, but I didn't have cause to be. Lachlan was right, whatever he and Cassie did was up to them. I wasn't into dominating her anymore, so she had to find that elsewhere and I'd wanted it to be Lachlan. I just hadn't known it would take *this* form. It went to something far past a Dom/Sub relationship. It was deeper and would hold something exclusive to them within it that no one else could touch. That *I* couldn't touch. I hated to admit it to myself, but I was jealous. So jealous.

The thing with Rob was nothing. Cassie wouldn't enter into an arrangement with him, I was certain, especially after I'd what done to him. That, in Cassie's office earlier, was the tip of the iceberg. I had done far worse to others for less where she was concerned. But never in front of her. Never, ever, while she was watching. It was the *only* thing that had made me pull back, or I would have beaten him to death for even daring to suggest that she be unfaithful to us.

I hunched my shoulders and shoved my hands into the pockets of my black denim jacket. I was walking through the throngs of people, trying to clear my head in the crowd. It was controlling the rage. The rage that I had towards Lachlan for doing this to me. He, of all people, should have known better than to, not only blindside me with this, but to ask Cassie to do it in the first place.

I was so absorbed in my anger that I didn't even notice that someone was stalking me, until I stopped at a crossing and he stepped up next to me.

"Rex," Derek said.

"What do *you* want?" I asked rudely, in no mood to deal with this asshole.

"My boss wants to see you."

"Tell her she can go and fuck herself. Or, is that your job?" I said, turning to him.

The sharp look he gave me had no effect. I *wanted* him to come at me. It would give me the perfect excuse to get rid of this feeling of needing to destroy that I'd had to pull back from with Rob. So, I gave him a challenging look that got his blood roaring. He was jonesing for a fight as much as I was.

The crowd moving forward tore our gazes apart and we had no choice but to move with it over the street to the other side, where he grabbed me by my elbow and pulled me to the side of a building.

"I would listen to what she has to say, if I were you," Derek snarled at me. "You already look like shit, but that won't stop me from dragging your ass to her if I have to."

I shoved him off me, ignoring the slice of pain in my ribs that had been throbbing in agony since I'd worked Rob over a little bit.

"You want me to go anywhere with you, you will have to drag me. Especially to see that bitch."

His face went really dark, which only proved I was right. He was doing her. I wondered what William would think about that. Obviously, Damien didn't give a flying fuck what she did.

"I know stuff about you, asshole. Information that I would happily pass along to that little slut you are shacking up with, so I would listen up real good..."

He didn't get to finish what he was saying, because, despite the crowded streets, I decked him so fucking hard, I was sure I broke my hand. He had a fucking hard head.

"Jesus," I muttered, but I would do it again. "No one talks about Cassie that way. I just smashed another man into the ground for it, don't think that you won't be next."

He smirked at me and rubbed his jaw. I'd hurt him, but not enough. He was a tough son of a bitch. It would take a lot more to get this asshole off his feet. Not for the first time that day, I wished for the heavy feel of my Glock shoved into the back of my jeans. I knew that if I still carried, Rob would be lying dead in Cassie's office right now and she would know all about me. It was one of only a couple of reasons why I kept it locked up now.

"Just move," he said and gave me a rough shove that made me bite my tongue as the pain arced through me. Fucking Lachlan and his steel-toed boots. He was next on my list of asses to kick.

The crowds had parted momentarily after my fist had connected with Derek's asshole face, but they soon forgot about us and swarmed around again, intent on making the most of their lunch break. We got lost in the throngs as Derek kept shoving me forward. I was in no fit shape to take him on, that much was clear, so I had no choice but to go with him. Besides, maybe this would all come to a head now.

I would find out for definite that it was Suzanne who was threatening me, and we could all move on and Cassie would never have to know what kind of a man I really was.

A few moments later, we stopped at a black SUV idling at the curb. Derek opened the door and shoved me inside. He attempted to get in himself, but Suzanne stopped him.

"Alone," she barked at him.

He glowered at me but slammed the door and climbed in the front.

"Thank you for joining me," Suzanne drawled at me.

"Like I had a choice," I drawled back, giving her a filthy look. It was uncanny just how much Cassie looked like her. Only Cassie's green eyes were full of life and love and passion. This bitch was cold, calculating and full of hatred.

She smirked at me. "I was so disappointed to learn that Cassandra wanted to remove me as her Power of Attorney," she said. "But that isn't going to happen. You see, I run her entire trust. I am the only one who can change the Power of Attorney and I am not removing myself."

"I'll pass it along," I muttered, wondering where the fuck she was going with this.

"Mm, I'm sure you will," she said, giving me a searching look. "Do you have any idea how much she will be worth when she turns twenty-five?" she asked suddenly.

"I don't care," I replied.

She laughed. "If that's the truth, then you will be the only man in the world who doesn't."

"Not true."

"Oh, yes. The other two," she said insultingly.

I shook my head at her. "What do you want from me?"

"Quite a bit. I'm getting to that," she said dismissively. "Cassandra will be worth three billion dollars in a little over a year. The rest of her trust will unlock, and she will be the sole heir to my father's estate."

I hadn't known that. Cassie never spoke about money. The bitterness in Suzanne's voice wasn't unexpected by this revelation and it actually explained a lot. Why she'd never wanted her daughter and why Damien had wanted even less to do with her. They were jealous that Cassie would be the sole heir to the Bellingham Empire, and probably worried that their gravy-train would come to an end when she did inherit the lot.

"I don't know why you are telling me this, but, as I said before, I really don't care. I am not with Cassie for her money, or her position. I love her."

"Love," she scoffed. "Are you even capable of that?"

"Are you?" I challenged her, to her amusement.

"Touché," she chuckled. "But you seem to be missing my point. The company she runs now is only the tip of the iceberg. She will be in charge of the entire empire that *my* father built from the ground up. She will be so consumed with work; you will never see her. *Trust* me on that."

Her sadness caught my attention, but it was gone as soon as it had appeared.

"She will be working 90-hour weeks, weekends, holidays, *birthdays.*" She counted them off on her perfectly manicured fingers. "Her child will never see her. Ruby will be brought up by nannies and you three lovesick idiots, when you are there. Is that any way for a child to be reared?"

"You tell me?" I asked her, her words hitting me hard in the stomach. "This is obviously about you."

I hit the nerve I was looking for and smirked at her.

Her eyes flashed dangerously. "No! This is about Ruby. That girl will grow up not really knowing her mother, because she will always be at work."

"Cassie would never do that," I said mildly, fully believing it. "She would never allow her job to take her away from raising her daughter."

"It isn't a *job*," she sneered at me. "It's a legacy. One that my father slaved over for decades so that he could pass it along to someone 'deserving.'" She used air quotes. "I am telling you this now, Rex, so that you will do the right thing."

"And what is that?" The dread was coiling its way around my guts, squeezing tighter and tighter.

"I am filing for full custody of Ruby," she stated, out of the blue. "That child is going to need full time guardians and Damien and I are able to give her that."

I couldn't help the gawk and then the snigger that escaped. "Are you fucking serious?" I laughed. "The two of you couldn't keep a houseplant alive and you expect, with your track record, to gain full custody of our child?" I was utterly incredulous. "You are seriously fucking deluded, Suzanne."

"Cassie turned out all right, didn't she?" she sniffed, not that hurt by my comments at all.

"Yes! Which was *nothing* to do with you, but your parents and her own fucking fortitude. If you think for even a second that this is going to happen, you are going to be very disappointed. Cassie will fight you to the death for her daughter. And so will I."

"That's where you come in," she said, holding up a folder. "You are Ruby's biological father. You will sign over your parental rights to me and Damien. That will prove to Cassie that you think it is the right thing to do and I will leave it to you to convince her of the rest."

"Not a fucking chance," I growled at her. "Why would you think I would do that?"

"Because of this..." She held up another folder.

I grimaced at it. I knew exactly what was in it.

"You do this for me, and I won't tell Cassie what a bad man you really are," she said in a voice so sickly-sweet, I wanted to vomit.

I needed time to think, to find a way out of this. I couldn't, *wouldn't,* do what she'd asked. However, I also knew that Cassie could never find out about my past. Suzanne had me well and truly over a barrel.

"What about the job?" I asked as a distraction. I knew that Suzanne was behind the threats.

"Oh, I still need you to take care of that," she said in surprise. "I will pay you now for your work. I hear you are the best, after all."

I gave her a level look. "Who is it?"

She gave me an evil smile that sent ice shooting through my veins. "Here," she said and chucked a third file at me.

I opened it and looked down at the photo and raised my eyebrow. "Oh?"

"I believe you know him."

"I've had the displeasure," I drawled, slamming the file shut. "Why?"

She laughed. "I thought you didn't ask questions?"

"I'm making an exception."

She took in a deep breath. "I'm protecting my daughter from that predator."

I narrowed my eyes at her. *Predator.* That was an odd choice of word. "You will have to do better than that."

"What's it to you, anyway?" She ignored my statement.

"He is currently on his way to the hospital for a beating that I just gave him for trying to take advantage of my wife. I want to know why you think he is a predator and why you want him taken out. Is he really a threat to Cassie?"

"Yes," Suzanne said. "I have known Rob Greenwood all of his life. We grew up together. He is a pig. How Beth put up with him all of those years is a mystery to me. She must've given him what he wanted in that area. No wonder she finally decided to call it quits. Filthy pervert."

"What has he done?" I asked quietly.

Her eyes flashed with something unexpected and it tore at me. "Why do you think we sent Cassie away to boarding school and conveniently forgot to get her all those years? Why do you think we insisted she attend university in England? Because that disgusting pervert wanted her from when she was a small child. You might think we were monsters, Rex, but we were trying to protect our little girl, the only way we knew how."

I gaped at her. "What?" I thundered at her. "He sexually abused her?"

"It never got as far as that," she said shortly. "We stopped it before it did. Cassie wasn't the only child of his father's patients that he went after. There were supposedly plenty that were left in the wake of that bastard. Nothing was ever mentioned, because of how hard it would've been to prove. He was squeaky clean. Not to mention...the *scandal*." She took in a steadying breath.

"Why did you let him get so close to her?" I asked, wondering the same of myself. I'd never found out any of this in my investigation of him. It was *very* well covered up.

"It wasn't our choice. She was an adult and wasn't going to listen to anything we had to say. Besides, we figured Rob had gotten over his predilections as things had gone quiet while he was with Beth. But we heard something a few months ago...He tried? Today?"

"Yes," I said quietly. "He tapped into something she wants and used it. I made sure he wouldn't do it again in a hurry."

"Fuck," she muttered, her eyes closed.

Then they flew open again and the sort of 'moment' we'd had was gone. "You will do this job to protect Cassie and then you will sign these forms giving your parental rights of Ruby to me and Damien, or I will tell Cassie everything. She will get rid of you so fast your head will spin if I give her this folder. She always was a bleeding heart, taking care of every living thing, from those stupid bonsais to stray cats and wounded birds. How do you think she will feel about you killing people?"

I gave her a look that would usually have someone backing down, but not this time, not this woman. She was as hard as nails and I thought I might've unlocked a small part of the reason why. It didn't change anything. She was still a bitch and I still hated her. I had a moment of clarity when the rest of the pieces fell into place. She didn't give a rat's ass about

Ruby. All she wanted was control of Ruby's trust. That was what all of this had always been about. Money.

"Never," I said. "I will do this job. Not for you, but for Cassie. No one will ever hurt her. Not him and certainly not you. Tell her, if you must, but I will never let my wife, or my daughter, think that I willingly abandoned her."

I shoved open the car door, hoping that I hadn't just made a grave error.

If Suzanne called my bluff and told Cassie, I was done for.

Chapter 15

~Cassie~

I breathed in deeply. I was nervous. It was Saturday night, the night of the Corsets & Collars Mistresses Ball.

After the incident in my office with Rex and Rob, I'd decided that perhaps I wasn't ready for a full time return to the office. I'd made the decision to work from home three days of the week and go to the office for two full days. The sharks could circle for all I cared. They wouldn't get their mitts on my company. I wouldn't allow it.

Aurora was still here full time, which left me to work when I needed to. She took on a lot more around the penthouse than was expected of her. She was a godsend who cooked, cleaned and took care of Ruby like a pro, all with a smile on her face. She had proved the men wrong and now they would be lost without her. As much as I liked to pretend I could cook, Alex was the expert in that area. But with his job, he had precious little downtime, so with Aurora taking that on, it made him happier than I had seen him of late. He'd been hitting the gym more often to work off his frustrations.

They were all frustrated, but tonight that would end. Tonight, I planned to take my men into a playroom at the club and fuck them all until they were happy. It'd been four weeks since my surgery, but I felt fine. Sure, I wouldn't be doing any gymnastic fucking for a few weeks yet, but I was fully capable of giving them a night they would remember. Especially Rex.

I had forgiven him for his actions in my office on Monday. I hadn't had much choice.

Alex and Lachlan had been firm in their convictions that he had done the right thing, and they'd made it clear that if I thought differently then, what the fuck? They were right. I didn't care about Rob. He was fine. He'd gotten patched up and walked out of my office and I hadn't heard from him since.

I expected that I would. He'd been adamant that he would press charges if I didn't reconsider his offer.

I wasn't taking it. Lachlan had stepped up and that suited me just fine, even though we hadn't yet played in that way, we would. Soon.

But tonight, was about *my* dominance. It was about Rex's submission to me and I couldn't fucking wait to show him off. I had a special surprise for him that I knew he would love. It was in the gym bag, along with my outfit. We had to get dressed at Corsets & Collars tonight. We couldn't very well leave here in full BDSM mode with Aurora holding our daughter, waving goodbye to us. Although, she had walked in on the display a couple of weeks ago and had not said a word, or judged us in any way, it wasn't appropriate in front of our daughter.

I took a moment to steady my nerves. I wasn't as nervous as I'd been last year. That'd been my first time and we had barely stayed long enough to enjoy it. I intended to make the most of this evening and, although I wasn't a Mistress to

Alex and Lachlan, they would still be there. Lachlan obviously needed to be there, but Alex had agreed to attend as Lachlan's plus-one. They were already there, so it was just going to be me and Rex in the car, alone for the first time since he'd beaten up my ex-doctor.

It'd given me a small insight into his head. Now, I just needed to smash the rest of that wall down. He would do anything to protect me. I was fine with that. I enjoyed it. The submissive part of me enjoyed that dominance in a man. I shivered every time I thought about it.

But tonight, I wanted to forget all of that. Forget work and how tired I was. I wanted to show off my husband and make sure that all those other women knew he was mine.

Lachlan had pulled me aside a few days ago and told me I needed to keep a tight leash on him. He was a hot commodity in this world, an alpha male that submitted to his woman. I knew I would never lose him, but I intended to keep him as close to me as possible. I couldn't risk someone getting close enough to him to offer him more than I did. I couldn't let him think that he needed things I wasn't prepared to do. Call me selfish, but this was my show and I wanted to run it *my* way.

"Ready?" he murmured from the doorway.

"Yes," I replied, with a smile.

He returned it and picked up the bag. His smile grew at the weight of it and he jiggled it.

"Nice," he whispered. "I can't wait to see what you've got in here."

"Patience," I chided him, then we walked to the elevator where Aurora and Ruby were waiting for us.

We both kissed our sleepy baby goodbye and then stepped into the elevator.

"Have fun," Aurora called quietly and waved to us as the doors slid shut.

"You okay?" he murmured.

"Yes," I said brightly. I was missing my baby already, but my husbands needed me tonight. Ruby was in good hands.

We were silent as we left the elevator and climbed into the SUV. Rex grabbed my hand and put it on his leg as he drove us to the club.

It was late out now. A light rain was falling, splashing onto the windows as I got lost in my thoughts, trying to push my nerves aside.

The club was already filling up when we arrived and pulled up around the back.

Alex was waiting for us at the back door, looking way more nervous than I felt. I didn't blame him. He was so far out of his comfort zone, it wasn't even funny. But he gave us a brave smile and bent to kiss me, before he stepped back and then did something that surprised both me and Rex. He gripped Rex's t-shirt in his fist and dragged him closer, pressing his lips to Rex's and slipping his tongue into his mouth.

"Oh," I breathed out, the desire slamming into me.

Alex drew back with a wicked smile that did nothing to quell the burning lust. "Hi," he said.

Rex was looking down at him with a look akin to amusement. "Hi," he said and then took my hand and we followed Alex into the club. We ducked into Lachlan's office and Rex dumped my bag on the desk.

"We'll leave you to get ready," he said and kissed me briefly, before he disappeared with his own bag slung over his shoulder and Alex on his tail.

As soon as the door closed, I opened the bag and pulled out my chosen outfit. It was new and very sexy. A sheer black top that showed off my tits, held together with black leather straps and black panties. That was it.

I slipped into my killer black heels and put my kitty mask on. I was ready to go. I reached into the bag and pulled out a long chain with a black leather collar on it. It was for Rex. Last year, I'd had him cuffed to me, but this year I wanted him on a leash.

He was waiting for me outside Lachlan's office with my other two husbands, dressed only in black leather pants. So was Lachlan, but Alex had decided to wear a tight black t-shirt with his black jeans.

They practically drooled when they saw me.

I smiled to myself. Oh, yeah. They wanted it bad, but they would have to wait until I was ready to give it to them. I wanted to parade Rex around for a bit and take in the atmosphere before I succumbed to it.

"You like?" I teased.

To say that they panted their reply would be an understatement. It made me giggle and then I crooked my finger at Rex, holding up the leash in my other hand.

His eyes filled with pleasure as he took it in. He smirked at me and then it disappeared as he bowed his head, his eyes on the floor. He had turned into my submissive and I wouldn't see my husband again until I told him to come back.

"Down," I ordered him, and he did as he was told. I leaned over and fitted the collar around his neck and then picked up the attached chain.

I gave Alex and Lachlan a small smile. "See you later," I murmured. I knew they wouldn't be too far away from us, but they would leave us alone. I started walking and met resistance when Rex remained where he was.

"Come," I barked at him and he stood up and followed me meekly.

The rush of power that I felt was intoxicating.

I could feel Alex's eyes on us as we got lost in the crowd, but it only served to turn me on more.

I could've used a drink, but I needed to remain clear-headed for Ruby. I was no good to her tipsy later, or hungover in the morning. Instead, I led Rex to the bar and asked for a club soda.

When it arrived, I took it and moved it to the side. "And a bowl of water for my pet," I added wickedly.

The bartender didn't even flinch as he put it in front of Rex.

I dragged Rex a bit closer. "Drink," I said to him.

I half expected his alpha side to rear its head and refuse, but, without even a look at me, he leaned over and lapped up the water.

I ran my hand into his hair, scraping my nails over his scalp. "Good boy," I murmured, and then the music pumped out so loud, it nearly deafened me. I was used to quiet, calm, lullabies these days, not hard-core techno. I grimaced as I realized I had turned into a 'mom'. Not that it was a *bad* thing. I adored my baby and I wouldn't be without her, but I felt, in that moment, that I'd lost a part of myself, which was only exacerbated by the fact that I hadn't had sex in forever and rough sex in even longer. That had to change. Tonight. I was ready and if it hurt just a little, then that was fine as well. I wasn't wasting another second worried about my scar. It had healed and I was fine.

I roughly pulled on Rex's leash, dragging him away from the water and snapping my fingers at him to pick up my glass.

He did and I led him to the dance floor. It was already heaving with gyrating bodies. Tits and asses and cocks were all on display, bouncing around, and it made me smile. I took the glass from Rex, took a few deep swallows and then left it on a table to drag Rex as close to me as I could with both hands on the leash.

His body pressed into mine, firing up my libido like I had never felt before. I moved against him, keeping one hand on his leash. The other, I ran up his rock-hard chest, enjoying the feel of his well-defined abs and pecs.

"You are magnificent," I purred at him, before I pulled hard on the leash, forcing him to lower his head. I licked his lips, slowly and seductively, as I ground against him, feeling his hard cock pushing against me. I slid my hand over it, and he groaned.

He stood stock-still as I rubbed my hand over the bulge in his pants, all the way up his stomach and chest again. At the same time, I licked my way down his throat, suddenly biting down over the sensitive spot on his neck. He gave me no reaction, other than breathing in deeply. He was mine to do whatever I liked with and, right now, I just want to lick him, taste him, and feel him like I hadn't done in so long.

I felt eyes on us, knowing it was Alex and Lachlan, but also a handful of strangers that had stopped to watch this slow seduction that had me so wet already I was almost dripping.

I pushed Rex to his knees, my hand on the back of his head, as I pushed his face to my pussy.

He breathed in the scent of my arousal and awaited my next instruction. "Suck me," I said to him, wondering if he would even hear me over the thump of the music.

He did, because he pressed his mouth against the fabric of my underwear and then sucked so hard my clit twitched.

"Ah," I cried out, throwing my head back, keeping my hold on the leash to keep me steady.

He ground his teeth together, nipping me gently, before he sucked again, causing a rush of wet heat between my legs.

"Fuck," I breathed.

I was completely aware that everyone on the dancefloor had stopped what they were doing to watch us now. The music was still pumping out the bass and I was lost. Only Lachlan coming up behind me and whispering in my ear, made me come back to planet earth. "You sure you want to do this?" he murmured.

I opened my eyes and caught everyone watching me. It made my heart thump.

"Yes," I said, needing to do this. I threw every last inhibition I had to the wind and reveled in the power I now had over everyone on the dance floor. "Touch me," I demanded Rex.

He wasted no time in sliding his fingers past my panty line and onto my clit, before he delved into my hole with three fingers, making me cry out at the invasion.

"Fuck," I heard Alex mutter in my other ear.

He had joined us, and I wondered what he was going to do.

Watch, or join in?

~Alex~

I LOOKED DOWN AT REX finger fucking Cassie in the middle of the dance floor and my dick went so hard, I thought it was going to break. I was highly aware of several pairs of eyes on us, but, if I didn't do anything, that would be worse than having everyone see me do *something*. I followed Lachlan's lead and moved in even closer to her, nuzzling her neck and twisting her other nipple. She squirmed in our arms, her breathing heavy. She turned her face to me. I could see her eyes behind the sexy kitty mask. They were shining with triumph. She wanted this and there was no way I would let her down now. I looked up as a chair came skidding over to us, which someone had kicked in from the sidelines. I grinned and sat down. I pulled Cassie down onto my lap. She allowed Rex even more access to her as he pulled her panties off and she opened her legs wide. I was glad that he was shielding her from all of the prying eyes. I was just able to stand her having her tits on display, but her pussy was different. That was *ours*.

I felt her wiggle over my dick, so I slid my hand down and fumbled with my jeans. I was free within a few seconds and inside her a second after that. I just couldn't wait any longer and the opportunity was right here.

She gasped at the invasion of both my cock and Rex's fingers. She started to move, and I groaned. She was soaking wet and so hot. It had been so long. I knew I was being a selfish prick, but I got here first. It really was as simple as that. I reached up and dragged Lachlan closer to me by his hand. He looked down at me in question and then grinned when I undid his leather pants and dipped my hand inside, pulling his cock free.

"Tempted as I am by this, Suits, we are here for her," he said to me.

"I know," I retorted, grabbing her hips as she moved up and down on me. "Put your cock in her mouth. Let her suck you off in front of all of these people."

"Oh, you don't need to ask me twice," he murmured, and guided his cock into her already open mouth. She was skilled enough at this to ride me and give Lachlan a blowjob at the same time without missing a beat. It was such a turn on, that I couldn't hold on any longer. I dropped my head back as she fucked me, using me to please herself and I unloaded into her with a loud groan.

The crowd moaned with me, as Rex withdrew his fingers and went back to licking her clit so that she could follow.

She did within moments. She clenched around me, saturating me. I kept my dick inside her, willing it to get hard again so that I could keep pleasing her.

Lachlan had his hand on the back of her head as she sucked him off. I watched her mouth, her lips, her teeth grazing him.

"Fuck," I murmured as she drew back with a wicked smile on her face.

I knew what she wanted. So did Lachlan. He jerked himself off for a few seconds and then he came on her face, on her tits, in her mouth.

The beat of the music was making my heart pound in time to it. The throng of people drew in closer. All eyes were on us.

It was the most hedonistic thing I had ever done, and I loved it. I hadn't thought that I would. But here, in this atmosphere, there were no inhibitions. No one was judging. All they wanted to see was a live sex show and it was up to us to give them the best one they would ever see.

Sure, they were only really looking at Cassie. We were just her props and that was fine by me. I would do anything right now to please her.

Rex made her come again. She milked my cock into a hard enough state for her to be able to ride me again.

She slowly tugged on Lachlan's cock, a sensual movement that had me and everyone else, mesmerized.

He was thoroughly enjoying being the center of attention and I envied that. I was glad that most of me was hidden.

When Cassie turned to me and whispered, "Suck him," and guided Lachlan's cock to my mouth, I hesitated, but only for a second. The low noise of the crowd suddenly went up a notch and all eyes landed on me.

They were waiting for me to do it.

I had no choice.

I didn't want one.

I was all in.

I'd been half out of it with pain when Lachlan had made me do it last weekend. I'd just gone with it. This time, my head was completely clear. It was a conscious decision to open up and grab his cock, sliding my tongue over him, tip to balls, and then, back up. I closed my mouth over him, and he let me take the control this time. Cassie stood up and turned around, straddling me as she watched us, leaving Rex behind her.

I didn't know how he did it. How did he just sit there and not ravage her? I couldn't do it. I had no restraint with her. I was already so hard and ready to come again as she fucked me, watching me give her other husband a blowjob, that he was definitely enjoying by the heavy breathing and the hand he slid into my hair. It encouraged me to up my game a bit. Suck him that bit harder, reach up and squeeze his balls until he moaned.

"Fuck, Suits," he groaned. "You're fucking killing me."

"Let go," Cassie murmured. "In his mouth. I want to watch him swallow every last drop." Her eyes were on me, challenging me.

I raised my eyebrow at Lachlan, my mouth full of his enormous cock.

He closed his eyes, and, with a quick thrust and a loud grunt, he came, flooding my mouth with his salty taste.

It was a reflex to want to spit it out, but there was no way I was doing that. Cassie wanted me to swallow, so I did.

"Fuck," she murmured at me and pulled me away from Lachlan to her mouth, kissing me deeply, swishing her tongue around, tasting him in my mouth.

"Jesus," I muttered as I came again inside her.

She gave me a sassy smile and then she turned away from me again, grabbing Rex's head and guiding his mouth back to her pussy.

I was spent. My role here had been fulfilled. All that was left for me to do was to sit and watch and wait to see what she would do next.

Chapter 16

~Cassie~

I was in ecstasy. Pure and unadulterated.

This was the most erotic experience of my life and I was reveling in the power of having all eyes on me. I scanned the crowd and saw a few of the men were jerking themselves off as they watched us. Even more were servicing their Mistresses as the women couldn't tear their eyes from us either.

I was about to come again, but I didn't want that yet. I wanted to savor the anticipation.

I put my foot up and, digging my heel into Rex's shoulder, I pushed him away from me.

The loss of his mouth on my clit was savage. A brutal tearing of pleasure away from me by my own foot made me grunt with dissatisfaction.

I panted, needing it back, but also wanting to give the voyeurs a heightened experience.

Rex sat back on his heels; his head bowed. He amazed me in that moment. I knew he could do it. I knew he could deny himself an orgasm as I had demanded it more than once from him, but here, like this...I'd half expected him to quit being my bitch and jump me. I was glad that he didn't. In a Mistress-y type of way. I needed all of these women to see that I had an alpha male that did what *I* fucking told him to.

It was enthralling.

He was enthralling.

I could see the envy, feel the jealousy directed my way.

It made me smile a slow, almost evil, smile as I grabbed Rex's head and moved him back to my pussy.

His eagerness to please me again was so hot, I had to force myself not to thud against his mouth. He added three of his fingers again, twisting them around inside me, before he finger fucked me. He drew his mouth back and added a fourth finger.

I gasped as he stretched me, but I was so slippery with Alex's cum and my own juices, that he slid his fingers in and out easily, his thumb teasing my clit every now and again.

I felt myself on the verge again, but, again, I didn't want it. I shoved him away to the gasps from the voyeurs.

I laughed. I couldn't help it. They wanted to see me come and I was denying, not only myself, but all of them. It was so empowering. I didn't think I would ever come down from this high.

I touched myself then. I rubbed my clit, my eyes on Rex. He was waiting to touch me again, waiting for my permission. I denied it to him. I was being cruel, but a part of me loved this wicked side.

I waited a few more seconds and then I nodded at him, letting him thrust his fingers back inside me, as I continued to play with myself. I drew my eyes away from him and looked out at the crowd. They knew I was going to come this time and they knew it was going to hit me like a freight train, having denied myself twice.

They held their breath, furiously masturbating, as they watched and waited. One man, in particular, caught my eye. He was in a gimp mask and leather pants. His dick was in his hand as he pumped furiously, fixated on me. He stepped closer and closer, his hand working even more to bring him pleasure.

I indulged him. I pinched and twisted my clit, gasping as I felt my blood start to race. I flicked and circled, and then it was on me, sweeping me up in its wave, as I kept my eyes on the man. It was mutual masturbation with someone other than my husbands and it had got me off something good. I felt only a slight tinge of guilt as the blood rushed straight to my pussy and I clenched tight around Rex's fingers, moaning out loud as the man took his loosened mask off and came as well, all over his hand.

My eyes went wide.

Rob?

He flashed me a dark look, as I sat up suddenly, but then he was gone. Lost in the press of people that had watched our sex show.

Lachlan told me he'd banned him from Corsets & Collars. How had he gotten in here?

I felt ice cold all of a sudden.

The moment had swept me up and I had been encouraged by his attention. But the fact that he had been standing there the entire time, jerking off to me having sex with my husbands, made my skin crawl. I don't know why. It was just a sudden and awful feeling that I had that was insidious and menacing.

I stood up and hauled Rex to his feet, grabbing my abandoned drink off the nearby table. I downed it quickly, quenching my thirst.

Alex and Lachlan, sensing the change in my mood, quickly followed me as I stalked off the dance floor, still underwear-less, but not really caring. It wasn't like covering up now was going to hide anything. They had all already seen what I had to offer.

I dragged Rex into a playroom in the back and let go of the leash. Alex and Lachlan joined us, and Lachlan closed the door.

"Time for Rex," I barked out, hiding my creeped-out feeling behind my Mistress mask. "Get on the bed," I ordered him. "Strap him down," I added to Lachlan.

I didn't think Alex would get involved in this. He had once before. He'd held Rex down while I'd tormented him, but he hadn't done it since, and he'd made it clear that he just wanted to watch.

They both did as I commanded, and, minutes later, Rex was on the narrow bed, his arms stretched out to the sides, cuffed in place by Lachlan. I gave him a challenging look to see if he wanted to dominate Rex now that he was in such a submissive position. He gave me a mild look back and stepped away.

Good. That wasn't a problem that needed addressing. I had been growing increasingly concerned about what I had witnessed between the two of them the day Rex had said he was leaving me.

Feeling that pain and humiliation and insecurity fired up my cruel side. I was going to put Rex through the ringer before I gave him a fucking he wouldn't forget in a hurry.

I sauntered over to the array of whips on the far wall. The low, red lighting was messing with my vision after the intensity of the sex show. My head was fuzzy, but I brushed it aside and reached for a cat-o'-nine-tails.

I spun back to Rex, ignoring my slight lightheadedness and approached him, flicking the whip against my leg.

"You've been a naughty boy," I purred at him and lashed him across the chest, slightly harder than I meant to.

He flinched but made no sound.

"You denied me," I pouted, placing the blame on him for my own actions. "Twice."

I wanted him to bite back at me, but he didn't. I didn't know why I was suddenly feeling so hot and sweaty. I felt claustrophobic.

Lachlan frowned at me and handed me a bottle of water after he uncapped it.

I drank deeply, feeling my head clear a bit. I thrust it back at him and lashed out at Rex again.

"So, so naughty," I sighed and laid the whip down.

I leaned over and undid his pants, dragging them down, so that his cock sprang free. He was rock-hard, and it pleased me.

I licked him once and then pulled back, picking up the whip again.

"Don't you want to make your Mistress happy?" I asked him, trailing the whip over his cock gently.

"Yes," he murmured. "Always."

"Good," I said appeased, but then lashed out at him again with the whip so hard, I saw the red welts pop up on his skin.

I felt sick.

But I didn't stop.

My head was going fuzzy again.

"Why won't you let me in?" I shouted at him out of the blue, whipping him again.

"Uhm," Lachlan said, stepping forward.

"Stay out of it!" I snarled at him, turning on my husband.

He narrowed his eyes at me.

"You aren't his Master. He is *not* your sub. He is *mine!* Got it?"

"Got it," Lachlan gritted out.

I spun back to Rex, feeling dizzy. I put my hand to my head and whipped him again. "Why? Why won't you tell me about yourself? Why do you make me feel like this? Do you want me to be insecure? Do you?"

"Cassie," Lachlan said, but I ignored him.

Rex was staring at me, eyes wide, caution swimming in them.

"Tell me everything!" I screeched. "I need to know!"

"Peaches," Lachlan hissed at me, grabbing me by the arm.

"What did you just say?" I hissed back.

"Enough, Cassie. Peaches."

"Not for you to decide," Rex growled at him.

"What?" Alex asked, staying where he was over in the corner.

Lachlan glanced at him. "It's the safe word. I'm calling this."

"Not for you to say," Rex said quietly.

"Fine," I told Lachlan, chucking the whip down and pulling away from him. "If you're going to be a pussy about it."

"Cas," he warned me, but, again, I ignored him.

My blood was pumping through my veins.

I had gone from being angry at Rex to wanting him so badly, I was practically drooling.

I pushed aside the pounding in my head and climbed onto the bed with Rex. I straddled him, leaning over to kiss him.

"I'm sorry," I murmured, the guilt killing me now.

What the hell was wrong with me?

"Don't be," he murmured back. "Everything you've said is true and I'm sorry, Cassie. I'm no good for you."

"Please," I begged him. "Just let me in."

He looked away and the tears sprang into my eyes and fell onto his chest.

The silence that descended was awkward. There was only one way to break it. I reached down and grabbed Rex's cock. It was still rock-hard, so he was still turned on by what I'd done to him. What I'd said.

I slipped him inside me and started to ride him.

My confidence grew again as he moaned softly, feeling me encase him for the first time in weeks.

"Oh, Sweetcheeks," Lachlan sighed at me, coming up behind me and stroking my hair. "You are so precious." He kissed me and I forgave him for his actions. I'd needed to be stopped, that much was clear to me.

Alex didn't join us. He sat and watched, probably re-thinking the entire thing. I'd acted like a paranoid lunatic. I'd let the seeds of doubt that I had about Rex fester and grow into something huge. It wasn't right.

Something wasn't right.

I let Lachlan kiss away my tears as I concentrated on bringing Rex to a perfect climax that had him bucking underneath me for more.

"I need a minute," I muttered, climbing off him and escaping the playroom. I fought my way to Lachlan's office, still half-naked, cum dripping down my thighs, and ducked inside, drawing in a calming breath. I was shaking and the nausea had returned now. I headed to his office en-suite and splashed water on my face. I leaned heavily on the sink and then looked up as I heard someone behind me.

"What are you doing here?" I asked, drying my face with the hand towel.

He didn't answer me as he pressed me into the counter-top.

"Stop," I said, struggling uselessly. I was suddenly tired, so very tired.

I felt a sharp prick in my neck, and I slapped weakly at it.

"Come with Daddy now, my princess. I will make everything all better," Rob whispered to me, before everything went black.

Chapter 17

~Lachlan~

"Where is she?" I mumbled to myself, apparently, as Alex was uncuffing Rex from the bed and not listening to me.

Cassie had been gone for several long minutes that were ticking away, slower and slower as each one passed.

"Something's wrong," I blurted out, turning to the other two men.

Rex was rubbing his wrists to get the blood flowing again and Alex was looking shell-shocked. It was the first time he had seen Cassie have a meltdown.

It was not *my* first rodeo with her. When I'd first met her, she'd been volatile. Her parents' abandonment of her had fucked with her head so badly, that at times, I didn't recognize her.

"You don't say," Alex drawled, indicating Rex's chest.

"No, I mean, she should have come back by now," I insisted. "She is wandering around here half-naked. I don't like it."

I was dragging the door open before the other two men had taken in what I said. I was shoved out of the way by Rex, who stormed the corridors, pushing people out of the way.

"Where would she go?" he demanded.

"The office bathroom," I shouted back.

He headed in that direction. I grabbed Alex's hand and led him after Rex. He was white-faced and quiet.

"She's okay," I said to him, more as a platitude than fact.

She wasn't okay. Something had snapped in her before we'd gotten to the playroom. I had no idea what it was, so I didn't know how to help her. Although, judging by what she'd said to Rex, whatever it was wasn't the root of the problem. Rex was. Or, rather, his lack of forthcoming. I glanced at Alex trailing behind me. He'd said it at Finn's the other night.

We needed to come clean.

It was the only way.

If she refused to accept Rex after that, it would be up to us to change her mind. Make her see that he was still the man that she loved. That his past didn't have to define him, if *she* didn't see him that way.

He'd said all along that she was his redemption.

We had to trust her enough to let her in.

Rex was already barging into the bathroom in my office as Alex and I caught up with him.

"She isn't here!" he said, desperately looking around.

"Her bag is still here with her street clothes in it," Alex said, finally pulling himself together. "Wherever she is, she is still naked!" His frantic look matched my own, I was sure.

"Fuck!" Rex roared. "What the fuck happened in there?"

"She doesn't trust you," Alex spat out. "I said it before, I'll say it again. We need to come clean."

"Agreed," I said, firmly. "You saw what that doubt is doing to her."

"That wasn't just about her doubts," Rex gritted out. "It was paranoia. It's like she was drugged, or something."

We all looked at each other and then two accusing glares were aimed my way.

"Not in my club," I growled at them.

"Then, what?" Alex asked.

Rex was already rooting through Cassie's bag for her phone. He pulled it out and dialed.

"Who are you calling?" Alex asked.

"The Captain," he snapped. "Who else?"

I nodded my approval. Teddy had resources that we didn't have to scour New York for his niece. The three of us going out there would be like trying to look for a needle in a pile of needles. We were too scared. Too emotional.

Alex looked like he was about to cry, and Rex looked like he was about to kill someone.

Not necessarily a bad thing if Cassie had been hurt, of course.

I shoved Alex into a chair and thought back. I'd watched as Cassie had put her drink on the table near the dance floor, but then I was with her, so I hadn't seen if anyone had slipped anything into it. Of course, it *was* possible. I didn't allow drugs in here. Everything had to be about consent. Dub-con and, most especially, non-con, didn't fucking fly in my house. I insisted on clear heads and anyone caught holding was banned immediately.

Banned.

Banned.

Banned. Banned. Banned.

I don't know why, but suddenly I knew who was behind this.

I pulled out my own phone and brought up the app that was linked to all the security cameras in the club. I scrolled down to the one in my office and tapped it. I saw the three of us standing around like idiots and then I sent it back a few minutes. I saw Cassie enter and go into the bathroom. I went back even further and saw *him*. Only a few minutes before Cassie had come in here, a man had entered. The door was usually locked, but I'd left it open for Cassie, not really that bothered about theft as everything was locked away and on camera anyway.

I felt my stomach drop as I saw his face.

"Rob," I croaked out and they both looked at me, Rex stopping mid-conversation.

"What?" Alex snapped.

"Rob. I banned him, but he snuck in tonight. I mean, security knows not to let him in, but with everything else going on...he slipped by. He didn't leave the office. Neither of them did."

I stormed into the bathroom and shoved at the window. It was unlocked. He'd abducted her through the fucking bathroom window.

"What does he want with her?" Alex asked, as I went back into the office and Rex relayed the information to Teddy and then hung up.

"He's on his way," he said grimly.

"We stopped him from getting what he wanted from Cassie," Rex said, his face ashen. "There's...shit...fuck. I was going to tell you, but I was trying to find the right time, when we were alone..."

"We're alone now," I shouted at him, grabbing his arm. "What do you know?"

He swallowed and started to recount what Suzanne had told him a few days ago about Rob and his disgusting predilections and her plan to have him killed.

When he finished up, Alex leaned over the wastepaper basket and threw up.

I didn't blame him.

Cassie had been on that pervert's radar for years. She was sent away because of him. I suppose, under the circumstances, Suzanne and Damien had done the right thing, but it hadn't helped Cassie then, or now. He must've thought she would be open to an arrangement with him now, and he could do things on the up and up. Only, it was anything but that.

"He wanted a daddy kink arrangement with her," I said quietly. "You know why now, don't you? He is twisting it to mean something it doesn't. Something sick."

"He's taken her to make her his Little Girl," Rex said, also looking like he was going to vomit. "We have no way of finding her. There is *nothing* on this guy. He is as solid as a rock. I have dug and dug and found nothing. Every house, car, credit card he has, is in his wife's name. If he has an alias, who the fuck knows what it is?"

"So, he can fly under the radar and get away with this sick shit," Alex said. He stood up and went to Rex. "You should've killed him the minute you found out about this. What the fuck were you waiting for?"

"The right time to leave for a few days to do the job, asshole," Rex snarled at him. "I might be cold, but I can't kiss my wife and child goodbye and walk out of the door in the morning and come home later that night after shooting someone in the head! I'd need a day or two to process it."

Alex backed down and so did I. I had been fully supportive of Alex's demand, but now, yeah. We were the ones being dicks here. Rex wasn't a machine, as much as he liked to pretend he didn't have feelings.

"This isn't helping Cassie, or anyone," I said, always the voice of reason, it seemed. "We need to stick together. We know more information now. We know Rob probably took Cassie. And, if anyone can get her back, it's Teddy."

"What if it's too late?" Alex asked. "What if he has already...done stuff to her."

I didn't have an answer for that.

No one did.

Chapter 18

~Cassie~

I woke up with my head pounding and my mouth as dry as sawdust.

I put a hand to my head and then my eyes flew open as I remembered seeing Rob in the bathroom at Corsets & Collars.

I sat up and groaned. I felt ill, but I pushed that aside as I took in my bright surroundings.

"What the fuck?" I muttered, my eyes going wide at the little girl's room that I was in. It was lit by bright lights. There was pink and white everywhere. A huge dollhouse in the corner. A tiny table and chair set with a tea party set out. Teddies a-plenty. A clock that ticked away and told me it was eight o'clock. I assumed that was in the morning.

I was dressed in a pair of short pink pajamas with no underwear, I noted. He'd abducted me and dressed me up in this while I'd been unconscious. I gulped as the reality of my situation sank in. Had he done anything else to me while I'd been out?

The nausea got worse as I climbed off the bed and rushed to the door. Of course, it was locked.

I spun to the drapes, racing over to them, I pulled them back, but faced nothing but a concrete wall.

"Shit," I muttered. "Shit."

The panic started to set in.

The room started to spin.

I started to sweat.

I wrung my hands as tears welled up.

I was locked in, away from my baby, away from my husbands. They must've been frantic, knowing I was gone. It was morning already, so I had been gone a few hours. They hadn't found me yet. Would they ever?

I was close to melting down, but then thoughts of Ruby pulled me back to myself.

No, I wasn't going to let him take me away from my family. My daughter needed me. My husbands needed me. I was not going to sit around waiting for someone else to find me. I had to get out of this myself.

I was used to taking care of myself. I'd done it for years. Now was no different. I needed to stay calm and play along with whatever this was, while I took in everything I could about my surroundings. If I could get him to let his guard down, I could escape. I just needed the layout outside. Racing out of here the second he opened the door would be beyond foolish. I needed information first.

My heart raced as I heard a key in the lock.

Rob opened the door and saw me standing by the bed. "Oh, good. You're up," he said, with a smile, coming into the room and shutting the door behind him. He didn't lock it, but he didn't move away from it either.

I swallowed, trying to get my tongue off the roof of my mouth.

He was waiting for something from me. I *had* to play along. It was my only way out of here.

I gave him a sweet smile and lowered my eyes. "I'm thirsty," I pouted, knowing what was required of me. "Will Daddy get me some water?"

I heard him catch his breath and I knew I was doing the right thing. I just hoped I could get out of here before he wanted anything physical from me.

"Yes, princess, of course." He held out a bottle of water that had been hidden behind his back.

I went quickly to him and took it, uncapping it and drinking deeply. I didn't think it was drugged. He already had me here. What would be the point in keeping me co-matose? I hoped, anyway, as I finished the entire bottle and then dropped my eyes again. "Sorry," I said. "I was really thirsty."

"That's okay, princess," he crooned at me, coming to me and reaching for my hair. It was only then that I noticed it was in two braids.

He wrapped his hands around the braids and gently pulled me towards him.

"Are you happy to be here, Cassie?"

He gave me an expectant look.

"Yes," I replied, my stomach twisting into a small knot. "Very happy."

He nodded, a happy smile on his face. "I knew you would be," he said confidently. "I knew getting you away from those men was the right thing." His face went dark and I gulped. "Watching them maul you in public last night made me sick," he spat out. "Their hands and mouths all over you. His cock inside you while everyone jerked off as they watched...We need to get you clean," he declared and let go of my hair to take my hand. "You are dirty, you need a bath."

I nodded, feeling ashamed, even though I knew I shouldn't. His words had gotten to me. I had to remember what I'd done last night had been exhilarating. It hadn't been *dirty*. It'd been in the moment, in the appropriate setting, with the men that I loved. There'd been nothing wrong with it. He seemed to have forgotten that he'd also been there jerking off, as he'd watched us.

However, his words drove home the fact that he hadn't touched me since I'd been here. He was disgusted by my 'dirtiness'. That was a relief, at least.

He gripped my hand tightly and turned towards the door. He opened it and my eyes went everywhere, trying to see anywhere I could escape from.

My heart sank as it appeared, I was in a big warehouse.

It had been decked out to look like a dollhouse and I was sure that if I opened the drapes, there wouldn't be any windows and I couldn't see a door.

I didn't let it dishearten me. It was the first time I was seeing it. There had to be a way in and out, or we wouldn't have gotten in here in the first place.

Rob led me to a bathroom and locked the door behind us.

He turned from me to run the bath.

The sound of the water suddenly made me need to pee. Badly.

I wasn't that shy about peeing in front of my husbands now. It was something that I'd had to get over, because there were four of us sharing a bathroom. Up until a few days ago,

I probably would've peed in front of Rob because he was my doctor.

Now, it was humiliating.

But I *had* to go.

He still had his back to me, so I quickly lifted the lid and pulling my shorts down, I sat and peed as quickly as I could.

To my utmost relief, he didn't turn around as I wiped and pulled my shorts back up. I flushed and only then did he turn with a smile on his face.

"Ready?" he asked, beckoning me over to him.

I nodded and slowly walked over to him. The bath was full of bubbles and rubber duckies.

He turned me towards him and started to undo the buttons on my pajama top.

I braced myself to be touched, but he didn't even graze a finger over me. He looked, his eyes going dark, as he saw the daisy chains around my nipples, but that was all. He slipped the top off my shoulders and then slowly pulled my pants down, his fingers skimming me as little as possible, it seemed.

"Get in," he ordered me.

I did as I was told without complaint. The bubbles would cover me up.

"Do you want Daddy to wash you?" he murmured.

I knew he wanted me to say yes.

I didn't know if I could.

I gulped and then whispered, "Yes, please."

The idea was to keep him happy and for him to let his guard down. I could handle anything he did to me, as long as I got out of here and back to my family. Soon. I was strong. I knew that about myself. I would deal with it just to get back to my daughter and my husbands.

He picked up a washcloth and lathered it with soap. Then he started to wash my back and under my arms, down my chest, barely touching my breasts. He dipped lower, under the water and rubbed in between my legs quickly and then down my legs to my feet.

It was over in a couple of minutes and then he was holding out a towel for me.

I stood up and stepped out of the bath. He wrapped the towel around my shoulders and held it together as he drew me closer and closed his eyes as he drew in a deep breath.

"Much better," he murmured, and dropped a kiss on my forehead. "You like to be clean for your Daddy, don't you princess?"

"Yes," I murmured back.

"Good girl. Dry yourself now and put this on."

He handed me a short, white nightgown that would barely cover my ass and it looked way too small to handle my abundant breasts.

I was right. I busted out of that thing like it was at least two sizes too small.

I peeked up at him, but I still didn't see lust in his eyes. He was completely clinical about all of this. I had my hopes raised a tiny bit, that this was just what he wanted. A Little Girl to take care of.

But then they were dashed as I mentally kicked myself. If I thought that, then I was a bigger fool than I looked in this get-up.

He handed me a capful of mouthwash. "Rinse," he said.

I did. My mouth felt like shit and my breath was probably disgusting. He didn't offer me a toothbrush, but this was better than nothing.

"Come," he said, taking my hand and leading me back out of the bathroom. "You are being a very good little girl," he commented. "Daddy is very proud of you, Cassie. You are such a special princess."

I simpered at him, *detesting* the fact that I enjoyed hearing it. He knew it was what I wanted, and he was giving it to me.

"Thank you," I said, squeezing his hand and wishing that I hadn't suddenly lost control of myself.

He smiled down at me, knowing he had pleased me.

He led me back into the bedroom and sat me down on the bed. "Now, if you are a good girl and stay here until Daddy comes back, you can watch TV for a bit later, okay?"

"Okay," I said meekly.

He kissed the top of my head again and then he left, locking the door behind me.

My positive attitude deflated a bit.

I was a prisoner here.

I would never see my family again.

"No," I ground out. "I will get out of here. Do what it takes, Cassie. *Whatever* it takes."

~Alex~

I LISTENED AS TEDDY was *still* on the phone. It seemed like he hadn't put it down since he'd arrived hours ago.

It was 10am now. Cassie had been missing since midnight. Anything could have happened to her. Rob could've done *anything* to her in that time.

"Let's go," Teddy said, finally hanging up and gesturing for us to move forward.

"Where to?" I asked, following him, along with Rex and Lachlan. Neither one of them had said a word in hours.

"Damien and Suzanne's," he replied. "I'll explain on the way."

I nodded and stepped into the elevator with the other two men.

Rex looked so desolate it broke my heart even more and Lachlan looked angry and guilty. Cassie had been abducted from *his* club. It had to be eating him up.

I didn't have any words for him though. I was going through my own shit and I couldn't drum up much sympathy for him. Not yet.

Anything spare I had was going to Rex. We couldn't let this drive him over the edge. He looked like he was about to fall and plummet straight back into his old mindset. I brushed my hand against his.

He glanced up; his dark eyes full of pain.

"We'll get her back," I murmured.

He gulped and nodded and then turned from me to seek comfort from Lachlan.

It hurt, but I got it. They had something between them.

As we stepped out of the apartment building toward the SUV idling at the curb, I stopped dead, with Lachlan crashing into me from behind with a muffled curse.

Rex suddenly came to life as he spotted what I had.

"You!" he spat out, marching over to Ella.

Teddy also stepped forward and cleared his throat. He took Rex by the arm and pulled him away. He leaned down to kiss Ella on the mouth.

"You shouldn't be here," he said to her. "You know the rules."

"I wanted to make sure you were okay," she pouted. "I wanted to see if I could help."

"Go home," he ordered her.

"I thought you took care of this?" Rex demanded. "She isn't supposed to be anywhere near Cassie, or our home."

"I did take care of it," Teddy said calmly. "So that *you* didn't have to. She knows she isn't supposed to be here. She'll be punished."

"Ugh!" Rex spat out. "You took her for yourself."

"What better way to keep an eye on her?"

I barely registered their exchange that occurred with Ella standing right there, because I was still staring at what was in her hands. Or, rather, what her hands were clutching.

A stroller with a baby in it.

I gulped as she stared at me unblinking.

I stared back at her.

Then she dropped her eyes as Teddy told her to get going.

I watched her push the stroller away with an awful feeling in the pit of my stomach.

I'd had unprotected sex with her. Twice. She'd said was on the pill, but I'd only had her word to go on.

Teddy had completely ignored the baby. If that had been Ruby, I would've cooed and tickled her, bent down to kiss her. He couldn't be the father, could he? Cassie had never mentioned it, but then would she even know if her uncle was shacking up with her ex-stalker?

Rex was still growling at Teddy for being a complete asshole, when Lachlan snapped.

"Shut the fuck up and get the fuck in the car!" he roared, his hands clenched into fists.

Rex and Teddy stopped their arguing over Ella and did as they were told. So did I.

Lachlan was about to blow a gasket and I, for one, didn't want to be in the firing line when he did. He was so laid back usually, I knew that his still water had to run deep. When things got too much, enough was enough and he erupted.

Good to know.

I slid in last, casting one last look back at Ella. She had stopped further down the sidewalk and was looking back at us.

She pointed to the baby, then to me, and spun on her heel and marched off.

What the fuck was she saying?

Was she fucking with me?

I couldn't deal with this right now.

Cassie was missing and finding her was the *only* thing that mattered.

"What exactly are Suzanne and Damien supposed to do?" I asked into the silence that had fallen. Lachlan and I were sitting opposite Rex and Teddy.

"Suzanne practically grew up with Rob. She knows him. If anyone can shed some light on his activities, she can," Teddy replied.

"She doesn't know anything," Rex chimed in. "When I spoke to her the other day, all she said was that they'd heard something a few months ago about him."

Teddy went stock-still and then turned to his former employee with a face that went so dark, even Rex shifted uncomfortably.

"You knew about him?" he asked so deathly quiet, Lachlan and I stopped breathing.

"Yes. Suzanne asked me to kill him. Which, by the way," Rex suddenly spat out, "I am sure I have *you* to blame for her finding out about me!"

Teddy blinked. "How dare you?" he hissed. "I would never betray you, and thus myself, you little shit. Don't give me that bullshit. However she found out, it wasn't from me."

"Well, she knows. She wants me to kill Rob and I agreed to it. I was waiting for the right time. How the fuck was I supposed to know he'd do this?" His desperate look made Teddy's face soften slightly.

"You should have come to me immediately," Teddy said. They shared a knowing look that excluded me and Lachlan.

I looked out of the window and tuned them out.

Lachlan grabbed my hand and laced our fingers together. I was grateful for the support. I needed it, or I was going to crumble. If that pervert hurt my wife in any way whatsoever,

Rex would have to get in line, because *I* would kill that bastard without a second thought.

"You okay?" Lachlan mumbled to me a minute or two later.

"Yeah. Are you?"

He shrugged. "The guilt is eating me alive. If she gets hurt by this prick, it will be all my fault."

"No," I said, squeezing his hand. "We all let her go off on her own. We should have protected her. She is our *wife* and we all abandoned her when she needed us the most."

A morose silence descended on us then as everyone reflected on my words. I blinked back tears of fear and anger. I would be of no use to Cassie if I fell apart. She needed us to be strong for her and for Ruby. She needed us to find her and bring her home.

I wouldn't let her down ever again.

Chapter 19

~Rex~

"I hope this works," I muttered as we stopped outside a palatial mansion in the suburbs. I had never been here before. I suspected that Lachlan had, as this was the house that Cassie had grown up in. Well, supposedly. I'd thought she'd spent more time at school than here, but in light of the recent revelation, I didn't think that was such a bad thing now.

However, it'd also become clear during that conversation, that this was being paid for by Cassie's trust and that Suzanne and Damien needed Ruby's trust to keep this place once Cassie inherited her full trust.

I hadn't come clean to the other men about that part of my conversation with Suzanne. I wasn't sure that I ever would. It was a non-starter, as far as I was concerned. If Suzanne went through with her threat, then so be it. I wasn't giving my parental rights away for anything. If it cost me everything, then I would have to deal with that when the time came.

I looked across at the two men, silently staring out of the windows. I had to trust that, just maybe, they would have my back and help me to keep my wife and child if it came to it.

The gates slid open and we swept up the long driveway, pulling up outside the front doors.

Suzanne was waiting for us.

Damien was nowhere in sight.

"Teddy!" she cried, the tears flowing freely. "You have to get her back!"

He went to her and took her by her upper arms. "We will, Suzanne. But, right now, you need to calm down and tell me anything you know."

She cast a cursory glance at us, but then ignored us, as she turned and went into the house.

We followed her further inside until she stopped and grabbed a half-full glass of Scotch off an end table. She took a long, steadying sip and then handed the glass to Derek the Dick. He glared at me and I glared back, but now wasn't the time for a confrontation.

"This is all I can think of," she said and scooped up a business card. She handed it to Teddy.

He peered down at it.

I snatched it off him and read the name.

"Jay Armstrong. Attorney at Law. Who the fuck is this?" I asked.

"Rob's lawyer," she said to Teddy, still ignoring me.

"How can he help?" I asked, moving to stand right in front of her face so she would have to acknowledge me.

Derek stepped up and gave me a rough shove, which I returned, hoping he would react to it then so that I could finally beat on someone and take out my fear and frustrations. They were building up by the second and I was ready to snap.

He gave me a bland look, but that was it.

"I don't know if he can," she said. "However, if Rob has been hiding this side to him, you can bet that any woman he has been involved with was forced to sign an NDA. Jay would've arranged it. If you can find a woman, you might be able to find where Rob has Cassie."

"He won't talk," Alex piped up.

"That's why you are going to take Derek when you go," she replied, putting her hand on her henchman's arm. "He is useful."

I cast a critical eye over him. "We don't need him," I scoffed. Fuck's sake. We had *me.*

Suzanne's cold green eyes landed on me. "I would've thought that getting Cassie back was a priority, that you would do anything to ensure her safe return."

I glowered at her. For once, her barbed comments made sense.

"Take Derek," she said firmly and shoved him at me, in so much as a slight woman who was half-cut could shove a man the size of Derek.

"Fine," I drawled. "Maybe he can be useful for kicking down doors and stuff."

The slight insult hit home like I'd intended.

He came at me, fists clenched. "Just give me a reason, asshole, to kick *you* down."

I gave him a cocky smile. "Try it," I snarled back, totally ready this time to take him out. My ribs were feeling marginally better, but I had what I'd been lacking the other day. My gun.

I reached around my back, flicking my leather jacket out of the way, my hand closing around the grip.

"Stop," Lachlan hissed at me. "We don't have time for a pissing contest." He gave me such a vicious glare that I let go of the gun. He shook his head at me, his face grim. He knew I had it now, something that I'd been trying to hide to save myself the lecture and judgment. He also knew that if I came face-to-face with Rob, I was using it. No one, not even him, could stop me.

Alex's ashen face also clued me in that he'd come to the same conclusion.

I didn't give a fuck.

Rob was dead.

Even if Cassie was unharmed when we got her back, I was going to shoot that fucker in the head. If he *had* harmed her...then God help him and have mercy on *my* soul for what I was going to do to him.

"Let's go," I said and turned on my heel, leaving that house, hoping never to return. If Cassie ever said she wanted to move to a place like this, I would be vastly uncomfortable in it. But I suspected she would one day. Especially, if we had more children. She wouldn't want to raise them in the city. Despite what Suzanne thought, Cassie was a good mother and she would never allow her work to take precedence over her family.

My heart ached for her. She had to be missing Ruby so much.

"Don't worry, baby girl," I muttered under my breath. "We'll get your mommy back."

"Of course, we will," Lachlan said, sliding back into the SUV next to me. I should've known that he would have taken it upon himself to be my babysitter for the duration of this hell we were going through. But there was no way he, or any of them, would stop me from doing what needed to be done.

Teddy climbed into the car with a grim look, pocketing his phone.

"What is it?" I barked at him.

"Jay is on a plane, flying back from Tokyo. He won't be available to speak to until tomorrow," he said.

"Great!" Alex shouted. "Just fucking great! The only lead we had is a million miles away."

He dropped his head into his hands. Lachlan leaned over to pat his knee, but it was a useless gesture.

We had nothing.

No lead had panned out so far. The CCTV in the area had been good enough to track them all of a mile down the road and then we'd lost them under a bridge. Rob had switched cars and we'd lost her. He had planned this meticulously.

We were screwed and we knew it.

~Cassie~

I'D BEEN SITTING ON this bed for hours. I'd read a few storybooks on the bookshelf, just for something to do.

My positive attitude had plummeted the longer I'd sat there. I was close to tears, but I knew that once I started, I wouldn't be able to stop and that wasn't going to lead anywhere. First and foremost, Rob would know that I didn't want to be there, and my whole escape plan hinged on him believing that I did, so that he loosened the leash enough for me to get away.

I flicked the ears of the teddy that I had taken a liking to and sighed at it. It was brown. The only brown bear in a sea of pink and white ones. He'd looked as lonely as I felt, so I'd picked him up and hoped we could comfort each other.

I jumped as I heard a key in the lock, glancing at the clock before I fixed my eyes on the door.

It was 5 o'clock. Rob must've gone to work, like nothing was wrong with his head, and come back here to me, his prisoner.

He smiled at me as he sidled into the room and saw me sitting exactly where he'd left me.

He nodded his approval and I smiled at him.

His eyes dropped to the bear and lit up. I found that odd. *More* odd than this whole situation.

"You like that one?" he asked softly.

"Yes, Daddy," I purred at him.

He rushed to me and dropped to his knees, startling me as he placed his head in my lap, his cheek resting on my legs.

I had no idea what to do.

I hovered my hand over his head and then gently started to stroke his hair.

It was the right move.

He sighed happily and fisted his hands into the fabric of my nightgown. "I bought that for you for your sixth birthday," he whispered to me. "I wanted so desperately to give it to you, but your parents had sent you away. It broke my heart that I didn't get to see your face when I gave it to you."

I stilled, my blood turning to ice. What was he saying?

"You did?" I croaked.

He nodded, turning his head so that he was face down. "You were such a pretty little girl," he crooned. "I missed you so much while you were away, but I had to move on, Cassie. You understand that, don't you, princess? I didn't know when I would see you again."

He clutched desperately at the nightgown, tugging on it as he looked up at me.

I gulped as all of this just became a whole hell of a lot more sinister. This wasn't just about him wanting me for some daddy kink. This ran to a place that was *sick* and *twisted* and it made my skin crawl.

"I understand," I said, pushing my other hand into his hair, wishing that I could pull his head back and knee him in the nose. But if I did that, I had nowhere to go. I had no idea how to get out of there yet.

"I love you, princess," he whispered to me and nestled his head back into my lap, breathing in deeply.

I had to think quickly. I had to say something to him that would keep him on my side. But there was no way that I could tell him that I loved him too.

Fortunately, he didn't even notice my silence as he carried on. "You are happy to be here, aren't you, princess?"

"Yes," I said. That was easy. One simple word. One syllable that I used all the time.

"Good," he said and stood up. "Now, I promised you that if you were a good girl, you could watch some TV." He held his hand out for me and I grabbed it. Anything to get out of this room and out there where I could plan my escape with more information.

He led me over to the sofa in the living area, and sat down, pulling me down with him. He clicked the remote and a show about a hospital came on. He settled down to watch, as he kept my hand in his.

I pretended to watch, but my eyes were darting out as far as they could without me moving my head. It was pointless. I couldn't see *anything*.

My stomach rumbled and I put my free hand on it. I'd been trying to avoid thinking about food. I was starving.

"May I please have something to eat?" I dared to ask him.

He looked at me. "Yes, of course. When this finishes."

I glared at the screen as he turned back to it. Was that his plan? To starve me into submission so that I was too weak to escape?

Luckily, the show was already halfway through, so I didn't have too long to wait.

Rob let go of my hand and looked at me. "Would you like some cereal?" he asked.

I nodded enthusiastically. Anything would do.

He frowned at me and I realized my mistake instantly. "Yes, please, Daddy," I murmured, eyes lowered.

"Good girl," he murmured back, and then stood up. He went to the kitchen, which was open plan, directly behind the sofa. I wasn't sure if I should join him or wait until he called me.

I decided to wait, trying to push the warm feelings aside that his words had given me.

Right move.

"Come, princess," he called to me, the pleasure in his voice noticeable.

I was knocking this shit out of the park at the moment. But that could end in a second, if I did anything he didn't like. It was exhausting being on alert every minute I was in his presence.

I stood up and approached the round kitchen table. He'd placed a bowl of Lucky Charms with too much milk in it, on the table. He pulled a chair out for me and I sat.

I waited, hoping he would hurry up and sit as well so that I could start.

"Such pleasant manners," he crooned as he sat opposite me with his own bowl.

I gave him a small smile and then I couldn't wait any longer. I dived into the bowl, spooning up the cereal at a rapid rate.

I was finished before he had even gotten started.

I put my hands in my lap and waited silently for him to finish.

"Go and clean up," he said to me when he stood up to clear the dishes away.

I blinked at him. *On my own*?

He had his back to me, so I assumed that, yes, he meant on my fucking own.

I stood up quickly and rushed to the bathroom. Not only was I bursting for a pee again, but also something else. Something that I was not prepared to do even in front of my husbands, never mind this sicko.

A FEW MINUTES LATER, I was washing my hands, feeling a world better just for having been given the opportunity to go to the toilet. It was humiliating and pathetic and it destroyed my soul just a tiny bit. I wallowed in it for all of a second, before I pushed my shoulders out and headed back to my captor.

"Tomorrow, Daddy has a friend coming over," he said when he saw me hovering on the edge of the kitchen part of this weird, human-size dollhouse.

"Okay," I said meekly. I did not like the sound of that one bit.

"You need to wash your hair in the morning, okay, princess, make yourself all pretty."

I nodded, swallowing my fear.

"Go to bed now, it's late," he instructed.

It couldn't be more than 7pm.

"Tuck me in?" I asked coyly.

Right move again.

His eyes lit up. "Of course."

I let him take my hand and lead me back to the bedroom. As I trailed behind him, I looked everywhere. I had been too focused on getting to the bathroom before to look for anything else.

It was then that I spotted a narrow hallway that led off behind the kitchen. I didn't know how I didn't see it before. My heart started to pound. That *had* to be the way in and out.

Rob looked back at me and I smiled at him, feeling my spirits soar again. Yes, the door would be locked, but at least I knew where it was.

It was a start.

ROB LOOKED UNCERTAIN as he hovered by the bed. I climbed on and patted next to me. I had a plan. When he was asleep, I would do some recon. I doubted very much he would lock us in here if I could distract him into forgetting.

"Stay with me, please, Daddy. I'm afraid," I whispered to him.

He was on the bed like a shot, gathering me to him.

He stroked my hair. "You don't have to be afraid, princess. I'm here to protect you."

I snuggled into him and bit the inside of my lip to stop myself from retching at his closeness.

"You are so precious, Cassie. You don't ever have to be afraid. Daddy will always look after you," he murmured.

I nodded.

After a pause, he said, "Don't worry about tomorrow. You won't be required to do anything."

I looked up at him. He was frowning and that wasn't good.

"Daddy won't let anyone hurt you," he added and kissed the top of my head.

It didn't reassure me at all.

But I couldn't think about that. I had to focus on the matter at hand. Waiting for him to go to sleep, so I could sneak out of the bedroom and do some snooping.

Chapter 20

~Cassie~

I must've fallen asleep waiting for Rob to, as I awoke suddenly by a familiar sound. The light *slap-slap* of a masturbating male reached my ears and I froze. I wanted to block it out, but I also wanted to make sure that it *was* Rob and not some weirdo that he'd let in.

I cracked an eye open and saw Rob jerking off as he looked at me.

"Go back to sleep, princess," he panted quietly.

I slammed my eye closed again, but then I opened them both and looked at him. I knew somehow it was what he really wanted.

He groaned softly as he looked into my eyes. He didn't tear them away from me as he came suddenly in hot splats on my nightgown.

He didn't say a word as he put himself away, and then climbed back onto the bed with me, holding me close to him and closing his eyes.

I shut my eyes again and leveled out my breathing. I was sure he was going to sleep now, I just had to make sure that I didn't again.

As it turned out, he didn't sleep. He stayed awake all night, holding me and, eventually, I had to succumb to the exhaustion that was dragging me under.

HE WOKE ME UP WITH a gentle shake.

"Cassie," he whispered. "It's time to get up, sweetheart. We need to get you ready."

I moaned softly and stretched. I felt like I'd been hit by a truck. Little food and sleep had taken its toll on me.

He helped me get off the bed, eager to get me moving.

I rubbed my gritty eyes and glanced at the clock as I trailed out of the bedroom. It was the crack of dawn. I cursed my predicament and that I *still* hadn't found a way out of there. I was letting my daughter down; I was letting my men down and I was letting myself down.

I hoped that a bath would liven me up a bit. I needed to be on full alert for this mystery friend of Rob's that was turning up so early, for who the hell knew what?

Rob was turning on the shower in the corner of the bathroom. I stood there wondering if he was going to get in with me or let me get on with it myself.

He turned and smiled at me, approaching me cautiously.

He reached out and started to undress me, pulling the messed-up nightgown over my head.

I wanted to run and hide to cover up my nudity from his raking gaze. But he didn't touch me. His eyes lingered once again on the daisy chains and then he turned away.

"I will leave you to shower. Get dressed in this when you are done," he said and indicated a navy-blue slip dress with a long-sleeved, white t-shirt underneath it, hanging on a hook.

I nodded and stepped into the shower, just to hide the shudder that was threatening to go over me. There was still no underwear in sight and still no shoes either.

He left me alone then. I took my time unbraiding my wet hair and then washing it slowly and carefully. I felt like I needed it to boost my self-esteem, which was plummeting to great depths the closer the time got to the friend arriving.

I methodically washed myself, dried myself and got dressed.

I looked for a toothbrush, but still nothing, so I grabbed the mouthwash again and took a big capful of it in my mouth. I rubbed my teeth with my finger, hoping it would clean them up a bit.

I spat it out and ran my tongue over my teeth. Better. Not great, but it would do.

What I wouldn't give for my mother's crappy, mono-grammed toothbrush gift right now.

I drew in a deep breath and opened the bathroom door.

Rob looked up and beckoned me over to him. He was placing a stool in the middle of the living area.

"Sit," he said.

I did.

He arranged me how he wanted me, with my knees to-gether and pushed to the side and my hands in my lap. Nice and demure.

Then, he braided my hair again, even though it was wet through. I would look like I'd been dragged through a hedge if it dried like that.

"All you have to do is sit," he murmured to me. "Daddy wants to show you off, okay, princess?"

I nodded, unable to speak. He had put me on display like a doll and it was creepy as fuck.

A few moments later, I heard a buzzer. Rob glanced at me and then told me to close my eyes.

I did, but then as soon as I heard him move away, I cracked them open. I saw him disappear behind the kitchen, knowing I was right about the location of the door.

I held my breath as I listened. I heard four beeps, which indicated a keypad. The door was locked with an electronic lock, not a key.

Dammit.

How the hell would I figure out what the code was? My heart sank, but then it thumped as a wiry, middle-aged man entered the room with Rob following him. The man was balding, dressed in a drab, gray suit with brown shoes and wire-rimmed glasses. He was slight and looked like a weasel.

His eyes shone when he saw me sitting there.

He approached me carefully, like I was a rabbit about to bolt. He stopped in front of me. He reached out and placed his cold hand on my cheek.

"So perfect," he muttered as Rob hurriedly slapped his hand away.

"No touching!" he snarled.

The man shrugged and turned away, putting his briefcase down on the sofa and opening it. He pulled out a neatly folded hand towel and sat down, placing it on his lap.

I watched in horror as he unzipped his pants and pulled out his very unimpressive dick.

I gulped but remained motionless as he started to jerk himself off while he looked at me.

It was exactly what Rob had done last night.

It was relatively inoffensive as non-con sexual acts go. It could *definitely* have been worse. But I hadn't agreed to this in the slightest. It made me feel dirty and used. It made my insides shrivel up with disgust.

I wasn't going to risk making a run for it, because, firstly, where would I go? And secondly, it might escalate this to something far, far worse.

I forced myself to keep a neutral expression on my face, my eyes on his as he tugged on himself with fervor. His lips parted as he came with a soft grunt, all over the hand towel.

I risked casting my gaze to Rob now that this was over with. He was watching us from the corner of the room, his arms folded, his face pale, but his eyes were flashing with desire.

"Go now," he croaked out to the man, who did as he was told silently.

Rob followed him down the corridor and let him out, then he returned to me with a smile.

"Oh, princess, you *are* perfection. Daddy is so proud of you. You did just as Daddy told you, good girl. Don't ever worry about anyone hurting you, okay? Daddy will protect you."

I swallowed back my acerbic comment that *he* was hurting me by keeping me there and gave him a small smile instead.

"Now, Daddy wants to look at you. Sit still while he shows you how pretty he thinks you are."

I blinked at him as he proceeded to do everything the man had done, minus the towel.

I wanted to cry.

I wanted to scream at him that he was so mentally unhinged, he needed serious psychiatric help.

He was a sociopath that functioned perfectly well in the high society in which he worked. He hid it so well. I hadn't a clue that there was anything off about him in all the time I'd known him. However, his recent behavior and admission to me last night, made it very clear that he was dangerous.

I wondered what his trigger had been? He had been treating me for months since I returned from university in England, and he'd not once made a pass at me or even given me a flirty smile. The other night in the penthouse, something had changed for him. I racked my brain to think what I did, or said, that made him suddenly act this way.

I felt so lost and alone as I watched him come all over himself with my name on his lips. I didn't think I would ever get out of there.

I would never see my daughter again. I would never see my husbands again.

I was trapped with no chance of escape.

I bit back the sob of absolute desolation that was threatening to come out and forced myself to get a grip and smile at him. I asked, "Are you happy with me, Daddy?"

He beamed at me. "Oh, yes, darling, so, so much. Daddy loves you."

I nodded in relief. He hadn't seen my mental falter. All I had to do was keep making the right moves for him and I could get myself out of there.

I had to.

AFTER THAT HUMILIATING experience, Rob locked me back in my room with a plate of toast and a bottle of water. I had no idea when he was going to come back. I knew he would though. He was living out his sick fantasy with me as his prop. My attitude had taken a beating this morning. Was this going to be my life from now on? Put on display for men to look at me while they masturbated? Or would it eventually get worse? I was waiting for it to. It had to at some point. Rob wasn't going to sit around here, happy with jerking off when he could get his kicks the proper way.

All of those thoughts, swimming through my head all day, had made me a mess by the time Rob came home at 5pm again and unlocked the door.

I didn't care that he saw me crying under the covers.

He glared at me as he came into the room.

"Is princess not happy to be here?" he asked coldly.

It was the wrong move. So totally the wrong move, but I hadn't been able to help it.

I sniffled and sat up, dropping my eyes to my lap, trying to figure a way out of it as the silence grew even icier.

"I missed you, Daddy," I said eventually, daring a risky move that might well backfire, somehow. "You left me all alone in this room. I want to be with you."

I didn't look up as he slowly approached me.

"Oh, princess," he murmured. "Daddy missed you as well, but he needs to work."

"Please don't leave me," I begged him. If he was *there*, I wasn't locked up. All I needed was him to fall asleep so that I could attempt my escape.

"Oh, baby," he crooned, stroking my hair. "I won't. I won't ever leave you. You are mine now, just mine, and I will make sure that you know every day how pretty you are and how much I love you."

I nodded, holding back the tears. I couldn't afford to lose this progress that I'd made, small as it was.

I forced myself to beam up at him.

He sat down next to me with a serious look that made my blood run cold. "We need to get rid of those markings on you," he said decisively. "They make you look cheap and like a whore. Daddy doesn't want that." His eyes were on my tits as he said that, so I knew exactly what he was referring to...my daisy chain tattoos. "I will arrange it." He patted my hand and stood up. "Do you want something to eat?"

"Yes, please," I murmured. This was going downhill quickly. After that, I was reasonably sure that my tattoos were the reason he wasn't touching me yet. He wanted me 'pure'. It meant he would be arranging their removal very soon and then, all bets were off.

It was the necessary mental kick up the ass I needed after my self-pity had gotten the better of me. If he even touched the angel wings on the back of my neck, I would kill him.

I knew I wouldn't actually *kill* him, but that anger and the thought of his painful demise, got me on my feet and trailing behind him to get something to eat.

LEAVING THE ROOM CLEARED my head, and I was a delight to be around for him, putting him at ease. When bedtime came around, I asked him to stay with me again.

He must've been exhausted. He didn't sleep a wink the previous night, that I was aware of.

As we settled on the bed, he handed me the brown teddy. I wanted to rip its head off but took it and squeezed it tightly.

I closed my eyes as he cuddled me, hoping to just feign sleep and not actually go to sleep.

To my surprise, he fell asleep quickly. I sat up carefully, making sure he was asleep and not pretending like I was.

It was my chance. I'd racked my brain all day to come up with four digits that would open the lock. I'd heard the beeps twice. I wasn't sure if I could match them off the bat, but I had a few options to go through. His birthday, the number on his office door and *my* birthday, which I sincerely hoped it wasn't. It wasn't much, but I was flying blind. I didn't really know anything about him.

I climbed off the bed and crept out of the room. I paused at the door to make sure he was still sleeping. He was snoring quietly, so I turned my back on him and scampered across the warehouse to the narrow corridor behind the kitchen.

First, I tried his birthday. It was the same as mine, with a different year. We'd laughed about it a couple of years ago, but now I felt disgusted by it. I cringed as the beeps sounded like foghorns in the silence.

It wasn't right. But I was clueless whether the beeps were the same or not.

"Shit," I muttered and looked behind me.

I tried mine, but the lock remained in place. I quickly tried the office number, but that too failed. I was close to tears because I had nothing else.

I would have to go back to him, and that stupid bear, and think of something else.

I blinked and bit my lip. That bear.

I looked over my shoulder. It was desperate, clutching at straws, but I had to try.

I punched in the date of my sixth birthday and held my breath. The light turned green and so did I. I wanted to hurl, but the door was open.

I had to move.

I had no money, no car, no *shoes*. I had no idea where the hell I was. All I could do was run and hope that I made it far enough away from him that he didn't catch up with me.

I lunged forward and ran, straight out onto an abandoned car park, surrounded by a barbed wire fence and a huge electronic gate that was not made for climbing over.

"Fuck," I muttered, but there was nothing for it. I would tear myself to shreds rather than go back in there. I ran to the fence and looked up. I wasted precious few seconds removing the t-shirt from under my dress and then I scaled the fence. My scar ached as I pulled it with this climb, but I ignored it. If I did damage to it, then I would deal with that later.

I just needed to escape.

That was all.

I threw the t-shirt over the barbed wire and winced at it. It was less than useless, but I dug my hands in anyway and hauled myself to the top. My palms were slashed to ribbons, my thighs scraped, my feet aching, but I had to keep going.

I gritted my teeth and got over the top of the barbed wire. Then, I dropped quickly down the other side, my hand pressed against the right side of my scar as I hobbled away. I looked around, but I had no idea where I was. I could be any-where. I ran towards the tree line that I spotted in the dark, on the other side of the road leading up to the warehouse. If I went in there, I was doomed. I frantically looked right and left, needing to make a decision.

I landed on left. It went behind the warehouse and in the opposite direction that my instincts were telling me to go. Hopefully, he wouldn't think that I had gone that way when he woke up and found me gone.

"Cassie!" I heard a roar in the darkness.

I ran as fast as I could to the left, hoping that I wasn't running right back into trouble.

Chapter 21

~Lachlan~

I stared at the bathroom door and winced.

It didn't sound good.

"I'm going," Rex declared, storming into the bedroom.

"We have to wait for Alex," I pointed out.

"We have the address of this woman who knew Rob. We need to go. Now!"

I didn't back down from Rex's ferocious gaze. Alex was just as much a part of this and he would want to be there.

"Give him a sec," I muttered as the bathroom door opened and Alex staggered out.

He was wearing his glasses, his hair was wet and sticking up, his face was green. "Sorry," he mumbled. "I'm ready."

"Such a lightweight," I teased him and grabbed onto his arm. He was looking a bit unsteady on his feet.

He wasn't a big drinker, none of us were, but he had succumbed to the bottle of bourbon before we had last night, trying to drown our sorrows. Teddy's contacts in the police department were drawing as big a blank as we were to the whereabouts of our wife.

Aurora had been good enough to stay with us to take care of Ruby for the last couple of days. We were less than useless as fathers right now. Cassie was going to kick our asses when she discovered just how pathetic we were in her absence.

I clung to that as we headed for the door. We had locked up the elevator last night, in preparation for leaving Aurora alone with Ruby this morning. Nothing could be left to chance. If someone wanted in, they had to go through Security Guard, Pete, downstairs, who was on Rex's payroll. He was as badass as the man I loved, and we all trusted him. Hell, he'd chased Alex up to the penthouse a few months ago at gunpoint, trying to protect Cassie.

I couldn't help the chuckle that escaped. Even though it got me a filthy look from Rex, I needed the laugh to break the tension.

I had never been so anxious about anything before. There was a good chance this woman knew where to find our wife. She had no idea we were coming. We couldn't risk her running. She was going to be reluctant to talk, but there was no way we would be leaving without the information we needed to find Cassie.

"Call if you need anything," I said to Aurora as she gave us an encouraging smile.

"We'll be fine. You go and bring your wife home," she said.

I gave her a nod and bent to kiss Ruby nestled in Aurora's arms. As I straightened up, there was a commotion in the doorway.

Rex was there, yanking the door open, quicker than a shot, and Cassie tumbled into the penthouse, with Pete right behind her.

She fell with a sob into Rex's arms.

He scooped her up, practically crushing her as his hands went into her unnaturally wild and wavy hair. He set her down and kissed her wet face.

"Found her outside," Pete said. "Haven't been able to get a coherent word out of her."

I moved quickly over and took her from Rex. I needed to hold her, make sure she was unharmed and actually here and that is wasn't a dream. She was shaking, cold, filthy. She had no shoes on and her feet were dirty and cut. She had deep scratches on her hands, arms and legs. She was half naked and sobbing, but she had never looked more beautiful.

"Fuck," I murmured to her, sliding my hand to the back of her neck, my hand covering the angel wings, and drawing her even closer. "You're here."

She nodded, sniffing and sniveling into my t-shirt.

Alex was just staring at her in shock.

"How did you get away?" he croaked out; his voice hoarse from throwing up half a bottle of bourbon.

She started crying even harder, but then she drew in a deep breath and pulled away from me. She went straight to Ruby and took her from Aurora, holding her so close and smelling her sweet baby scent.

She ignored us and turned to the hallway, disappearing with our baby girl into the nursery.

"I'll..." Aurora started, but I put my hand up.

"Give us a minute," I said and then followed Cassie, as did Rex and Alex.

We stood like spare parts in the doorway of the nursery, watching our wife in her pitiful state, cuddle her daughter and get a hold of herself like nothing I had ever seen before.

She'd been a mess a few seconds ago, but Ruby had brought her back to herself. She knew she needed to be strong for her, so she put her own issues aside and stepped up.

It was awe-inspiring.

She was truly the most amazing woman I had ever met.

"Are you hurt?" Rex asked, more briskly than he'd probably meant to.

She kept her eyes on Ruby as she answered carefully, "Nothing you can't see."

He gritted his teeth. That wasn't an answer and we all knew it.

"Did he hurt you?" he asked, going to her.

She glared up at him. "No, he didn't," she replied and then went back to cooing to our daughter.

After an awkward pause, in which none of us even breathed, she sighed. "I will tell you everything in a bit. I need to spend time with Ruby, then I need a shower. Give me twenty minutes. I'm okay, I promise. Just please, give me twenty minutes."

"Of course," I said.

Alex, having finally gotten his act together, went to her and kissed her forehead. "I love you," he murmured. "I am so glad you're home safe."

She nodded; her nose wrinkled up. "You smell like a distillery," she commented, with just a dash of her usual sass.

He snorted, kissed her again, and then left the room, Rex hesitantly followed him. I hovered and her eyes found mine and her strength wavered. She was my oldest friend. She had come to me countless times with her pain and her problems. I fixed things, but this time, I wasn't so sure that I even knew how. She wasn't as okay as she was making out. I knew that and she knew that I knew.

"Give me twenty minutes," she whispered and then turned from me to sit with Ruby in the rocker, calmly and steadily rocking our daughter as she murmured to her.

I had no choice but to leave them alone. I was encroaching. As much as I wanted her to look up at me and tell me she loved me, she didn't even know I was still in the room. It stung for a minute before I got over it. Her daughter was what had gotten her through whatever hell she'd endured at the hands of that asshole. Only her daughter could help heal her now.

~Cassie~

AS I ROCKED MY DAUGHTER, she started to fall asleep in my arms. Her little mouth went slack as her eyes closed. I held her even closer, but then I had to relinquish her to her crib. I needed to clean up and my husbands needed answers. I had abandoned them for long enough as it was, but I'd needed the peace and calm that came with holding my baby.

I carefully stood up, ignoring the pain in my battered feet, and placed her gently in the crib. I stood and watched her for another minute and then, with a heavy sigh, I crept out of the nursery and down the hallway to my bedroom. I closed the door and stripped off the stupid dress that left absolutely nothing to the imagination since I'd removed the t-shirt underneath. Pete had gotten a right eyeful as I'd raced into the building several minutes ago.

I pushed the escape to the back of my mind for now. I would recount it to my husbands when I had to and then I didn't want to think about it ever again.

I climbed into the shower and turned on the jets.

I savored the hot water beating down on me for a moment, before the sting hitting my cuts made me hiss. I washed my hair, first and foremost. It had dried in the braids and I must've looked like a wild thing with it all wavy. I was so glad that I hadn't looked in the mirror before I'd climbed into the shower.

I navigated the scratches that I'd gotten from the barbed wire with the washcloth and then I turned off the shower and went straight to brush my teeth.

Nothing had ever felt so good in a long time.

I would never take dental hygiene for granted again.

My stomach grumbled and I was thirsty, but all of that could wait now. My husbands needed me.

I pulled on a white satin robe and tied it tightly. Then, I brushed out my hair and, leaving it loose, I pulled open the bedroom door and marched into the living room. The men were waiting for me, lined up on the sofa, and Aurora was making coffee and toast in the kitchen. She looked up as I approached the coffee pot with gusto.

She gave me a solid smile and then poured me a mug and left it on the counter.

"I'll leave you guys alone," she said.

I frowned at her. "Don't go far," I muttered.

"I need to go home. I'll be back in about two hours," she said.

I nodded at her, forcing a reassuring smile on my face, which left as soon as she turned from me to gather up her bags and leave the penthouse.

I drew in a deep breath and turned to my husbands. They were all looking expectantly at me. I picked up my mug and went to sit in front of them on the coffee table.

After shooting down their offers of joining them on the sofa, I looked down into my mug and took a sip. It was scalding hot, but I didn't care. I hadn't had coffee in three days. I thought it was three days.

"Three days?" I asked my thought out loud.

"Yes," Alex replied.

I looked at him. He looked dreadful. Clearly, he hadn't found solace in the bottom of that bottle last night.

I looked at Lachlan seated in the middle. Guilt was written all over his face.

Then I shifted my eyes to Rex. The anger and pain in his eyes nearly made me start sobbing again.

"He didn't hurt me," I said. "He barely even touched me."

Three sets of eyes were riveted to me as I told my tale of what Rob had done to me while I'd been with him.

Saying it out loud actually helped to make me see that it wasn't as bad as it could have been. In fact, it wasn't that bad at all, really. Sure, it was creepy and weird and the not knowing if it would get worse, was awful. But I hadn't been mistreated in the way that would damage me permanently. I probably wouldn't want to go near a locked room full of teddy bears for a while, but I was convinced that I would be fine. I hadn't convinced my husbands of that, though. Their expressions told me that much. They were furious, sad, worried, sick at the mental image I had put in their heads of the masturbating experiences.

"I'm fine," I said firmly.

"I will kill him," Rex growled.

I patted his hand, trying to reassure him. He seriously looked like he was ready to commit murder. But, then again, that was nothing new. He was a force to be reckoned with and I loved him more than I could say. He would protect me and our daughter as best he could. In this instance, he had been handcuffed to a bed by *me*. Hardly in a position to do anything about it, but I knew he was blaming himself. So was Lachlan. It was his club that I'd been abducted from. But it wasn't his fault either,

It was Rob's. He was the one where all of the blame fell.

"How did you escape?" Alex asked, before I could get the thoughts out into words.

I finished off my coffee before I answered that.

How would they feel, knowing that I had lain in the arms of my captor as he'd fallen asleep? Would they understand?

"You did what you had to," Lachlan blurted out. "Don't be afraid to tell us."

"I played into his fantasy," I said eventually. "I gave him what he wanted from me. He bought it for long enough to let his guard down sufficiently for me to risk running."

I heard Alex gulp, but I kept my eyes on Lachlan. He was probably the one that would understand the most.

"You did what you had to do to survive," Lachlan choked out. I was pretty sure he was trying to convince himself, not me.

"He didn't touch me," I reiterated and saw the relief flood his eyes. I also saw something else. I'd wondered if it would enter his mind during this conversation. I'd had a lot of time to think about it. Did I still want a daddy kink relationship with my husband? The answer wasn't just a simple 'yes'. It was a yes, but with stipulations. But that was something we could discuss between the two of us. I couldn't, and wouldn't, deny that the feelings Rob invoked in me were ones I needed to deal with. I needed to feel that fatherly approval and admiration. I needed to know that just by existing, I was doing the right thing in his eyes. Everything that my own father had denied me, I needed. I craved it and, despite the situation, despite the man who'd brought those feelings forward, they were there.

"We'll talk about that later," I murmured to him, registering his surprise that it wasn't an outright 'no'. I bit my lip, worried that he would think I was a weirdo that had severe issues, but he just nodded, his eyes swimming with nothing but love for me.

I relaxed.

"Once I got through the door and over the fence." I winced as I remembered that horror, "I ran in the opposite direction to which I wanted to go. I'd hoped it would throw him off my trail. I assume it did as he didn't catch up to me." I glanced at the door. Or maybe he'd actually been in front of me, due to my diversion. I'll admit, I was surprised he hadn't shown up here yet. Would he dare risk it? Who knew, he was *that* deranged? "Then I ran until I reached a road. It was pitch black, I couldn't see a thing, but I just kept going. I couldn't stop. I knew that if I stopped, I was never going to see any of you again. If he caught me, I would never get the opportunity to escape again."

"Oh, Cassie," Alex moaned, grabbing the mug off me so he could take my hand. "We should have protected you."

"I'm okay," I said again. "When I hit the road, I slowed down to see if I could figure out where I was."

"Where were you?" Rex asked.

"Greenwich," I replied. "Connecticut. Once I stopped running. I don't really know where I was before then."

He clenched his jaw. "We should have found you. You shouldn't have had to escape like that."

I stifled my laugh. It was inappropriate, but very 'Rex' to brush past the fact that I shouldn't have been abducted in the first place, just that he should've found me before I'd made a run for it.

"So, dressed as I was, I was reluctant to seek help. I didn't want to end up in even more trouble, but eventually, after I walked until dawn, I was tired. I had no money, no phone, I didn't know what to do. I knew I had to get off the road, though, soon. It was then that I saw a bike propped up against a lamppost. I had no idea whose it was, or why it was there, free to ride away. I stole it and made my way back home."

They blinked at me.

"From Connecticut?" Alex asked slowly.

"I realize that it doesn't sound that harrowing..." I start-ed.

"Are you kidding?" Lachlan interrupted me. "Cassie, you are amazing. You risked everything to get home. If he'd caught you..." He gulped and went pale.

"Please can you call the police and tell them everything I've told you. I'll write down what I can remember about when I got to the road."

The men exchanged a look that chilled me.

"I'll call Teddy," Alex said decisively and stood up to do exactly that.

I narrowed my eyes at him. Why would Alex call my uncle? Lachlan was the one who'd known him the longest.

I looked back at my other two husbands. Lachlan was gripping Rex's hand in a death grip.

"Write it down, Cassie," Rex said to me quietly.

"What are you going to do?" I asked, licking my lips, my blood running cold at the blank look on his face.

"Teddy is on his way," Alex interrupted. "He'll be about an hour."

I nodded my thanks and stood up. "That's enough time," I declared, deciding to ignore my own question to Rex. I didn't want to think about it anymore. Nor did I intend to let this experience interfere with my time with my husbands.

I stripped off my robe to shocked looks.

"Cassie," Alex started, placing his phone down carefully.

"I want this. I want you," I said huskily. "Look at me."

All eyes came to me, roved over me, filled with lust and love. It ignited the spark that Rob had tried to snuff out. He had tried to take me away from the men that meant everything to me. He had tried to separate me from my daughter, but I wouldn't let him. I needed to ride the wave of power that was suddenly coursing through me.

"Take me," I whispered.

Alex was the first to swoop down on me. I knew he would be. He didn't have the restraint of the other two men. He kissed me fervently, his hands twisting around my wet hair as he devoured my mouth. His cock was so hard, it dug into me. I wanted it in my hand.

I reached up to unzip his jeans and pulled him out, stroking his long length with a delicious shiver.

It was too much for Lachlan just to sit and watch. He needed action. He was the only one of my husbands who hadn't had sex with me yet. A blowjob didn't count, really.

"Fuck, I love you," he murmured.

Alex dropped his mouth lower, sucking my nipple into his mouth so slowly, I felt my clit pulsate in response.

Lachlan lowered his mouth to mine and gave me a sweet kiss, sweeping his tongue around my mouth, tasting me, claiming me.

"I love you," I breathed as he let me up for air. "All of you. Show me that you love me."

Lachlan moved me towards Rex, still sitting on the sofa, watching us with hooded eyes. I knew he wanted to ravage me, but he also wasn't sure if that was what I wanted.

I crawled onto his lap and ground down on him, enjoying the soft moan that escaped his lips. I unzipped his jeans and then crawled off his lap, taking him in my mouth as I lowered myself to my knees in front of him.

"Cassie," he groaned, sliding his hand into my hair. "I missed you."

My heart pounded at his admission. He never made them in front of the other men. He hated feeling vulnerable. I smiled up at him, knowing he had come so far from the man I'd first met.

I popped my mouth off him as Alex sat next to him and Lachlan pulled me up by my elbows.

"Sorry, wife. I'm fucking desperate," he groaned as he turned me and lifted me up. I chuckled, finding him completely naked already and sporting a hard-on that would take your eye out. He picked me up and I wrapped my legs around him. I gripped him hard in my hand and guided him into me, relishing the feel of his stiff cock deep inside. I threw my head back, clenching my thighs tighter around him as I rode him in the middle of the living room.

He came quickly, flooding me with his desire.

I barely had a chance to take my next breath, before Rex had a hold of me, dragging me off Lachlan and onto his cock as he sat back down.

"Need you," he murmured into my hair, before he kissed me.

I felt Alex's hands on me from behind, his fingers working my nipples into hard peaks that I wanted clamped so badly, I moaned into Rex's mouth.

I rode Rex's cock like it was my last day on earth. I needed him as well. The last time I had taken him was like a bitter taste in my mouth.

Alex's hands dropped lower, finding my clit and gliding over the slippery nub as I worked hard to bring Rex to a climax.

Alex flicked and pinched as I pumped up and down and, in a sweet, blissful moment, we came together. He shot his load into me as I milked him, not ready for this to end. But I had one more man to wear out before I was done. I let Alex take me from Rex and lay me back on the sofa. Then he slid into my wet heat as his lips landed on mine. He pounded into me, giving it to me hard, for both himself and me.

"Fuck," he roared as I came around him in a wave of pure ecstasy. "One more, just one more," he panted, slamming his hips against mine. I wrapped my legs around him tighter and easily gave him what he wanted. My blood raced through me as he made me climax again, his long, even strokes, stoking the fire deep inside me.

"Yes," I cried out, arching my back and feeling him unload into me.

His breathing was heavy in my ear, his arms wrapped tight around me. "I will never let you go again, Cassie," he whispered to me. "None of us will."

It was the right thing to say at the right time.

Things couldn't have been more perfect in that moment.

But, of course, perfection never lasted.

Chapter 22

~Rex~

I watched Alex finish and mutter words of reassurance to our wife. I wanted to take her again, but she was getting up and putting her robe back on. Lachlan was already re-dressed so it was clear this moment was gone. I reluctantly put myself away.

"I'm going to shower," Cassie murmured, but then frowned as there was a knock at the front door.

She blinked at me and moved forward.

I was with her in under a second. Had she learned nothing?

"Wait," I said to her.

"It's Aurora...I forgot something," came through the door and Cassie smiled.

"See? It's just Aurora."

"Why didn't Pete buzz her up?" I muttered, but Cassie was already pulling the door open.

"No!" I roared, but it was too late.

Rob shoved Aurora into the room, a gun pointed at her.

Cassie stilled, her hands clenching into tight fists, before she slowly raised them in front of her.

"You are a naughty girl," Rob spat at her. "Why did you run? I thought we were happy?"

It made me sick. Not only that his delusion had led him to believe that, but also that Cassie had played into it. I knew that she'd needed to do it. It'd been smart. It'd been the only way to survive and get out of there, but it still tapped into the rage that I was holding onto for dear life.

"Rob," she said calmly. "Let Aurora go. She has nothing to do with this."

Rob glanced at Aurora and gave her a rough shove forward, but kept the gun leveled at her.

Then he took in the rest of the room. Alex was only half-dressed and Cassie in just her robe. It was a bit obvious what had happened in here.

Rob completely lost it.

The rage in his eyes as he looked at Cassie and turned the gun on her wasn't something that you saw on a regular basis.

"You whore," he hissed at her. "I gave you what you wanted. I was taking it slowly with you to show you how much you mean to me, yet you come back here to fuck these assholes so wantonly. It is cheap and disgusting."

Cassie licked her lips. I knew she was biting back a comment that was also on the tip of my tongue. This was our home. We were married. How could any of this be seen as cheap, or wanton?

"Rob," she started and moved a bit closer.

What the fuck was she doing?

"Cassie," I growled at her and reached around to grab my own gun, still stuck in the back of my jeans. She was in front of me and didn't see it at first, as I flicked off the safety and aimed it straight at Rob's head. Aurora whimpered, but I didn't look at her. I was focused solely on the prick in front of me. Even Cassie had faded into the background. My old mindset flooded back to me in that instant. I knew what I was going to do, and I was completely fine with it.

"Drop it," I said to him calmly.

He looked at me, his gaze going back to Cassie erratically. He stepped to the side; his gun still pointed at my wife.

Out of the corner of my eye, I saw Cassie take in my own weapon. I also saw her take a step back. I wasn't sure if she did it because she was afraid of me, or if she was giving me space. Either way, it didn't matter. Rob was going down. I just needed him to get that gun out of Cassie's face first.

Alex and Lachlan approached slowly; hands also raised. Lachlan's hand snaked around Cassie's wrist and he dragged her back behind him.

"You deal with us," he said to Rob. "You won't ever get this close to Cassie again."

It raised the question in my mind, how he'd gotten past Pete.

"Cassie!" Rob called out, his frantic look going even wilder. He was about to lose it and he needed neutralizing.

I stepped up closer.

"Rex." I heard the plea in Cassie's voice, but it was no use. This was happening. I cocked the trigger and that was when all hell broke loose.

Rob aimed his gun at me and fired while Lachlan and Alex tackled him, knocking him to the ground.

Aurora screamed and dived behind the kitchen island as Cassie let out a roar of her own.

"Ruby!" she screamed and ran from the room.

I heard the baby wailing as I looked down. I was hit, but it was just a graze. The tackle had changed the trajectory of the bullet and instead of burying itself in my chest, it'd grazed past my arm.

I grunted and clicked the safety back on the gun, shoving it back into my pants. I'd had worse.

"Move," I said to Alex and Lachlan.

They did as I asked, and I hauled Rob to his feet. I punched him in the face, needing that skin-to-skin contact with him before I snuffed him out of existence.

"What made you think that you could take Cassie from me?" I asked him quietly. "Did I not hit you hard enough before?"

"You don't deserve her," Rob spat out, along with a load of blood.

I hit him again and then again.

"You don't know her," I said to him quietly, trying to ignore the hurt his words had caused. I knew they were true, but I had to focus.

I wrapped my hand around his neck and squeezed.

He gagged.

"Did you touch her?" I whispered to him. Not that I didn't believe Cassie, but I knew that she had brushed over the trauma that this had caused her to protect us. It was who she was. She would rather suffer in silence than think she had caused us any pain.

"Yes," Rob choked out, his eyes flashing. "I fucked that little slut until she screamed."

I knew he was lying, but it was what I'd wanted him to say. It made this easier.

I mentally shook my head at myself. Since when had I grown such a conscience? Or, maybe it had always been there, but I hadn't noticed it, because I'd been *that* dead inside.

Cassie had changed all of that.

She had changed me.

But not enough.

I dragged him closer to me so that he was inches away. "I'm going to kill you, you sick bastard. If you think Cassie will care, then you are wrong. She will celebrate, knowing that she doesn't have to live her life knowing a sick fuck like you is still breathing the same air as she is."

I spun him around and got him in a chokehold that knocked him unconscious.

With a look back at Lachlan and Alex, I hauled him over my shoulder and headed for the elevator. Alex stepped forward to unlock it.

The doors slid open and I walked into it.

He looked at me before the doors closed.

I expected to see hesitation or disapproval on his face.

I was surprised to see determination and a brief nod as the doors slid closed.

~Cassie~

I WAS HOLDING RUBY in a grip so tight; she was squirming against me. My ears were still ringing from the explosion of the shot, but Ruby had settled down now after being woken up by it and screaming for several long minutes. I jiggled her a bit and risked putting her back down. I needed to get back out there to see if anyone was hurt. Rob's gun had been aimed right at Rex. I gulped as my blood ran cold. Rex's gun had been pointed at Rob. I hadn't known that he carried one, let alone had it to hand. It was too dangerous to have around the baby.

What was he thinking?

I had no idea which one of them had fired. It was all a blur. All I knew was that I'd needed to get to Ruby.

It was too quiet as I peeked back out into the living room.

Rex and Rob were nowhere in sight, only Alex, Lachlan and Aurora.

Lachlan was consoling Aurora, but she seemed remarkably okay for someone who'd just gotten caught amid a shoot-out.

"Where is he?" I demanded, as Alex spotted me and came over to take me in his arms.

"Is Ruby okay?" he asked, full of concern

I gave him a tight smile that covered up my insensitivity. Of course, they needed to know about Ruby first. "Yes, she's fine. She was just shocked."

Lachlan let go of Aurora. She scrunched up her tissue and threw it in the trash. "You okay?" I asked her.

She nodded.

I bit my lip. "Look, I understand if all of this is too much for you. I will have a glowing reference ready for you in the morning," I said, wearily. I was sad to see her go.

She shook her head. "I'm okay, seriously. It's not my first gun fight."

All eyes turned to her in surprise.

"Wh-what?" I coughed in amazement.

She shrugged. "All in good time. But, for now, I'll leave you. You have...stuff..." She trailed off and an awkward silence fell.

"No, you can't leave," I said to break it. "It's not safe."

"Stan is on his way," she reassured me.

I blinked at her.

"My boyfriend," she explained. "He works security at CoCo."

"Oh," I said, surprised but then frowned. "Still...maybe you should wait for the police?"

Lachlan made no attempt to stifle his cough. "Stan can take care of himself and Aurora," he said.

I glared at him. He'd known this all along about our nanny? Not to mention...why weren't we calling the cops? Plus, where the hell was Uncle Teddy?

"It's my biggest regret that he wasn't working the other night..."

He gave me a look full of sorrow and guilt.

I ignored it and focused on Aurora instead. My questions could wait.

She gave me a solid smile back, which then turned to a frown. "Sorry, I should've mentioned this before...that guy...Rob, is it? He knocked out the security guy downstairs with some kind of drug."

"Thanks," Lachlan said. "We'll take care of it. I'll walk you down to wait for Stan."

She nodded her thanks and then she hesitated for a second, before she rushed at me, crushing me in a hug that took me by surprise. She was strong.

I hugged her back and then she and Lachlan were gone.

"Where is Rex?" I demanded Alex as soon as the door closed behind them.

Alex looked a bit shifty. "He and Rob left," he said lamely.

"You don't say?" I drawled at him, rolling my eyes to convey my annoyance at his vagueness.

Alex looked back at me sheepishly, knowing that ambiguity wasn't going to work. "I don't know," he said eventually.

"Is he hurt?" I asked, folding my arms across my chest as a defense mechanism.

"He'll live," he said and then he grimaced.

I narrowed my eyes at him. "Did you know he carried a gun?"

"I knew he had one and kept it locked in his safe in the office. As far as I know, he only started carrying it since you..." He looked down.

I nodded, taking all of this in. It wasn't the first time that I'd thought I didn't really know the man I was married to and it probably wouldn't be the last either. The fact that my other husbands knew him better than I did stung like a bitch. It wasn't supposed to be that way.

"Was Rob alive when they left here?" I asked quietly.

"He was," Alex answered, just as carefully.

The tension that built up was interrupted by Lachlan. "Stan was already there when we got downstairs. Aurora will be fine."

I nodded at him. "Good."

He looked at me and then at Alex and also folded his arms across his chest. *His* defense mechanism. I wasn't sure which one of us learned it from the other. "Everything okay in here?"

"Apart from the obvious?" I snapped at him. "Where the hell is Rex?"

He shrugged. "I don't know."

"I see," I said stiffly, making it very clear that I was pissed off with both of them. All three of them. They were keeping secrets from me. Again. "I need a minute. Please go and sit with Ruby."

To my surprise, they both bolted from the room as I'd asked. I'd expected them to try to linger. It only confirmed to me that something deeper was going on.

I sat down and put my head in my hands.

Rex had a gun.

He'd pulled it out and aimed it at Rob.

Did he fire it or was it Rob?

I racked my brains to try to remember exactly what had happened.

I will kill him.

Those words of Rex's said not that long ago, echoed through my thoughts.

I will kill him.

"I will kill him," I whispered. I always knew that Rex was capable of a darkness that put most people's own to shame.

I'd hoped that being with me had let a little light into his life. I'd hoped that Ruby, his daughter by blood, had lit up the shadows even more.

Was I wrong?

Did I have it all wrong?

Did I have no effect on him at all?

Didn't Ruby?

The secrets.

The evasiveness about his past.

The knowing glances between the men.

Lachlan's words in the nursery the day Rex said he was leaving me. *I know all about your darkness.*

These thoughts swam around and around until I landed on the only conclusion that I could.

Not only was Rex capable of killing Rob. I was sure that he had, and that my other husbands were covering it up.

AN HOUR PASSED.

I'd shut myself away in the office once I'd reached the conclusion that I had.

I heard the men whispering and moving about. I heard Ruby, but I knew she was fine, that her daddies were taking good care of her.

I didn't want to speak to anyone until Rex returned.

I heard the elevator doors open and my heart thumped. I quickly stood up and dragged the door open, hesitating in the doorway as Rex looked at me. He had a blank look on his face, and he turned from me to walk further into the penthouse.

"Don't walk away from me!" I barked, following him, only now realizing that I was sweating and probably looked a right mess. But I didn't care. I needed answers.

He slowly turned back to me. I saw the bandage on his arm, seeping blood. I wanted to ask him if he was okay, but the words got stuck in my throat.

"Ask your question," he said, glaring down at me as Lachlan and Alex flanked him.

I felt outnumbered and overwhelmed, but the gnawing in my stomach had to go. I needed answers and I needed them from him now.

"You killed him, didn't you?" I whispered.

His eyes searched mine. Those black depths that ran so deep, I felt myself getting lost in them.

"What if I did, Cassie?" he whispered back, after a long moment. "How would you feel about that?"

It confirmed it for me.

He'd done it.

My stomach twisted into a tiny ball that squeezed up the coffee that I'd consumed hours ago. I swallowed it back.

"I love you," I said quietly. "You can tell me anything, Rex."

"Will you still love me, if I told you that, yes, I killed that motherfucker and I feel absolutely nothing about it?" he spat out.

Tears sprang to my eyes. "Yes," I bleated, knowing it was true. Rob had hurt me, hurt who knows how many other women, other *girls*, far worse. He needed putting down. I shocked myself at how okay I was with this line of thought.

When did this happen to me?

When keeping your daughter safe is the only thing that matters.

If Rob had ever come for her, I know I would have killed him with my bare hands. How was this any different for Rex? A man that I knew would protect me at all costs. He had told me enough times. It had finally sunk in and I was just fine with that.

"Yes," I said, lifting my chin higher. "I still love you and I understand, Rex. You don't ever need to hide yourself from me. We are in this together. All of us." I looked at my other husbands to include them. "We don't need secrets, because we don't judge here. We love each other and that is all that matters."

The relief that flooded Rex's eyes was short-lived and replaced with a lot of resigned determination. "If that's the case, then there's something else I need to tell you," he said.

"Rex, man," Alex said. "Think about this for a second."

Rex spun to him. "Didn't you want this a few weeks ago?"

Alex looked down and kept quiet.

Rex looked back at me. "When we met, Cassie, I didn't work in I.T."

"Oh?" I prompted when he stopped for a long pause.

Lachlan's hand landed on his shoulder and he took a deep breath. "I worked for your uncle."

My eyebrows went up at that. Where was he going with this?

"As a killer for hire," he said in a rush. "I killed people for money."

The world stood still for just a moment, before it came rushing back, the blood roaring in my veins, making me feel light-headed.

"I see," I said, the room spinning around and around. "I see," I repeated before the spinning stopped and everything went black.

The End

Stay tuned for book 3 of the Enchained Hearts Series: Lives Encaptured — Coming Early 2020

About the Author

Eve Newton

Eve is a British novelist with a specialty for paranormal romance, with strong female leads, causing her to develop a Reverse Harem Fantasy series, several years ago: The Forever Series.

She lives in the UK, with her husband and four kids, so finding the time to write is short, but definitely sweet. She currently has two on-going series, with a number of spin-offs in the making. Eve hopes to release some new and exciting projects in the next couple of years, so stay tuned!

Start Eve's Reverse Harem Fantasy Series, with the first two books in the Forever Series as a double edition!
Newsletter Sign up for exclusive content and giveaways: https://emailoctopus.com/lists/ a0f1e6a3-7a21-11e9-9307-06b4694bee2a/forms/subscribe
Facebook Reader Group: https://www.facebook.com/ groups/2042198485818170
Facebook: http://facebook.com/evenewtonforever
Twitter: https://twitter.com/AuthorEve
Website: https://evenewtonauthor.com/

Other Books by Eve Newton

T**he Forever Series:**
Forever & The Power of One: Double Edition[1]
Revelations[2]
Choices[3]
The Ties That Bind[4]
Trials[5]
Switch & The Other Switch[6]
Secrets[7]
Betrayal[8]
Sacrifice[9]
Conflict & Obsession: Double Edition[10]
Wrath[11]
Revenge[12]

---

1.   http://viewbook.at/FTPO

2.   http://mybook.to/RevelationsFS

3.   http://mybook.to/ChoicesFS

4.   http://mybook.to/TTTBFS

5.   http://mybook.to/TrialsFS

6.   http://mybook.to/SwitchFS

7.   http://mybook.to/SecretsFS

8.   http://mybook.to/BetrayalFS

9.   http://mybook.to/SacrificeFS

10.   http://mybook.to/ConflictObsession

11.   http://mybook.to/WrathFS

Changes & Forever After: Double Edition[13]
Arathia[14]
Constantine[15]
The Dragon Heiress (Delinda's Story)[16]
The Dragon Realms Series:
The Dragon Heiress[17]
Claiming the Throne[18]
The Early Years Series:
Aefre & Constantine 1 & 2[19]
The Bound Series:
Demon Bound[20]
Demon Freed[21]
Demon Returned[22]
Enchained Hearts: Contemporary Reverse Harem:
Lives Entwined[23]
Circle of Darkness Series:
Wild Hearts[24]

---

12.   http://mybook.to/RevengeFS

13.   http://mybook.to/CFAFS

14.   http://mybook.to/Arathia

15.   http://mybook.to/ConstantineFS

16.   http://mybook.to/DragonHeiress

17.   http://mybook.to/DragonHeiress

18.   http://mybook.to/CtT

19.   http://mybook.to/AefreConstantine

20.   http://mybook.to/DBound

21.   http://mybook.to/DFreed

22.   http://mybook.to/DReturned

23.   http://mybook.to/ENLivesEntwined

24.   http://mybook.to/WildHeartsK

<u>Savage Love</u>[25]

Printed in Great Britain
by Amazon

75374537R00173